The False Countess

MICHELLE MORRISON

Ingram ISBN: 978-1-9-53100-27-6

Cover Design: Rebecca Poole-Dreams2media

Editor: Penny Brandon

First Trade Paperback Printing by Scarsdale Publishing: January 2022

10 9 8 7 6 5 4 3 2

www.scarsdalepublishing.com

One

London, 1817

IF NOT FOR his mother's plea and a promise to his dying brother, Robert Carlisle could have remained out of range of his father's vitriolic ranting.

He clenched his jaw and wished he were anywhere but here. Not just this damned crowded drawing room, but England. The guests, who included actors, opera dancers, playwrights, poets, and courtesans, had gathered to celebrate the opening of a new play at the Theatre Royal Covent Garden. Many noblemen and wealthy gentry mingled with the members of the *demimonde*—those not-quite-respectable-but-still-wildly-popular members of London's society. Tonight, even members of the royal household shared in the laughter, ribald jokes, political debates, and overt flirtations that filled the room.

Robert should have been enjoying himself but couldn't muster any interest. The weeks since his return to England after a three-year absence had been anything but tranquil, and he was done in. Life as the Marquess of Dunsbury was not the life of leisure most people imagined. He considered joining the play at the card table, but that appealed to him as little as any of the other amusements offered at the party.

"Gads." He downed the last of his drink.

"I quite agree." His friend, Lord Noel Wayland, shook his head. "I think Mrs. Wilson waters her drinks. Not a terrible idea considering the amount this crowd is likely to consume, but it does leave one in want of a decent brandy."

Mrs. Wilson was a rather notorious courtesan, her favors so sought after that she could afford a luxurious townhouse where she hosted glittering parties.

Robert glanced at his empty glass and realized he hadn't even tasted its contents.

"Shall we head to my club? We can get a decent drink there," Wayland said.

"I suppose so." No amount of alcohol could dull Robert's ill humor. He sighed, feeling like the very type of man he disdained—the one who constantly sought new amusements, only to be unimpressed by any of them. It was quite fashionable to sport an air of ennui—but having spent the last three years traveling through war-ravaged Europe, he found such an affectation as ineffectual as it was annoying. Still, he could think of no other word for the mild restlessness that refused to let him enjoy the evening.

Wayland grinned. "Don't grow too excited, old man. I shouldn't want you to overexert yourself."

Robert smiled. "Sorry. I'm not good company this evening. Tell me, Wayland, what's worse, to be suffused with boredom or to realize you've become the very thing you've always abhorred?"

His friend laughed. "My, you *are* in a state tonight." He flagged down a footman and took two glasses of champagne. "Here, drink up. It's not brandy, but there's no way to water down champagne. The bubbles will tell."

Robert sipped the sparkling wine and tried to push aside his melancholy.

"Now tell me what's nagging you. The Robert Carlisle I've known since Eton is *never* bored and would throw himself into the Thames before being classified as a pampered aristocrat."

Robert's attention snagged on the crowd across the room. Someone or something caused a stir, but he couldn't see through the press of bodies.

"It's your mother, isn't it?" Wayland asked.

Robert frowned. "My mother?"

"She's pushing you to marry, isn't she? It's no surprise seeing as you've been gone for so long."

"What? No! Well, I mean, she's mentioned it, but she's not forcing the issue."

"Gads, I envy you. My mother practically invites young women into my bedchamber."

Robert choked on his champagne. "Are you saying your mother is a madam?"

Wayland laughed. "Certainly not to her face. Still, I can't believe you've escaped the daily reminders about duty and preserving the title and all."

Robert avoided his friend's gaze. "Yes, well, my father is still alive, so the need is not as pressing as it is for you."

"Oh, I'd heard— Well, I don't mean to be indelicate, but my mother was under the impression your father was…on his deathbed."

Robert's stomach clenched at the mention of his father. It was a common enough feeling that he should be able to ignore it, but somehow, the sharp pang of betrayal never dulled. "Your mother is not wrong. It's just that he's been there for the better part of a year, and I suspect he'll stay around to torment us all for years to come."

He glimpsed Wayland's sympathetic glance, though thankfully, he let the matter drop.

Robert returned his attention to the knot of people across the room who were laughing uproariously and cheering. "What is going on over there?"

"Perhaps something to cure your boredom."

They wove their way through the room, trying to find a gap in the crowd. One young buck gasped, and as another stepped aside to take a flute of champagne, Robert ruthlessly stole the man's spot. Though still at the back of the gathering, Robert could see a chess match between the Duke of Newcastle—Lord Chamberlain to His Majesty—and a woman.

Robert's breath caught. He'd long scoffed at the poets who claimed love at first glance. To experience such a visceral and instantaneous reaction startled him. He studied the woman more closely. Light chestnut hair, gray eyes, a scattering of freckles, and a full mouth curved in a wry smile. She was pretty, to be sure, but there were a dozen ravishing beauties in the room, and none of them had captured his attention. He couldn't understand why she had such an effect on him. She wore an elaborate gown, its red and white velvet bodice embroidered in gold that hugged her body more tightly than the high-waisted dresses currently in fashion.

He dragged his attention to the chessboard for a moment, conscious of how the woman played the game.

"I'll be dammed!" A surprised smile creased Newcastle's face. "She's got me trapped!"

"I believe you call that checkmate, no?" the woman said in a throaty Russian accent. She didn't quite successfully repress a smile.

Victory and mischief lit her eyes, and a hectic flush stained her cheeks. Robert's body tightened, and for the second time in as many minutes, he found himself confounded at his reaction to this unknown woman.

The crowd erupted into cheers and good-natured ribbing of Newcastle, who was purported to be a master chessman.

The mystery woman stood and wound her way through the well-wishers. She passed Robert, and he caught a whiff of lemon verbena, a scent so quintessentially English it caught him by surprise.

He wanted to introduce himself but knew he would only be one of many fawning admirers. Instead, he let her pass and watched while she circulated through the guests, skillfully disentangling herself from the more eager men until she disappeared down the hallway leading to the retiring room. Robert bided his time, positioning himself where he could see all entrances to the room.

Wayland stepped up beside him. "Well, I fear your boredom is contagious. I suspect that chess match was the highlight of the evening. Shall we find a livelier diversion?"

"Boredom?" Robert asked. "I'm not— Oh." He flushed.

"Ah, she's intrigued you, has she?"

"Who is she?"

"Apparently, she's a Russian countess, recently arrived in London. At least, that's what Penny said."

"Penny?" Robert asked, confused.

"The actress. Of the play that just opened. I say, are you drunk? You appear dazed."

The countess in question re-entered the drawing room and paused just inside the doorway as if unsure of herself.

"Why is she in London?" Robert asked.

"No idea. As far as I've heard, this is the first event she's attended."

"A patroness of the theater, then?"

Wayland chuckled. "I'm sure I don't know. Why don't you ask her yourself?"

"I shall." Robert handed his empty glass to his friend then strolled through the crowd in her direction.

She watched the party with wide-eyed wonder as if she'd never seen such a glittering assortment. Her childlike air belied her confidence when she'd beaten the Lord Chamberlain at chess. Robert had heard tales of the opulence of the Russian court but wondered if perhaps she'd never attended. Certainly, this collection of London's *demimonde* was colorful, but nothing compared to a formal ball. Robert had the absurd desire to take her to such an event just to enjoy her reaction.

One eye on her, he paused to exchange a few words with the hostess, then continued a few more paces to watch a card game before taking another glass of champagne from a waiter near the countess.

Gaze on the action in the center of the room where a young man loudly recited bad poetry to one of the actresses, Robert sipped in silence for a moment before saying, "You could have ended that game earlier."

The countess turned to look at him. "I beg your pardon?"

He faced her and raised his left eyebrow. "The chess game. You could have had him in checkmate two moves earlier."

She chewed her lip as she stared at him, and he wondered if she was not as fluent in English as he assumed. He started to repeat himself more slowly, but she inclined her head.

"This I know, but it is not always enjoyable to end things early."

He grinned. "Indeed."

She put a hand to her chest and blushed as she clearly grasped his meaning. So, she was not as sophisticated as he'd first thought. How had an ingénue come to be at a party such as this? While the crowd was certainly not of the lowest order, actors tended to be a rather bawdy bunch.

"I imagine this party must seem quite shocking to you," he said to put her at ease. "Not all of London's events are as indecorous, I can assure you. Perhaps your host should have taken you to a dinner party for your introduction to the *ton*."

"The ton?"

"London's high society."

The countess studied him for a long moment—long enough for him to see that her gray eyes held no flecks of hazel but were the clear, soft color of a dove's wing, framed by lashes and brows several shades darker than her ginger hair. Her gaze lost its expression of naïveté, and she lowered her lids, looking at him through the fringe of her lashes. While the color stayed high in her cheeks, he had the impression her reaction was more excitement than embarrassment. It was almost as if the countess had pulled off a mask—or put one on—so great was the transformation.

"On the contrary. My only surprise with this gathering is it seems so much tamer than the artist's parties in my home country."

Her Russian accent sent an erotic thrill through his body. He huffed a short laugh. "Do tell, Countess."

She narrowed her eyes. "For example, an—how did you say —indecorous party in Kursk would not allow a chess game. Unless, of course, it was *disrobe* chess."

"Disrobe chess?" He lifted a brow, pretending not to understand.

"*Dah.* When you lose a chess piece, you must remove an article of clothing."

"Interesting. Such play must make for uncomfortable games in winter."

She waved a hand. "An Englishman may find it cold. A Russian has vodka."

"And what happens in the case of checkmate?"

The countess shrugged. "The loser must remove his remaining clothes."

"Of course."

She frowned, and her accent thickened. "You do not believe me?"

"To the contrary. I simply imagined it would be an incentive to master your strategy. So, tell me, how often have you found yourself in checkmate?"

"I am a very good strategist," she replied, her tone coy.

"Perhaps you could teach me this Russian version of chess."

A flicker of wariness crossed her face. "Sadly, we are not in Russia. We must abide English customs here, *dah*?"

Robert smiled at her sidestep. "*Dah*."

She frowned. "Is it not an English custom to introduce oneself to a stranger before making unseemly propositions?"

"Unseemly? Well, if we're being proper..." He executed a bow. "I am Robert Carlisle, Marquess of Dunsbury."

"I am Countess Alisa Borodinicha, recently from Novogorod."

She extended her ungloved hand. Robert swallowed at the erotic sensuality of her small hand in his.

She inhaled sharply and jerked her hand as if she intended to pull it back. Instead, she left it in his grasp, and he lightly ran the pad of his thumb over the softness of her skin. With a small shake of her head, she freed her hand.

"A marquess?" she asked, clearly trying to regain her composure. "Is that terribly important? I do not know your English ranks of aristocracy."

A renegade curl slipped from the countess's coiffure and dangled over her brow. He ignored the disconcerting urge to smooth it back then trace the curve of her cheek.

She arched a brow, and he realized he hadn't answered her.

"How important can a title be when it's simply bestowed upon you at birth?" he asked.

"This is an unusual belief for a man with a title, is it not?"

Robert grinned. "Perhaps I'm an unusual man."

"Perhaps," she said, though her suppressed smile and tone implied otherwise.

She didn't flirt at all like other ladies, and he found he quite enjoyed it. The Russian countess intrigued him. She teased him, challenged him, and represented something he'd long ago forsaken. "Perhaps I'm simply trying to pique your interest."

She frowned. "Why would you wish to do that?"

"Russian countesses are few and far between, especially beautiful ones. I'd wager you could have any man in this room at your beck and call with a mere snap of your fingers."

"Do you think so?" Russian accents didn't lend themselves well to expressions of delight, but the countess appeared enchanted despite her harsh Slavic pronunciation. She glanced around the room then caught her lower lip between her teeth. The abused flesh reddened, and Robert wondered how it would taste and feel if he had a chance to nibble on it.

He smiled. "I do."

"And what would it do to beckon any of these men?" She flicked her fingers at the increasingly rowdy gathering. "They are nothing but drunkards."

"A harsh critique from a Russian."

She shrugged. "A Russian man who cannot hold his alcohol is no use to anyone."

"Thankfully, I keep my wits about me even at the bottom of a bottle."

The countess sniffed. "So you say."

"Another challenge? Let's see, according to my tally, we must play your disrobing version of chess whilst I drink my weight in alcohol."

"I have challenged you to nothing," she replied.

"Nonetheless, I feel the need to defend my honor."

"If your honor is so easily impugned, perhaps you are too high in the instep."

"High in the instep? You speak like a born Englishwoman, Countess."

She lifted her hand to her neck, and a frown marred her brow.

He took a small step toward her. "Countess?"

She dropped her gaze and took a breath. When she looked back up at him, her bravado had returned. "I would not wish you to think me rude, my lord."

He wanted to ask what had changed her mind but was more curious as to what she had to say. "Why would I think such a thing?"

She plucked at her elaborate skirts. "I am unaccustomed to your...English custom of coquetry. A consequence of the language difference, I am sure, but your style of flirtation is..."

He grinned. "Is?"

"I am uncertain how much of what you say I should take to heart and how much to dismiss as balderdash."

"Balderdash, eh? Well, I can certainly see how disconcerting that would be."

"So, I may, in my Russianness, seem very—what is the word —brusque."

It was a very English sentiment to apologize for the possibility of appearing rude. Yet Robert could well remember the trouble he got into with his rudimentary German on his travels.

"I shall endeavor to be more straightforward, so you needn't question my meaning," he vowed. "Perhaps, we could retire to a quieter venue. I can provide you better refreshments than our current hostess, and you can teach me how to flirt in a proper Russian manner."

Just then, a half-dozen rowdy young men, clearly deep in their cups, barreled into the room. One tripped and threw out a hand to catch himself, but he only found the countess for purchase. She gasped as she stumbled against Robert, who caught her before he snapped out a sharp reprimand to the drunkard.

Robert returned his attention to the woman in his arms and found her staring at his shirtfront. His heart pounded in awareness of her scent, weight, and warmth, which made him lightheaded.

She panted as if frightened.

"Are you all right?" he asked.

When she looked up, her pupils had dilated, so they nearly eclipsed the pale gray of her irises. She pressed her hands against his chest, the pressure a distraction. Robert glanced at where she touched him, but his attention snagged on her cleavage. His mouth went dry at the overt display of her breasts, and he drew her closer, moving his hand from her elbow to the small of her back. He returned his gaze to hers and stood in a sensuous cocoon that muffled the increasingly rowdy party. Alisa dropped her gaze to his mouth and licked her lips—an action that caused already hardened parts of his body to stiffen further. He didn't need a second invitation to kiss her. He lowered his head to hers, then jerked back when a woman laughed loudly, its shrillness reminding him they were not alone.

"Shall we go?"

Before Alisa could reply, a crash sounded behind them, followed by a squeal of outrage. When the countess pulled her hand from his, Robert frowned but spun to see one of the actresses standing amid the ruins of the punch bowl in a soaked gown. An inebriated young man—another poet by the elaborate sweep of his hair and the effusive display of lace at neck and wrist—tried ineffectively to mop up the mess with his handkerchief. The drenched actress let loose a tirade of Cockney-flavored curses upon the young man who still dabbed at her ruined gown.

"I'd say no translation is necessary for her—" Robert turned to the countess, only to find her gone. He scanned the room, didn't see her, then ducked into the hallway. A flash of red going out the front door caught his eye, but by the time he reached the front stairs, her carriage was pulling away.

"No translation needed for that meaning either," he muttered. "Damn."

He turned to re-enter the townhouse as Wayland emerged, their coats in hand.

"Party's over," his friend said. "Turns out some young fool spilled wine all over one of the lead actresses."

"And that ended the party?"

"No, but the actress had borrowed the gown from our hostess, who was also quite put out that her favorite Aubusson rug was stained."

"Ah, well, if the rug was ruined," Robert said with a half-laugh as he gathered his coat, his mind still buzzing from his encounter with the Russian countess.

"Hmm, and I'd begun to really enjoy myself once I got Penny all to myself," Wayland complained.

"So, it appears neither one of us was successful with the ladies," Robert said. "The Russian countess abandoned me."

Wayland's coach pulled up to the front steps. "Speak for yourself. I've Penny's direction and will call to take her to Gunther's tomorrow for a flavored ice. I say, aren't I giving you a ride?"

"I believe I'll walk off my heartbreak. It's a lovely evening. Besides, you'll just gloat the whole time about your date."

"Too right you are." Wayland climbed into the coach then slammed the door shut.

Robert waved his friend off then crossed the street to make his way home. The distance was longer than advisable to walk at night, but he was restless and knew he needed the physical exertion to settle his mind even as he replayed the encounter with the Russian countess. His palm tingled as he remembered the touch of her bare hand, and as he inhaled, it was her scent, that disconcertingly English lemon verbena, which filled his nose, teasing him with a fresh innocence at odds with the smoldering gaze she had given him when she'd pressed against him. He laughed, the sound a little hollow. In one short night, he'd gone from dissatisfied to a full-blown, all-consuming attraction for a woman who clearly had little interest in him. He turned up his collar as a light spring rain misted the night. It was no less than he deserved, considering the state of his life.

Two

CATHERINE PURCELL GROANED as the morning light fell on her face. She pried open one eye as her maid, Sophie, threw back the heavy curtains a split second before a small figure hurtled onto Catherine's bed, knocking the breath from her.

"Mama! You slept so late! Grandmama said she may have to call the doctor to check on you."

Catherine shifted her son's solid weight off her stomach and sat up. "Surely it's not that late."

"It is! Breakfast is gone, and you'll starve until dinner."

Christopher's horrified tone made Catherine smile. "Perhaps *you* would starve, my growing boy."

"Give your mother a chance to wake up," Sophie said, urging Christopher off the bed.

"But why did she sleep so late?" he demanded.

Catherine glanced at Sophie, who pressed her lips together to keep from smiling.

"Perhaps you wore me out yesterday playing hide and seek," Catherine said.

Before Christopher could question her further, Sophie tutted.

"Leave your mother be until she's dressed." She took the boy's hand and tugged him to the door.

"But Mama promised we'd go to the museum today," he said, his voice now a whine.

"We will, but she can't go in her nightgown now, can she?"

As soon as the door closed, Catherine fell back against her pillows, the previous night's adventure returning in a rush. She couldn't believe she'd done something so outrageous and out of character by sneaking into a party hosted by a notorious member of the demimonde.

She thought of the actresses who had boldly drunk champagne and the ridiculous young men who had heaped extravagant compliments on her. It had been years since she'd had such lighthearted, exhilarating *fun*. Certainly since before she married Jasper.

A pang of guilt hit her as she thought about the husband she'd barely known before he died in a hunting accident two years ago. Despite still living with his parents, she rarely thought of him. Theirs had been an arranged marriage, instigated by her dying father so she wouldn't be alone and impoverished at twenty. Jasper was a good man, but they'd had nothing in common, and their brief interactions were always awkward and formal. Now she was facing another marriage of convenience, and the thought of another such union made her feel like she couldn't breathe.

As if she could escape the uncomfortable emotions, she scrambled out of bed and splashed water on her face at the washstand. She briskly rubbed her face with the linen towel, her skin tingling at the abrasion, which reminded her how her entire body had tingled last night as she'd pressed up against Robert Carlisle's chest. She'd stared at his finely molded lips and wanted to kiss him, then when he suggested they leave the party together, she had *agreed*! Were it not for the commotion across the room jolting her back to her wits, who knew what might have happened? Even as she ignored the surge of disappointment that she hadn't discovered how far she'd been willing to go last night, she had to admit she had a lucky escape.

Catherine sighed at fate just as Sophie returned to help her dress.

"Well, miss?" the maid asked after she pulled Catherine's gown over her head.

"Well, what?"

"You snuck into an actress's party—with *my* invitation, I might add—and didn't return until nearly two in the morning."

Catherine couldn't help but smile as she sat at the small dressing table. "You didn't have an actual invitation to the party."

"Billy Wainwright was going to sneak me in through the kitchen, so we could watch the goings-on. Without me, you wouldn't have known about the party, miss," Sophie said.

"I'm sorry." When she'd devised her plan to escape the inescapable constraints of her life just for one night, Sophie had instantly agreed to help, even forgoing her own evening off to take care of Christopher and cover for Catherine should the Purcells ask after her.

"It was…very colorful and…crowded."

"*Miss!*" Sophie dropped the hairbrush she'd begun to pull through Catherine's hair.

Catherine let out a short laugh as she realized Sophie would not give up until Catherine had shared every sordid detail.

"It was exciting and thrilling and unlike anything I've ever been to," she said. "I played chess against—"

"You played chess? I gave up an evening with Billy Wainwright so you could play chess, miss?"

Catherine laughed again. "No, it was—" She gave up, knowing Sophie would never see chess as anything but a waste of time. Though Catherine had enjoyed matching intellect with

Lord Chamberlain, what she remembered most was her bold description of "disrobe chess." She'd tried to seem worldly and sophisticated but had ended up amazed that she'd come up with something so…naughty. Her wickedness, however, was entirely Robert's fault.

Hoping her cheeks didn't betray her thoughts, she toyed with the hairpins on the dressing table before handing one to the maid. "I met someone. A gentleman." She glanced in the mirror and watched Sophie smile.

"Handsome bloke?"

Catherine nodded, picturing Robert's dark hair and eyes, strong jawline, and aquiline nose. Not to mention those lips.

"Did he take any liberties?"

Catherine blinked away thoughts of Robert's lips. "What? Certainly not. He was a gentleman. A marquess, even." There was no way she was going to confess to her bold consideration of leaving the party for a "quieter venue" before she'd come to her senses.

"You were no less than a countess. At least for the night," Sophie said. She finished with Catherine's hair and turned to put away her nightdress.

Catherine hadn't considered that. Perhaps she wasn't the only imposter at the party. She found the thought vaguely disconcerting. She wanted to keep her brush with the handsome marquess as a cherished memory, not taint it with the realization Robert Carlisle was no doubt as much an imposter as she was.

"So, you're saying he didn't even kiss you?"

Catherine shook her head.

"Billy Wainwright would have at least kissed me," Sophie said, her voice heavy with disappointment.

Catherine continued to grin at her maid's reaction to Catherine's lack of scandalous adventure in the arms of a false marquess as she headed downstairs in search of her son.

"Oh, there you are, dear," her mother-in-law called from the small front parlor. "I was afraid you'd fallen ill after all of our excitement these past weeks."

Catherine smiled as she joined Jasper's mother in the cheerfully decorated room. Since coming to London a fortnight ago, they'd attended what small social events the Purcells' new status as Baron and Baroness Tutley afforded them. Considering the state in which the previous baron had left the title and its lands, which included the debts he'd incurred, she was amazed she and the Purcells had received invitations to anywhere. Two small dinner parties and an afternoon of callers who hoped to hear gossip about the previous baron had scarcely constituted the whirlwind Mother Purcell had anticipated.

"I'm quite well, I assure you. Have you seen Christopher?" As a distraction, mentioning her son always worked. The Purcells doted on the boy; he was the only thing that had kept them going after Jasper's death.

"My darling Christopher! He was just here stealing biscuits off my tray. He didn't steal them, of course. I gave them willingly. He's so charming, isn't he? Just like his dear papa." Mother Purcell, who Catherine knew she had to get used to thinking of as the baroness, dug about her voluminous skirts until she found a handkerchief. She dabbed at the tears that welled every time she mentioned her son.

Catherine sat in the chair opposite and reached over to pat her hand.

Mother Purcell sighed. "You are so brave, my dear, holding your emotions in so our Christopher won't be sad. I know you must mourn Jasper as much as I do, for there never was a more perfect man, was there?"

Catherine gave her a wan smile.

"How you can bear the thought of marrying another man after Jasper is beyond me." Her mother-in-law must have realized how that sounded, for she quickly said, "Not that we're not incredibly grateful for your sacrifice."

Catherine stood. "I really must find Christopher. I promised him a trip to the museum today."

Mother Purcell, the baroness, held her handkerchief to her nose and nodded. "I think he's with the baron in the study," she said as Catherine left.

The study was an altered luggage storage room at the back of the Purcells' newly inherited house. The previous baron had converted every room into a place for gaming, drinking, and parties. The library had even become an indoor shooting range. The baron's lifestyle was no doubt part of why he died at such a young age and in such debt.

The new baron sat at a table laden with account books and stacks of papers that Catherine knew were overdue bills.

"Good morning," Catherine said. "I'm looking for Christopher. Is he in here with you?"

"Christopher?" her father-in-law asked with a twitch of his mouth. "No, no. Haven't seen him. No idea where he could be."

She heard a muffled giggle from beneath the table and raised her eyebrows at her father-in-law. He shrugged and lifted his feet so she could see her son, tucked under the heavy chair, his hands pressed to his mouth as he tried to stifle his laughter.

"Come along then. We've a museum to visit," she said.

THE WALK to the British Museum was a long one, but Weymouth was a busy street, and Catherine and Sophie had no trouble keeping Christopher's interest engaged. When he paused to investigate a dead beetle, Catherine glanced in a shop window that housed bolts of gorgeous fabrics stacked on shelves. The sign over the door indicated the shop was home to London's finest modiste.

"Fancy a new gown, miss?" Sophie asked. "I'm so glad you've finally given over your mourning gowns. It's unhealthy to wear such dull colors for too long, my mam always says."

Catherine smiled. Sophie was forever quoting her mother's wisdom, though Catherine suspected the maid offered quite a bit of her own advice under the guise of the older woman.

"I've enough gowns," she said, gazing back at rich jewel tones inside the shop.

"Aye, but none in those colors." Sophie glanced around. "They remind me of your grandmother's gown. The one you wore last night." She'd lowered her voice, though there was no one around to hear.

Catherine smiled. The red velvet gown had made her feel like a queen. It was far more ornate than the demure gowns she and Mother Purcell had chosen for Catherine's Season.

Christopher tugged at her hand. "Let's go, Mama!"

"Don't pull on your mother, you scamp," Sophie chided.

"But you're so slow!"

"Run ahead to the corner and look around," Catherine said. "But don't go into the street!"

"Will you go out again, miss? Like you did last night?"

"Of course not! It was… It was just a little adventure." Catherine sighed because the party had taken her from the quiet dullness of her life and given her a night of excitement before she committed to marrying another man she didn't love. Were she honest with Sophie and herself, she longed to sneak out again to find a party like Mrs. Wilson's and see Robert Carlisle once more.

"It was *almost* an adventure," Sophie muttered.

Catherine sighed again as they continued to walk. Since the maid's earlier disappointment that Catherine hadn't kissed the man, the notion had plagued her. She remembered how he had dipped his head last night and how her heart had pounded in wild anticipation. If only they hadn't been interrupted! Oh, why had she been so timid, running home when she'd been on the verge of experiencing a true kiss of passion? Could she manage another night as the countess? She shook her head. It was too risky. Besides, she wouldn't even know how to go about finding the man.

No, she had too many responsibilities. Robert's kiss would have to remain a fantasy. It was time to return her focus to finding a husband. A wealthy husband. When a solicitor had arrived at the small estate in Chippenham with news that Mr. Purcell was the sole heir to Baron Tutley, it was the first they'd heard of him. While the sudden rise to nobility had been a pleasant surprise, they soon discovered the baron's estate was nearly bankrupt and plagued with creditors.

"I hope your next husband wants to live in London, miss." Sophie had taken to big city living like one born to it. The noise, dirt, and traffic did not disconcert her in the least. She loved the bustle of London.

Catherine forced a smile. "Since our best hope for a match is a wealthy merchant who will overlook the need to help an impoverished estate in return for a connection to a title, I think it is likely his business will require we live here."

"You don't give yourself your due, miss. *You* are what will attract a man first. Didn't you see yourself last night in that red dress? That's why you should buy more colors like that. Green, purple, and gold! Not those pale shades Mistress Purcell—I mean the baroness chose."

Catherine watched her boots as they peeked from beneath her skirts as she walked. Last night she had been astounded at how the red dress had made her look and feel. The red should have clashed with her reddish-blonde hair. Instead, her hair had appeared burnished gold. Her complexion, aided by a bit of blush at Sophie's insistence, had glowed against the rich color. No one had ever told her she was beautiful until last night. She'd lost track of how many men had paid her that compliment in the short time she was at Mrs. Wilson's party.

There was no way she could ask the Purcells for more gowns, however, even if she could convince Mother Purcell to allow her to choose the colors. They were wagering what little capital they had left for this London Season in the hopes Catherine would be able to marry well and save the barony for Christopher.

Would she become a different woman if she had a closet full of gowns like the red velvet? Was she the quiet Widow Purcell, mother, and dutiful daughter? Or was she really the daring woman who'd breezed her way uninvited into a wicked party?

"Mama! Come *on*! I can see it!" Catherine allowed her son to grab her hand and pull her more quickly down the street. She forced a smile. She knew her place in life.

Three

Robert absently kicked the toe of his boot against the side table, where he sat outside his father's suite of rooms. If his sire was going to summon him to the family home like a miscreant to account for his wicked behavior, he would at least act like one.

He stilled as he considered the one sin his father routinely harried him about was the death of William, Robert's older brother.

He stood abruptly and paced the gloomy hallway, ignoring the censorious stares of his ancestors who marked his passage from their framed portraits. He awoke that morning still unsettled, still perplexed by the countess's abrupt departure last night, and his mood had not improved upon receipt of his father's summons, dragging Robert from his bachelor's residence shortly after dawn.

After several minutes, the door to his father's rooms opened, and his father's personal physician exited, his polished black shoes squeaking in the tomb-like silence of the hallway.

Robert smiled ruefully at his melancholy thoughts. Tomb-like, indeed. Ill as his father was, the man was cantankerous enough he would probably outlive all of them.

"He is ready for you, my lord," the physician intoned, appearing very much like a butler at that moment. Then again, the duke seemed to make everyone feel like a servant. As the fourth Duke of Dervinshire, Hammond Carlisle carried himself with an air of superiority that came to him as easily as breathing. Robert had never seen anyone best his father, nor had he ever seen his father's stoic demeanor crack but once.

Robert took a deep breath and entered his father's rooms. The drapes were open in the private sitting room, but as Robert crossed into the bedchamber, the only illumination came from a brace of candles on a side table and the fireplace in the already overly warm room.

"What did the steward's letter say?" his father asked without preamble.

"Good morning to you too, Father. How are you feeling today?"

His father coughed into a handkerchief and glared. "I've coughed up half a lung since breakfast, and I've no flesh left on my bones." He held up an emaciated arm. "How do you think I feel? Now tell me what the steward's letter said."

Robert dutifully relayed the estate news from Bosworth Manor. The doctor and Robert's mother had forbidden the duke from carrying on the business of his estates. Since returning to England, Robert had taken over the correspondence and management of the family holdings, but his father demanded frequent briefings and issued countermanding orders to Robert's decisions. In general, his father was such a pain in the arse it would have been less troublesome for everyone if the old man had continued to do the work himself.

"Why didn't that idiot of a manager evict that tenant as I instructed last month?" the duke demanded.

Robert forced himself to take a breath before answering.

"That would be because I did not include that instruction in my last letter to him."

"Why not?" the duke demanded.

"Those tenants have been on the land for three generations—"

"And they are a year behind on their rents!" Splotches of red mottled the duke's waxy complexion.

"Because Tom Forrester lost a leg to gangrene after breaking it while working for *you*."

"Is it my fault the man is a clumsy oaf?"

Robert scowled. The duke had always been a stern landlord but consistently fair, quick to show mercy, and ready to aid tenants in distress, claiming it benefitted the estate to cultivate good feelings from those who provided the family's wealth. But then, he also used to be a loving father, a fact that made his anger toward Robert all the more painful.

Since the death of Robert's older brother William, the duke had grown embittered, showing neither patience nor mercy for the rest of the world. Robert didn't know how his mother bore the man's company. The weekly visits Robert endured always left him with a splitting headache and a bad taste in his mouth that no amount of whiskey could wash away.

"William would never have made such a soft-headed decision," his father said. "He knew the importance of preserving the integrity of his legacy."

Robert stiffened. This was the same lecture in the four-page, vitriol-filled letter his father sent two months after Robert left. He should have burned it immediately. Instead, he had carried it as a reminder of how he had failed his brother. The damned thing was in Robert's breast pocket even now, itemizing his many faults.

Today, however, he'd had enough. "You're wrong," he said, his voice edged with anger.

His father, clearly on the verge of saying something else, froze. "What did you say?" he hissed.

"You're wrong. William would not have evicted a man so grievously injured in the service of our family. He would have had the decency to allow the man time to recuperate, time for his sons to grow old enough to aid him."

"You dare speak of William so? He was the best of men, the best of sons!"

"Indeed, I do dare." Robert ignored the sting of the duke's words. Frankly, it was a surprise he still felt anything at them. He should be inured to such hurt by now. "If you imply that William was not a good man to show compassion to those in his service, *you* are the one maligning his memory."

"You base cur," his father said. "You are not worthy to say his name!" The duke's voice rose until he was shouting. "Ever have you been envious of him. It is no doubt what led you to kill him. You could not bear to be compared—don't you turn your back on me!" He began coughing violently.

Robert's mother rushed into the room. "What is going on? Robert, what did you say to upset him so?" She gently pressed the duke back into his pillows then fetched him a glass of water. Hatred and pain filled the glare the man gave Robert, who turned and left.

The butler held the front door open and handed Robert his top hat.

"Robert!" his mother cried.

Surprised, for his mother never raised her voice in either anger or delight, he turned to see her quickly descend the staircase. He removed his hat then nodded for the butler to close the door.

"Why must you antagonize your father, Robert?"

He frowned. Though his mother never contradicted the duke when he was verbally accosting Robert, she had never spoken sharply to him, instead offering quiet support through a gentle hand on his arm or a sympathetic smile. To have her now blame him for his father's foul temper stung more than Robert cared to admit.

"As it seems my simply taking a breath antagonizes him, I fear there is no help for it, my lady."

Her strained expression softened, and she reached out a hand to him, which he pretended not to see.

"Forgive me, Robert. I didn't mean to sound so accusing. Your father worsens daily, and I fear the strain is taking its toll on my temperament."

Robert instantly felt contrite. Besides the burden of caring for his father, his mother constantly had to play peacemaker between the duke and him. He took her still extended hand and raised it to his lips.

"I'm the one who needs forgiveness, Mother. I fear I lose patience with his constant criticism. I can do nothing right in his eyes. I don't mean to add to your worries."

"He truly does approve of the work you've been doing," she said.

He smiled at her blatant falsehood. "You needn't try to make me feel better, Mother. I am quite used to him by now. He will always believe I maliciously killed William and will certainly never believe I could fill my brother's shoes." In truth, Robert knew he could never be as good a man as William.

A streak of pain marred the duchess's expression. "And you still blame yourself for your brother's death."

Robert shrugged uncomfortably. Though he had hardened himself to hearing his father rant about William's death, hearing his mother speak of it made him ill at ease.

Giving in to impulse, Robert kissed her brow. "Have a care for yourself, my lady, lest you fall ill as well. Then where would we all be?"

He turned to go but stopped at his mother's touch on his arm.

"There is one thing that may ease your father, perhaps even help mend your breach."

Robert knew nothing short of William coming back from the grave would mend fences between the duke and him, but he tilted his head in question.

"If you took a bride, started a family."

He frowned immediately, and his mother rushed on. "I know worry about the title weighs heavily on him."

"Because he thinks I will muck that up as well?"

His mother ignored his words. "You are of an age to wed and settle down. All I'm saying is don't let spite toward your father keep you from looking. I do believe a grandson would soften his grief greatly."

Robert kept his expression placid, though his emotions roiled. From the moment Robert was old enough to understand, his father had lectured him and his brother about the importance of carrying on the family dynasty and preserving the ducal lineage. Until William's death, Robert had gleefully ignored the lessons. It was his brother's duty to marry and produce an heir. Now, however, it was one more point of contention. The letter in his pocket reminded him that he was no fit replacement for William, and neither would any child Robert might father. The duke had implied Robert was *glad* his brother was dead.

Glad, when even now, the pain of missing his brother was like a knife in his gut. Losing his brother had been like losing a limb. Add the guilt of knowing he was responsible for William's death, that *he* was the reason William would never marry the girl he loved, have the houseful of children he wanted, and Robert would gladly have faced the hangman's noose or the French guillotine if it would have brought his brother back.

One night in Athens last year, drunk on ouzo, Robert reread his father's missive and came to a decision. He would never marry, never have a family. It was small recompense for what William had lost, but it was all Robert had to offer. His plan had the added benefit of denying his father's life's goal of seeing the next generation groomed as the Duke of Dervinshire. It was petty and mean, but it was the only power Robert had in the face of his father's hatred. For all Robert cared, the title could rot.

Looking at his mother's face, he noticed worry lines and threads of gray hair that hadn't been present three years ago. It was her letter, not his father's, which had returned him to England. She hadn't asked him to come home. She'd simply told him of her days spent caring for his father and trying to manage the estate. He'd read her exhaustion and despair in the wavering script, and his heart had clenched with guilt. She had also included a missive from Violet, the girl his brother had intended to marry. Violet's letter begged an audience as soon as possible as she had something vitally important to beg of him. William had asked Robert to watch over his love, and abandoning Violet was yet another way Robert had failed his brother.

He'd packed his bags that night and set out for England the next day, certain he'd return to find Violet destitute and heartbroken, wasting away. Instead, he'd found her healthy and radiant. She'd fallen in love and had begged Robert's forgiveness. Robert had felt another stab of grief for his brother, but there was nothing to forgive. There were too many years of life ahead for a young woman to spend those years in mourning. William would not have wanted that for her, and neither did Robert. He'd given his blessing, as much as it was his to give, and Violet had promised to always remember William.

Now, staring at the other woman who would never forget William, Robert found he did not have the heart to tell her of his intent to never marry. He had returned for Violet, but he stayed for his mother. For all that Robert had thought it would be easier to let the duke run the estate, the man *was* bedridden and weak of heart, and there was only so much he could direct from his bedchamber. Robert's mother had done her best over the last year, but the effort of caring for the duke as well as the business of the estate was simply too great. Robert had been shocked to see how much she'd aged during his years abroad, and there was no way he could leave again, even if it meant facing his father's hatred every day.

He could not tell her he would not marry, but neither could he lie to her. "I will attend some events," he said, knowing she would believe he would do so to meet the current crop of marriage-minded debutantes.

"That's all I ask," she said, her expression lightening with a smile.

R

ROBERT MOUNTED HIS HORSE, and as he urged it into a gentle canter, debated where to go. He needed something to take his mind off the encounter with his father. Robert had heard of a new ancient Greek exhibit at the British Museum and headed that way, hoping a few hours amongst the relics would restore his perspective on life because he knew from experience that relief did not come at the bottom of a bottle. He guided his mount to the private stable, where he rented a stall. It was halfway between his bachelor's lodging and the museum. He would leave his horse and walk the rest of the way.

His tight muscles loosened as he walked, and by the time he climbed the entry stairs to the museum, he felt more himself. His rank allowed him to take private after-hours tours, but he quite enjoyed visiting during public exhibition hours. He derived as much pleasure from people's responses to the arti-facts as he got from viewing them himself.

He spent nearly an hour in front of the Parthenon sculptures, but to see some of the very statuary he had marveled at in Greece sitting here in England was simultaneously satisfying and disturbing. While he liked that he could visit the sculptures more easily, it somehow seemed wrong to have taken the works from the country where they were made and had stood for thousands of years.

When his contentious visit with his father was but a remote thought, he decided to stop by the Rosetta Stone exhibit before returning to his scheduled appointments.

With the museum unusually crowded, Robert weaved through groups of visitors. Their hum of conversation added an air of excitement that infused his blood. Finally, he turned into the hall where the Rosetta Stone sat prominently on a low pedestal—and stopped at the sight of his Russian countess.

Well, not *his* Russian countess, of course, but *the* Russian countess. She had dressed very differently today, in a somber gray gown with a matching pelisse, the long coat hiding the curves he'd admired last night. She wore her hair pulled into a restrained knot low on her neck, its color seeming more red than gold next to the severe black bonnet perched on her head.

Despite her less-than-glamorous ensemble, to his eyes, she still glowed as when she'd worn her lush velvet gown. A sprinkling of freckles dusted her complexion, and lashes, several shades darker than her hair, framed her sparkling gray eyes. Once again, the fullness of her mouth drew his attention, and he couldn't help but want to feel her lips pressed to his own.

She smiled down at someone, and Robert dodged a few more bystanders to get a better view. A small boy stood beside her, holding her hand and staring intently at the Rosetta Stone. He frowned as if trying to decide what could possibly be so interesting about the dark slab.

A strange sinking sensation harried the pit of Robert's stomach. Despite the boy's darker coloring, he was clearly the countess's son, which meant a count existed somewhere. It was ridiculous to feel such acute disappointment. He'd spoken to the woman for a quarter of an hour at most. Nonetheless, he moved closer. He didn't intend to speak with her, but her radically different appearance intrigued him; it implied she had many facets, and he wondered how many other sides to her there were. Not that he was likely to find out now. He wouldn't pursue a married woman. Still, it could do no harm to look on her one last time, and if he heard her pouty Russian accent, well, he would have one more thing to cherish when he remembered her.

The crowds shifted again, and he ended up behind and to her left—enough to watch her in quarter profile. A quick glance revealed no man attended her, and Robert turned his attention back to her face. She smiled at something the young boy said.

"The words do look a bit like chicken scratches, but that's simply because we don't understand them. If we read"—she frowned and looked at the placard beside the stone—"ancient Egyptian or ancient Greek, it would make perfect sense to us." She spoke with no Russian accent. In fact, she spoke with a bit of a West Country lilt.

Robert frowned and wondered if he'd mistaken her identity and had perhaps responded to a woman with similar coloring. He'd spent so little time in the countess's company, it was conceivable he didn't remember her precisely, but then she laughed at something the boy said—that throaty, full-bodied laugh, and Robert knew it was her. Confused, he shook his head. Had she played him for a fool? Not just him, of course, but everyone at the party. Even the Lord Chamberlain.

The crowds around the exhibit thinned a little more, and the only people left were the mysterious countess, her son, and a maid.

Robert stepped forward and pretended to study the stone.

"Ah, for some reason, I thought it also had the text in Russian." He turned his head to the woman.

She gasped and quickly covered her mouth.

"Clearly, I was mistaken about the Russian." As he continued to stare at her, two bright spots of color bloomed high on her cheeks. After a moment, she dropped her hand and pressed her lips together in a flat line.

"Why, Countess, no cutting rejoinder to set me in my place?"

The young boy tugged at his mother's skirts. "Let's go, Mama. This is just an old rock."

"Sophie," the woman said. "Take Christopher to the next room, will you? I'll join you momentarily."

The maid cast a questioning glance at Robert before taking the boy's hand and leading him away.

The woman he knew as Alisa watched them go then turned back to Robert, though she kept her eyes downcast. Her entire demeanor was so different than the confident, sharp-witted person he'd met the night before that he would have thought he'd accosted the wrong woman until she looked up at him, guilt all over her expressive face.

As their eyes met, he again experienced that disturbing flutter in his chest—as if he had tripped and nearly tumbled in front of an oncoming carriage. He forced himself to ignore the flutter and lifted his brows in question, trying to stare her into submission. It seemed to work for a moment, but then she straightened her spine and lifted her chin. At the return of the confident countess, he had the sudden urge to sweep her into his arms and kiss her.

"My lord?"

If not for the tightening around her eyes or the way she twisted her hands, he wouldn't have realized how nervous she was. That she seemed worried and perhaps a bit scared should have pleased him—she had played him for a fool, after all. Still, he found he did not wish to cause her distress, nor did he wish to let her off the hook so easily.

"You are clearly neither a Russian nor a countess. However, I'm sure there is a logical explanation for your charade last night."

At his tone and words, she relaxed slightly. She still clutched her hands in front of her, but the tightness left her eyes, and a small, wry grin tugged at the corner of her mouth.

"No, I would say logic was the farthest thing from my mind when I put on that gown and accent, my lord."

"Then what *was* on your mind?"

"I—" She froze as if there were too many words in her mouth to choose only one or even a sentence of them.

"Come now," he said, trying to convince her to confess. "Surely your husband did not encourage such dangerous play, which leads me to wonder if he even knew about your little charade. Tell me, *Countess*, did you deceive him as you did all of us at the party?" He didn't mean to sound judgmental, but his words did not come across with the teasing implication he'd intended.

"My husband—" She took a breath and began again. "My husband passed some time ago."

He bowed slightly. "I'm sorry to hear that. I'm sure he would have offered you a bit of rational advice regarding your choice of entertainment. So, it begs the question, why *did* you pretend to be a Russian countess? Are you preparing for a role in Drury Lane? I daresay you have my endorsement." He offered an encouraging smile.

"No, I—" She glanced over her shoulder at the maid and the young boy standing in the doorway. The boy had clearly lost interest in the dusty offerings of the museum and tried to climb the leg of a bit of statuary.

"I must go," she said.

"I feel I must insist on an explanation. It's not every day I'm made to play the fool."

"I didn't— It wasn't about you. I didn't even know who you were."

"Then tell me your reasons."

At the door, the maid had to physically keep the boy from running to his mother.

"Another time, I promise," she said. "I must leave!"

He caught her hand. "The Haymarket Theatre. Tomorrow night, nine o'clock. You can join me in my box."

"What? I can't—"

She stared at her hand in his and then looked up at him. The pull of attraction he still experienced must have finally reached her, for her breath caught, and her pupils dilated slightly. The transition from nervous young mother to confident siren was nearly instantaneous.

"Please," he said.

She stared at his mouth for a moment before looking him in the eye. "Very well. I shall meet you there."

With that, she turned and fled, scooping up her young son before rushing out of sight.

ROBERT STOOD on the front steps of the theater, scanning the crowd for the Russian countess. Well, the *false* Russian countess. He was intrigued by the story behind the woman's double life—Russian countess by night, simply dressed English mother by day. He wondered if perhaps she was a courtesan. Very few "respectable" women attended *demimonde* events such as Mrs. Wilson's parties. One noblewoman, Viscountess Letitia Beaumont, was an exception in part due to her widowed state as well as her biting wit and sharp tongue; she generally cut down someone before they had a chance to malign her. She may well have been at the party two nights ago, though Robert hadn't noticed as he'd focused on other...entertainment.

However, something told him the Russian *countess*, though possessed of a biting wit and sharp tongue herself, was not of similar character to the viscountess. Besides, if the woman he hoped to meet tonight were of nobility, he'd surely have seen her before. On the other hand, if she were a courtesan, parties such as the other night would be quite common for her, especially if she sought a new protector. That thought gave him a strange thrill, though he'd never kept a mistress.

He spotted her as she stepped down from her hired coach. Even from afar, he found her breathtaking. He also found it hard to believe other men were not staring at her as she made her way up the shallow stairs. Relief flashed across her face when she noticed him.

"You came." He met her halfway and took her arm.

"I did not think I had a choice," she said, her Russian accent in place.

"Of course you did. I've no idea your real name or where to find you. It was sheer luck I visited the museum at the same time you did."

She nodded but did not answer as he led her inside and up the curving staircase to the level of his theater box. He'd expected a witty retort, but tonight she acted more like the young mother in drab gray despite her elaborate red and white embroidered gown—unveiled as he helped her out of her cloak. The gold satin cloak exhibited frayed edges and deep creases as if folded in a storage box for too long—information Robert tucked away for later.

Her gasp drew his attention.

"What is it?" he asked, joining her at the front of the box.

"It's— Well, it's the view. Look at all the people," she said in awe, her Russian accent evaporating.

"Haven't you been to the theater before?"

"Yes, but I've only sat down below," she said, indicating the main floor where patrons sat cheek-by-jowl. "You can see everyone from up here."

"And they can see you," he said.

Her smile faded, and she quickly stepped away from the opening, moving nearly to the back of the box where her face was in shadow.

He followed her to the dark recesses of the small booth. "Don't you wish to be seen?" he asked. "You portrayed yourself as a Russian countess at a somewhat licentious party. Surely the thrill of being seen in the Dervinshire box would appeal to your sense of drama."

"Who are the Dervinshires?"

He grinned, wondering if she were pretending ignorance. "My father is the Duke of Dervinshire."

"Duke? You truly are a marquess, then?" Even in the dim light at the back of the box, Robert could tell she was pale.

"Did you think I lied the other night?"

"I thought it likely," she said with a shaky laugh. "After all, I did."

"Ah, so you admit it?"

"I—"

She continued to stare at him, seeming even more nervous than when she'd arrived. Below, he heard the applause as the curtain opened.

"Are you going to expose me?" she finally asked.

"Expose you? I don't even know who you are, and why would I do such a thing even if I did know?"

She licked her lips then drew the lower one between her teeth. He tried not to stare as the plump bit of flesh slowly escaped her even, white teeth, but it was hard to ignore the intense urge to kiss said lip and judge if it was as soft and as sweet as it looked.

She parted her lips in a soft gasp. Glancing up, he realized she knew he'd been staring at her mouth. The heat between them was palpable—like he stood before a stove, though the fire burned inside him. His heart pounded, and his blood pooled in his groin, which made his tight breeches uncomfortable. He laughed softly. He was as aroused as a green lad with his first woman, and he'd not even kissed her.

"Tell me," he murmured. "Tell me your story."

She shook her head.

"Tell me." He stepped closer to her.

"There is nothing to tell. I have no story," she whispered.

The crowd below laughed uproariously at something on stage, but at the back of his theater box, it seemed as if he and his mysterious date were in their own little world. He realized that dim light or not, the people in the boxes opposite would still be able to see them. He turned to face her, so his body blocked hers from view.

"Everyone has a story. I confess to being excessively curious to hear yours. Come now," he urged as he sensed her wavering. "I've no reason to expose your secrets, however tawdry they might be."

At that, she laughed, some of the *countess's* spark visibly returning.

"My story is far from tawdry, my lord. In fact, it may put you to sleep from boredom."

"Then share it with me. I shall struggle to remain sentient."

"We are missing the play. Don't you wish to see it?" she asked.

"I find your character much more fascinating than those on stage. And you are clearly a better player than tonight's actors."

She pressed her lips together and stared hard. He resisted a smile at her obvious ire. Instead, he tried to keep his expression placid and encouraging. She glanced around him, and he realized the play was in full swing.

"Perhaps we might step outside, then? Surely you do not intend to lurk at the back of your theater box all night?"

At her clipped tone, he did smile. "An excellent notion," he said with a brief bow. "I should have thought of it myself." He gathered their cloaks and reached to open the door behind her. As he did, he caught a hint of her clean, fresh scent—part lemon verbena, part soft woman. He paused for a moment, inhaling her essence.

She tensed at his nearness, and he stepped back, allowing her plenty of room to exit.

He helped her into her cloak, and once downstairs, they stepped outside to find a heavy fog had rolled in, cloaking the street in a damp blanket that made it seem as if they were the only people in the city.

A footman appeared out of the mist and offered to fetch Robert's carriage.

The countess, as he knew her, shook her head. "I would prefer to take a walk, my lord."

"I give you my word you shall come to no harm in my carriage." Robert made his promise even as he could tell she was uncomfortable with the notion. At another tiny shake of her head, Robert inclined his. "Very well. I know of a small tavern near here. It was a famous coffee house twenty years ago, and one may still enjoy a cup if you don't care for ale."

She seemed to consider his proposal for a moment, then nodded. Robert smiled and tucked her hand in the crook of his arm before he guided her down the block and into the warm and welcoming pub. The establishment did not have a private room for ladies as most public houses did, but there was a bit of an alcove at the back that would afford them privacy and keep her from the noisier elements in the main room.

He caught the eye of the barmaid and ordered two coffees before he headed to a table. "You'll find it a stronger brew than tea, but—"

"I've had coffee before," she said, her tone curt. He dipped his head and held out a chair for her.

She was silent for a long moment, curiously glancing around the room, then she finally met his gaze. "I don't quite know where to begin."

"Perhaps you could start with your name."

"My— Oh!" she said with a wry grin. "You wouldn't rather simply call me Countess?"

"I would if you were one."

She raised a haughty eyebrow. "I may not be a countess, but now you're implying my manners are not the equivalent of a noblewoman's."

"Not at all. However, I've known very few noblewomen who didn't enjoy showing off their finery at the theater, fewer still who accompany their children to museums, and none who would dress as a governess, though gray does become you," he said, thinking of her somber, though well-fitting gown of the day before.

"Would a governess wear a gown such as this?" She sat back to display her tightly fitted and lavishly decorated bodice.

"Indeed not," he said with appreciation, glad her reticence was yielding to the drollness of their first encounter. "Nor does it appear to be of this century. Where on earth did you find it?"

She glanced down and fingered the heavy skirts. "That is part of the story." She appeared lost in thought for a moment, then looked up suddenly. "Oh very well, then."

While the barmaid placed the coffee before them, the woman seated opposite him remained silent, then she toyed with the cup, spinning it in its saucer. He waited patiently, studying the small cluster of freckles on her nose and the flush of color on her cheeks.

"I have to marry again. Rather quickly."

He froze, a dozen thoughts filling his head. Had she lied about not knowing who he was and contrived their meeting at the party with the hope of ensnaring him? It was a poor plan if that was her hope. Disappointment replaced his earlier interest. He'd so hoped her story was more interesting than that.

"I hate to break it to you, but I'm not your man."

She frowned. "What do you— Oh, no, that's not what I meant." She took a deep breath, clearly flustered. "Please let me begin again."

Her distress seemed genuine, and Robert relaxed back in his seat.

She took a small sip of coffee and wrinkled her nose. She set the cup down and pushed it to the center of the table.

"My husband died two years ago. It was unexpected."

"I'm sorry," Robert replied automatically.

"My son and I remained with the Purcells after my husband's death—we'd lived with them before, you see. Jasper was quite fond of his parents, and—" She shook her head as if telling herself this wasn't relevant. "The Purcells have a small estate in Chippenham, and we lived quite comfortably until recently."

"They're kicking you out?"

"No, no. You must understand, they have always been kind. I have no other family. They treat me as their daughter and provide everything Christopher and I could need. Six months ago, the squire learned he was the sole heir to the Barony of Tutley. I don't think he even knew he was related. Unfortunately, the last baron— Well, he was rather profligate with his money and had left a great deal of debt."

"I take it the property is linked to the debt?" Robert asked.

She nodded. "There is an estate and the house in London, but we can sell none of it."

It was a common story. One bad steward of a title could destroy what generations of his forebears had built and leave generations more to clean up the mess.

"What about the estate in Chippenham? Could your father-in-law sell it?"

"Well, yes, of course he can. It's not entailed, but it wouldn't be enough. At least that's what the solicitor said."

"So, you've come looking for a wealthy husband to bail the family out?" He sighed heavily, affecting a look of disappointment. "Joining the ranks of the mercenary husband-hunters." He shook his head though he struggled not to smile. He enjoyed teasing her.

"I'm not— It's not mercenary! It's— Well, yes, perhaps it is. But my in-laws have been very good to me. It is the least I can do, especially seeing as how my son will one day inherit the title and the lands."

He took a sip of coffee while he thought. Gads, it *was* awful. He pushed his cup away as well.

"All this is riveting, *Countess*," he said, the emphasis on the title to remind her she still hadn't given him her name. "It doesn't answer my question, however."

"What—"

"Why would a gently bred, respectable young widow such as yourself impersonate a Russian countess, venture into the not-so-respectable realm of the *demimonde*, and challenge the Lord High Chancellor to a game of chess?"

Four

CATHERINE RETRIEVED her coffee cup from the center of the table and pretended to drink it. Despite what she'd told this man, tonight was her first experience with the bitter brew, and she did not care for it at all. Having the coffee at hand did, however, provide a perfect reason to stall while she debated what to tell him. She'd only accepted the drink because he was having one, and she didn't want to seem provincial. Now she wished she'd asked him to order a mug of ale, though she'd never had one of those either. She set the cup down then patted her lips with the serviette, which at one point in its life had no doubt been white.

She glanced up to see him looking at her, and a pang of longing lodged in her chest. The man was too good-looking by half, and he talked *with* her. More than that, he listened. Yes, most of their conversation would never be deemed polite or appropriate discourse, but that made it all the more appealing.

Small talk with the men she'd met at the few social events she and the Purcells had attended had been awkward and stilted, at least from her perspective. She had so little life experience to share, and the men hadn't even appeared interested in where she'd lived before London, much less what she thought about anything.

Somehow, when she spoke with Lord Dunsbury, she never ran out of things to say. He made her feel interesting. Granted, in their first meeting, she'd simply invented things to talk about, but the novelty of the experience still acted like a powerful aphrodisiac that made her attraction to him disconcerting.

As she stared into eyes as dark as the liquid in her cup, she decided to lay bare her soul. "Have you ever found yourself wishing your life was drastically different than it is?"

His expression shuttered before he looked away and shifted in his seat. When he looked back, he'd pressed his mouth into a flat line, and Catherine experienced an insatiable curiosity to know what demons plagued him.

After a moment, he smiled, and in that instant, like a flower blossoming in the sun, her whole body reacted.

"Describe your life prior to the emergence of the Russian countess. What makes living as Alisa Borodinicha more interesting than life as… Well, as whoever you actually are. You still haven't told me your real name, you know."

She laughed. "I am Catherine Purcell." She picked up the coffee cup, thought better of it, and set it back down. "I shall have to tell Sophie about this strange brew," she said, forgetting for the moment that she'd pretended to be a sophisticated coffee drinker.

"Sophie is your maid I saw yesterday, right?"

Catherine nodded. "She's quite keen to try every new experience London has to offer. She's never been outside of Chippenham before, you see," she said, omitting the fact she was no more well-traveled than her maid.

"So, I now know your real name, your alias, and the fact your maid is of an adventurous bent. What you haven't told me is why."

"Why what?" Catherine asked, stalling as she reconsidered her impulse to bare her soul. It was one thing to tell him her name, even to tell him she was on a rather mercenary mission to marry a wealthy man. It was quite another to share her most closely held desires—those things she could certainly never share with the Purcells who represented her only family in the world. Even Sophie didn't really know what had propelled Catherine to don a costume and present herself as a Russian countess and infiltrate a party of London's more off-color members. To the maid, it was a simple lark, a peek into a world Catherine would never again experience, much like tasting coffee.

"Why, Mistress Purcell? Why risk your reputation, some might even say your very future, by putting yourself amid a chess game with the Lord Chamberlain at the home of one of London's most notorious courtesans?"

"The chess game was an accident. I only intended to watch the goings-on of the party. I tried not to even talk to anyone, but people kept approaching me."

Lord Dunsbury gazed at her in a way that made a heated flush sweep down her body, eliciting an awareness between her legs that made her breath quicken.

"It's easy to understand why."

Flustered, Catherine folded and refolded the linen serviette on the table. "Yes, well, once someone discovered I was Russian, the Lord Chamberlain insisted on testing his prowess at chess."

"And you, of course, couldn't let him win. You had to defend the motherland?"

"Actually, I was going to let him beat me until he implied that as a woman, I couldn't be expected to understand strategy. I still should have thrown the game—it drew far too much attention, but I found I simply could *not* allow him to think me unintelligent."

Lord Dunsbury smiled—another slow sensuous tilt of his mouth that made her feel self-conscious and bold all at once. He continued to stare, and after several long moments, raised his brows in question.

"Oh, very well," she said with an exasperated sigh. Though he might share her story and ruin her reputation, she wanted to tell him because there was a chance he'd understand. It was a ridiculous assumption, and yet his self-deprecating sense of humor the night they met and the fact he'd appeared intrigued rather than angered when he discovered her deception, allowed her to believe she could trust him.

"I grew up not far from Chippenham. My father was a scholar. He wrote histories but never managed to get them published. When I was eighteen, he contracted a wasting disease. He—" It was funny how four years later, talking about her father's death still made her throat catch. "He was gone within the year and my mother soon after."

"How did she die?"

She smiled, though she couldn't hide her sadness. "Grief, I suppose. The doctor could find no other cause."

He nodded. "Then the Purcells took you in?"

"My father arranged the marriage. I had danced with Jasper once at an assembly. I suppose he thought we would suit."

"Who thought that? Your father or Jasper?"

Catherine frowned. Robert's question was one she couldn't answer. She'd often wondered why Jasper had agreed to marry her. During their brief marriage, he was unfailingly polite but always so removed. Their relationship was one of distant acquaintances at best.

"After Jasper died, the Purcells, well, Mother Purcell, insisted we remain in mourning. We attended no social events after the usual year of seclusion, and we had very few visitors. I only had Christopher, Sophie, and the estate's library to occupy my days. Then the news came about the barony and the debt.

My remarrying seemed the best, the only, option. We thought perhaps a wealthy businessman would find the connection with the title appealing."

"How are your prospects?"

Catherine shook her head. "Thin. The Purcells have few acquaintances in London, and wealthy merchants have been scarce at the events we have attended. There is one gentleman who has come to call." She couldn't repress a small shudder.

"That bad?" Lord Dunsbury asked.

"He's older than the baron!"

As she tried to think of a way to explain the urge that had inspired her enactment, she stared at the table's grain, polished smooth by years of use. After a moment, she looked up.

"If I end up married to him, I will be safe and my son provided for, and some widows long for nothing more than that, but I felt that if I didn't do *something*, if I didn't see even just a tiny bit of the world beyond the safe boundaries of my life thus far, I would go mad. Or fade into nothingness, into a pale reflection of who I truly am. So, I had to have an experience that tested me, terrified me, and made me feel *alive*. Just one night to know who I could be. Then I could return to..."

She took a deep breath after her rush of words and realized she gripped the edges of the table. She forced herself to place her hands in her lap.

Lord Dunsbury sat still as stone, his expression stunned.

He must think me insane.

Five

In truth, he'd suspected an explanation along the lines of a bored young matron looking for a bit of a thrill, a peccadillo. What he hadn't anticipated was how much deeper her desires went than mere titillation. Though he'd certainly had more than enough excitement and adventure in his life, her passion and bone-deep desire to be more than she was, struck a chord within him. The feeling left him invigorated yet uncomfortable. Invigorated because it made him want to improve himself, and uncomfortable because it made him think of things in his life he'd rather forget.

He stared at her as she composed herself. Her flush of fervor disappeared, and her expression became wary. He didn't want her to retreat into herself, no matter his discomfort, so he smiled.

"You are quite an intrepid young woman."

She frowned even as a wry smile curved her mouth. "I'm not entirely certain that's a good thing."

"It is absolutely a good thing," he said before he signaled for a maid and ordered a bottle of claret.

"I really must return home," Catherine said.

"Spare me but a few more minutes. I have a proposition I believe will greatly benefit you."

Hot flags of color crested her cheeks, and she straightened her spine in earnest. "I realize my actions may have led you to believe—"

"That you are an extraordinarily intelligent young woman who would be wasted on the quality of men you are likely to encounter in your present situation."

She pressed her lips together, her expression puzzled. The barmaid returned with the wine and two glasses. Robert served, and Catherine took a cautious sip. From her exclamation of delight, she liked it. Robert smiled as he watched her, but then she glanced up at him.

"What do you mean?" she asked.

"I mean a woman with your *joie de vivre*, as the French say, should be introduced to more than mere barristers and fringe nobility." Worried she might think he criticized the Purcells, he shook his head. "Not that you couldn't make a splendid match in that realm. I simply propose to give you access to a greater pool of potential suitors."

"A pool? You make them sound as appetizing as fish."

Robert shrugged. "One might say the same of the entire marriage process."

"Are you not seeking a wife? Surely a man in your position—"

"No," Robert said, his tone brusque and final. "I am not the marrying type."

She nodded, studying him, no doubt wondering at his response. An awkward silence ticked by.

"How do you propose to give me access to this fishier pool?" she finally asked, no small amount of skepticism in her voice.

"For better or worse, *a man in my position*, as you adroitly described me, is not without some social consequence here in London. If I suggest to a few influential hostesses that the Purcells are delightful company, the invitations will quickly pour in."

Catherine frowned. "Won't they want to know why you are making such a recommendation?"

He waved his hand dismissively. "I'll let everyone know I met the family while taking the waters at Bath and was impressed with the baron's wit and intellect."

A short laugh escaped Catherine. "Dear heavens, don't say that!"

"Then perhaps I should mention the baroness's patronage of the arts?"

Catherine pressed her lips together, and he could see the amused dismay in her gaze.

"Not accurate either?"

She smoothed her expression. "They are very nice people. Any hostess would be pleased to have them as a guest."

"I will imply I knew the previous baron, then."

"Why?"

"I thought we settled that. I'll explain to the ladies—"

"Not the public excuse. The real reason. Why would you go out of your way for someone you barely know?"

"It's hardly out of my—"

"I won't become your mistress," she said, her flushed face betraying either embarrassment or indignation. Perhaps both.

"The thought never crossed my mind." It was a lie. He'd wanted her from the moment she declared some things were better when drawn out. His attraction to her had grown steadily since. Even now, sitting across from her in a noisy public house while talking about her marrying someone, all he could think about was unlacing her from that confining dress and exploring the treasures beneath. For the first time in his life, however, he wanted more than a woman's body. He was fascinated with this country widow false Russian countess. It was a startling realization.

"Then why, I repeat, would you make such an offer?" She put her elbows on the table and leaned forward, staring at him intently.

"Because I can," he said bluntly. "It costs me nothing to make a suggestion to some of my mother's friends, and I like to think I do have the capacity to aid my fellow man." When she continued to look at him with suspicion, he nearly smiled. "Besides, I find you interesting. Not many women in your position would dare assume a double life and attend a party of actors and courtesans."

This reasoning seemed to resonate with her as she relaxed back in her chair. "I wouldn't exactly call it a double life."

"No? What would you call it?"

"Merely a humble woman's wish for a tiny adventure," she said, her expression that of a prim spinster.

"In which you portrayed yourself as a Russian countess, affected a convincing accent, and defeated a member of the royal household at chess—a game, I must inform you, the Lord Chamberlain has long prided himself on mastering."

"Be that as it may," she said, her gaze full of mischief. "It was not a role I intended to assume more than once." She glanced down at her skirts. "Well, twice."

She studied him for a long moment while tapping her satin-gloved fingers on the table. It seemed she carefully weighed her next words. Robert inhaled and held his breath, waiting for her response.

Finally, she tilted her head. "It is a most gracious offer, and I would be remiss and ungrateful not to accept it. However, while I am not above accepting assistance, I should feel better if there was something I could do to return the favor."

A little jolt surged along his nerves as if he'd walked across a wool rug in winter and touched a doorknob. She hadn't meant a sexual favor, but his body responded as if she had. He forced himself to count to ten, affecting a look of concentration as if trying to think of a favor he could ask. He realized he had to carefully present the other half of his proposal lest she thought he had more nefarious motives.

"Well, now you mention it, I find myself in need of a bit of adventure as well."

A small crease appeared between his companion's coppery brows. "What type of adventure do you mean?"

"Oh, nothing as dramatic as impersonating a foreign noble, I assure you. It occurs to me, however, that I quite enjoy conversing with you. I find your outlook on life refreshing." At her disbelieving expression, he rushed to explain. "If for no other reason than because your background is so different from mine. In addition, I find Countess Borodinicha's company to be most...diverting. I should very much like to further my acquaintance with her."

"But—" She covered her décolletage with her hand in what he realized was a nervous gesture. "What is it you're proposing?"

"Only that on those evenings you and your relatives are not attending one of the more elite *ton* events to which I will see you invited, then I should like you to join me at an event such as the party at which we first met."

She frowned. "Why?"

"I told you, I find you fascinating. Your lack of regard for my title is refreshing, and I quite enjoy matching intellect with you. It is so very difficult to have a battle of wits with an unarmed person, you know. Also, you are clearly intelligent enough not to do something so silly as to fall in love with me."

Her lips twitched, and he knew she was trying hard not to smile.

"So, we would...converse during these outings?"

"Yes. Occasionally dance if the venue calls for it. Who

knows, we might even find the opportunity for a game of chess."

Watching her closely, he noticed the wash of color that suffused her from bodice to brow, and he suddenly remembered the Russian countess's *disrobing* chess. He bit his inner cheek in an effort not to laugh and embarrass her. "The English style of chess, that is."

She didn't respond to his comment, and he wasn't sure if she pretended not to understand or simply ignored the reference. The urge to grin was nearly unbearable.

"I shall wish to have some evenings at home. Christopher needs my attention, and I cannot sleep the day away after returning so late each night."

"Certainly," he replied, anticipation smoldering in his chest.

"We must not go anywhere I will be recognized. This... bargain is to help me find a suitable husband, which I will not be able to do if my reputation is in tatters."

"No one will realize the Russian countess on my arm is the respectable widow Purcell, I promise. That does bring up a consideration, however. Have you any other countess-suitable gowns. Not that I don't find this one delectable, but you will draw attention if you wear it every time we are out."

She smoothed the velvet of her skirts. "This was my grandmother's. She was Russian, though not a countess. She was a member of a noble household. Similar to a lady-in-waiting, I believe."

"That would explain your facility with the accent."

She smiled, and her expression softened as if lost in memories.

"Perhaps I might order some gowns—"

"No," she said, her tone sharp.

Robert held up his hands in acquiescence. He should have known a respectable woman would not accept such personal gifts as clothing.

"I will arrange something," she said.

"Then you accept my propo—my friendship offer?"

She took a deep breath and let it out slowly. "Very well. When shall our first assignation occur?"

At her choice of words, he inwardly chuckled, choosing not to show how she amused him. "I shall seek you out for a dance at the first *ton* event to which you and the Purcells are invited. We shall plan from there. However, there is—" He tried to phrase his next words with care. "There is one more requirement I must ask of you."

"I'll not attend a boxing match with you. If that's what you intend to ask, this agreement is over."

He smiled. "No, it's not that. I must insist our relationship remain exclusively platonic."

She stared at him as if trying to decipher his meaning. "I already said I would not engage in—"

"Let me clarify. I wish our relationship to remain on an intellectual level."

She frowned, clearly more confused. He sighed as he realized he needed to be explicit. "I mean, I should not like us to develop feelings beyond that of two friends enjoying each other's company."

"Oh!"

"It has nothing to do with you. It is simply that I cannot marry or fall in love. I am quite incapable of returning any such feelings."

She nodded, apparently lost in thought. Robert wondered if he'd just made her believe him to be impotent. About to clarify, though he had no idea how to explain without bringing up his father and William, she gasped and pulled at a chain around her neck, revealing a pendant watch. Catherine's dismay at the lateness of the hour didn't stop Robert from thinking how warm the small watch must be from its concealment so close to her breasts. His fingers actually *itched* to take the timepiece and feel that intimate warmth secondhand.

"I must return home," she said as she pushed back her chair. "I'm later than I told Sophie I would be."

Robert stood. "Ah yes, the adventurous maid. Perhaps at our next *assignation,* you can tell me how you managed to waltz into Mrs. Wilson's drawing room without so much as a by-your-leave from the footman." He offered his arm as they made their way through the emptying tavern.

"There's really nothing to tell. I was Countess Alisa Borodinicha, and no one tells the countess no," she said in her Russian accent.

He grinned down at her. "I shall have to remember that."

Outside, Robert turned to her. "May I offer you a ride home in my carriage?"

"No, thank you. I would rather…" She indicated one of the hired hacks that waited in front of the theater.

"Then I insist on paying." Before she could deny him, he slipped a coin to the driver then opened the door for Catherine to climb aboard. "I look forward to seeing Mistress Purcell soon. In the meantime, Countess, it was diverting as always."

A smile tugged at the corners of her mouth, but she maintained her regal façade.

"*Dah,* I shall relay your regards to her. Until our next meeting, *moy gospodin.*"

With that, she drew the door closed, and the coach took off.

Robert smiled as he made his way back to his own carriage. He looked forward to the next few weeks like he'd not anticipated anything in years.

Six

CATHERINE SQUINTED at the early morning daylight streaming in the window. She tugged at the covers to pull them over her head but met with resistance.

"Oh no, miss," Sophie protested. "You must rise. Master Christopher has been clamoring to see you for nigh on two hours, and Lady Purcell really *is* sending for the doctor since this is the second time this week you've slept late."

Catherine groaned as she sat up on the edge of the bed and rubbed her face, trying to force alertness into her skin.

"I heard her tell the baron that perhaps the *rigorous social schedule*"—Sophie snorted—"was too much for your delicate constitution, seeing as how you were still mourning Master Jasper."

Catherine laughed at Sophie's impersonation of Mother Purcell. As Catherine told Lord Dunsbury the night before, the Purcells had few acquaintances, and the small dinners and card parties they'd attended had been anything but "rigorous." She sobered as she thought of Jasper. Catherine knew Mother Purcell thought of her son daily and missed him constantly.

Catherine could fully understand a mother's grief now she had Christopher.

The mere thought of losing her son jarred her fully awake. She crossed to the washstand to attend her morning ablutions then hurriedly dressed with Sophie's aid.

"I suppose I'd better grow accustomed to less sleep. Our social schedule is about to become more rigorous."

"Do tell, miss!" Sophie's excitement showed how much she'd been dying to ask about the previous evening's adventure. "Did that man have wicked intentions?"

"Lord Dunsbury? Or am I supposed to refer to him as the Marquess of Dunsbury?" Catherine asked, trying to remember her crash course in England's peerage studies.

"Laws! A marquess? So, he didn't lie about that?"

Catherine smiled and sat at the dressing table to plait her hair. "Apparently not. The marquess is going to see we are invited to some events that may prove more fruitful in this quest to marry well."

"You mean rich," Sophie said as she spiraled Catherine's long plaits into an elaborate coil on top of her head.

Catherine bit her lip so as not to laugh. "To be explicit, yes."

"And why would he bother to do such a thing?"

Catherine took a breath and explained as succinctly as possible her agreement with Lord Dunsbury.

"It sounds like the devil's own bargain!" Sophie declared. "He'll mean to take advantage of you no matter what he says about liking your wits, miss." Though the maid scowled, Catherine saw an excitement not unlike how she felt when she considered the mad plan.

"I don't think so, but I really have no choice, do I? I'll never find a husband with the necessary requisites—"

"You mean money."

"Yes, well, I shall never meet such a man at the types of events the Purcells have been invited to thus far. Even the wealthiest men we have met could not undertake the saving of Tutley Keep."

Sophie was silent as she tucked the last pin into Catherine's hair. "It's too bad you told him about needing the money," she finally said.

"What? Why?" Catherine stared at the maid's frown of concentration in the mirror.

"'Cause now he won't marry you himself. If you could have kept that part secret, maybe he'd have grown feelings for you and wanted to marry you. No man with a title is gonna willingly take on that kind of headache unless he's so rich it don't matter to him. Is he that rich, miss?"

"I have no idea, and I wouldn't be so impertinent as to ask him." Not that it would make any difference as Robert clearly didn't want to marry.

"More's the pity. The bit I saw of him at the museum was awful nice to look at. A girl wouldn't mind waking up to that face every day."

Catherine's face warmed, not because of Sophie's suggestive words, but because she'd had the same thoughts since he'd put her in the coach last night. If she *had* to marry, which she did, it would be nice to be married to a man who actually found her interesting and whom she found completely fascinating in return. Not to mention a man who made her question if all marital intimacies were as tepid as hers had been.

As Sophie had noticed, Robert had a face Catherine would like to see first thing in the morning, his jaw rough with stubble, his hair mussed. She didn't know where such thoughts came from as Jasper had never spent an entire night in her bed, leaving directly after the few times they'd been intimate so he wouldn't "disturb her slumber." A flicker of a dream from last night made her flush. She had an impression of tangled limbs, firm lips, and a yearning for something she wasn't sure existed.

However, there was no denying his sincerity when she'd

asked him if he was looking to marry. She'd asked out of curiosity, not because she thought he might consider her, but his answer still stung. While he'd phrased it as a compliment, his comment that she was too smart to fall in love with him sounded more like a warning. Then there was his *actual* warning about not developing emotional attachments. She laughed humorously. Her fragmented dreams would become nothing more.

Catherine stood abruptly. There was no sense dwelling on fantasies. She needed to remember what was important—her son and his future title.

"Has Christopher had breakfast?" she asked.

"Nearly two hours ago."

"Good, then he shall be ready for a second one."

"He had that an hour ago," Sophie said matter-of-factly. "I've no doubt he'll be ready for a third, though."

Catherine laughed. Her son was clearly having a growth spurt, for he was insatiable whenever he was about to outgrow his clothes.

"I shall see if I can fill him up long enough to take a walk in the park."

ONCE AT THE PARK, Christopher ran to chase ducks, with Sophie sprinting after him. Catherine smiled but continued her sedate pace. Before their park excursion was over, both she and the maid would have stitches in their sides from chasing after the exuberant four-year-old.

As she watched Christopher and Sophie race about, Catherine turned her thoughts toward her excursion of the night before. Her time as the countess was simply too delicious a treat to indulge in more than a few minutes at a time, so she'd tried not to think of her adventure since telling Sophie of it.

Instead, Catherine had forced herself to think of the mending she needed to complete, the new shoes her growing son would soon require, and all her other mundane tasks.

Catherine slowed her steps and paused, staring at the toes of her walking boots that peeped from beneath her skirts. She smiled. No, it wasn't masquerading as a countess that was the treat—it was the company of Lord Dunsbury. Biting her lip, she could scarcely believe the bargain she had entered into, and yet, aside from the need to sneak out of the house every once in a while, impersonate a non-existent Russian noblewoman, and flirt with an outrageously handsome marquess, she felt she was receiving the better side of the deal.

Though Mother Purcell was sure they would stumble upon an eligible gentleman eventually, Catherine knew otherwise, and she suspected the baron did as well. Once the Purcells began attending the larger events of London's Season, Catherine hoped the chance to find and marry a wealthy merchant or businessman in need of a noble connection would improve.

It was not lost on her that she viewed the idea of marrying again, especially considering the reason behind it, with far less enthusiasm than the notion of her secret assignations with Lord Dunsbury. Perhaps that made her wicked, but her brief meetings with the handsome lord had fulfilled every desire she'd ever had for adventure and excitement.

Still, as she hurried to relieve Sophie, who clutched her side, Catherine knew she had to be careful. If the fragments of dreams she remembered were any indication, she could find herself behaving with more scandal than merely masquerading as a countess and attending events with Lord Dunsbury.

With a shake of her head, Catherine picked up her pace to join Christopher and Sophie. The maid would surely need to catch her breath by now, and it was Catherine's turn to chase the four-year-old.

SHE MANAGED to stifle most thoughts of Lord Dunsbury until the next morning when an invitation arrived.

At breakfast, the baron read the paper while Mother Purcell —there was no way Catherine would ever be able to think of the older lady as the baroness—opened correspondence. Mother Purcell gasped aloud at the crest on the back of one missive and shrieked when she opened it.

"Good heavens, Mother," the baron said. "Do contain yourself. What on earth should cause such a reaction?"

His wife handed him the heavy, cream-colored paper, and the baron lifted his bushy eyebrows as he read the missive.

"Why on earth would the Countess of Egerton invite us to her annual ball?" he asked, returning his brows to their normal perch.

"Perhaps they wish to welcome us to the nobility?" At her husband's frown, Mother Purcell frowned also. "Perhaps one of our acquaintances recommended us?"

Catherine buried her nose in her teacup to hide her expression.

"Or…perhaps word of our lovely Catherine has gotten out, and the countess wishes to meet her," Mother Purcell said.

Catherine pretended to look surprised. The baron, clearly believing none of those notions, nonetheless took pity on his daughter-in-law. "That must be the case."

He handed the invitation to Catherine and returned to his paper. Catherine glanced at the elegant note as Mother Purcell turned to her. "What shall you wear?"

The innocuous phrase made Catherine remember that she needed to figure out a new dress to wear on her next meeting with Lord Dunsbury, and how he'd kept stealing glances at the décolletage displayed by her grandmother's gown.

"Good heavens, child, are you ill?" Mother Purcell cried.

Catherine looked about the room, expecting to see Christopher. She'd barely turned back when her mother-in-law placed a hand on Catherine's brow.

"You are flushed as if with fever."

"Oh, it's... Well, it's merely excitement in attending a ball next week that has brought a flush to my cheeks."

"Well, you must not overexert yourself with interest. It will surely tax your constitution."

Catherine smiled at the older woman's concern and tried not to chafe at her words. Instead, seeking to distract Mother Purcell before the woman prescribed a day of bed rest, Catherine said, "The ball gown I have might not be fancy enough for an event of this magnitude. Perhaps I shall buy some trim today to add to the bodice."

The ploy worked, for Mother Purcell's eyes grew round. "You are absolutely correct, you clever girl. We must make our very best impression on Countess..."

"Egerton," the baron replied without looking up from his paper.

"Just so. Catherine, I shall go with you and perhaps select an embroidered shawl to brighten up my own gown."

Catherine forced a smile. She enjoyed her mother-in-law's company, but the woman had the most abysmal taste when it came to wearing anything other than her mourning clothes. It had taken every ounce of Catherine's persuasive skills to guide Mother Purcell on selections for both of their wardrobes for the Season.

THE NEXT AFTERNOON, Catherine and Sophie sewed trim and beads to Catherine's fanciest ball gown—a simple periwinkle blue muslin. The modiste had tried to convince Mother Purcell that a lady should have at least one silk ball gown, but Mother Purcell found the extra price too exorbitant.

Regardless, Catherine loved the new gowns, hats, gloves, stockings, and slippers. She was lucky and grateful to have the Purcells because without them, with no family of her own to turn to and no means to her name, life would be most uncomfortable. Still, Catherine wished she was allowed to decide the type of fabric to order or even how many gowns she would need.

"Are you all right, miss?" Sophie asked.

Catherine glanced up. Sophie had several pins pinched between her lips as she worked on the hem of Catherine's gown.

"Sophie, I told you that worries me when you hold pins such. Suppose you swallowed one?"

"Whyever would I do that, miss?" the maid asked, but she obligingly spat them out. "Is it your courses?"

"What?"

"You sighed heavy-like. If it's your time, I'll fetch you a hot towel."

"No, it's— I sighed?"

Sophie gave her best impression of a mournful sigh. "Just like that."

Catherine smiled at the maid's dramatics. "No, it's not my time. I'm just ruminating, I suppose."

"Eh? That don't sound pleasant, miss, if you don't mind my saying."

Catherine smiled again. "I was trying to figure out what I'm going to wear when I meet with Lord Dunsbury again. He was insistent that if I kept wearing my grandmother's gown, it would draw too much attention." She'd also been wondering what type of husband she might find herself married to if he was, in effect, buying her for her connections to minor nobility, but she didn't want to voice those concerns aloud.

"Miss, you've pinned that all crooked."

Catherine glanced down. She hadn't pinned the trim to her dress so much as stabbed it randomly about the neckline. "Perhaps I am not quite myself."

Sophie efficiently removed the jumble of pins. "I'll take care of it, miss." The maid paused with the length of trim in her hand. "Miss, what if we didn't put the trim on this dress?"

"Do you think it's too much? I thought the gown rather plain, but—"

"What if we use the trim to make you a new dress?"

Catherine laughed. "Scandalous wouldn't begin to describe such a gown, Sophie."

In response, the maid jumped up and ran to the wardrobe, digging in the back and finally emerging with her cap askew. In her hands was the gold satin cape that went with Catherine's grandmother's gown.

"What if I used this to make you a new dress? That gold trim there would look a sight better on this satin than it would trying to improve the muslin."

Catherine smiled slowly. "That's brilliant! It will mean ever so much work for you, though. I can't risk Mother Purcell seeing me sewing it."

"Bah," Sophie said as she sat on her stool and snatched up her embroidery scissors to begin opening the seams of the cloak. "I'll ask the footman, Danny, to play with Christopher a few afternoons. He's sweet on me, so he'll be happy to do me a favor. You'll have a new gown by your next meeting, miss."

"Thank you, Sophie. You're a— Well, you are a true friend."

The sensible maid looked up, startled. "Don't let her ladyship hear you say such a thing. She'll have us both out on our ears." She belied her statement with a grin.

Catherine smiled and shook out the muslin gown they'd decorated. It was very plain without the gold trim, but the small beads they'd added at the neckline made it more elegant, at least.

As she hung the gown back in the wardrobe, she thought again about the dream she'd had last night. She remembered even less now. As it often was with dreams, the more she struggled to recall it, the less she could. All she could evoke now was an awareness of her body that had long lain dormant. A sense of anticipation filled her, that and…something else, something primal and unsettling.

Catherine pressed cool hands to her heated cheeks. She would have to wear powder every time she was out with the marquess to disguise her tendency to blush. A sophisticated Russian noblewoman would not react so innocently to a simple dream. She smiled at her thoughts then shook her head. She was becoming as brooding as the heroine in the book she'd just purchased—a book that was unlike any she'd found in the Purcells' library. It was full of meaningful glances, foreboding characters, and a rather appealing heroine despite her propensity for staring out of windows, bemoaning her fate.

Setting aside thoughts of brooding heroines, she returned to Sophie and began helping dismantle her grandmother's cape.

THE NIGHT of Countess Egerton's ball, Sophie worked wonders with Catherine's hair, even weaving a strand of beads through the russet loops. Sophie had even convinced Catherine to dab a little of the *Pear's Liquid Bloom of Roses* on her lips and cheeks, and as she looked in the mirror, she was surprised to see an elegant young woman staring back. Catherine realized she looked rather lovely, much as she had when she'd dressed as the countess the first time.

"Laws, miss! You look beautiful!"

Catherine smiled at the maid's expression. "Thank you, Sophie. I feel…beautiful."

"Now, don't be going all shy tonight, miss. You must believe you *are* beautiful, or you'll end up a wallflower. Men like ladies who are confident. Gives 'em a bit of a challenge, see?"

"Speaking from experience, are you?"

Sophie did not suffer Catherine's unfortunate tendency to blush, but the maid did busy herself tidying the dressing table and generally avoided eye contact. "Ain't nothing but what my mam taught me."

Catherine smiled at the still-fidgeting maid. "Then it must be true. Very well, perhaps I can borrow a bit of Alisa Borodinicha's bravado."

"Who, miss?" Sophie asked with a frown.

"My alter ego. When I dressed up as the Russian countess."

Sophie nodded sagely. "That'll do, miss. Just don't forget and accidentally use that funny voice."

Catherine was tempted to use Sophie's favorite expression, "Laws!" at the thought of mistakenly using her Russian accent. Instead, she laughed. "Wouldn't Mother Purcell think I'd gone completely mad?"

The two women shared a giggle before Sophie shooed Catherine downstairs.

❦

DURING THE CARRIAGE ride to the Egerton house, Mother Purcell issued so many instructions on how Catherine should behave, speak, eat, and even excuse herself to the retiring room that Catherine felt the need to grit her teeth lest she ask just how many balls her mother-in-law had attended. She knew the older woman was simply nervous, but Catherine's own nerves already had her gripping the cushion beneath her and bouncing her heel in a most unladylike fashion.

Eventually, even the baron grew tired of his wife's incessant talking, for he laid his hand on hers. "Enough, Mother. Catherine is an intelligent lady. She will not embarrass us, and she will figure out all she needs to know."

"Yes, but I've heard those of the upper *ton* can be so unforgiving of the smallest faux pas."

"Catherine will be fine," the baron said firmly. Mother Purcell pressed her lips together as if the words inside her mouth battered to escape.

Catherine smiled at her father-in-law, but her smile faded as she thought of his assurance that she would not embarrass the family. If word ever got out of her masquerade— Well, she would simply make sure it didn't. That thought brought to mind Lord Dunsbury. Despite her attempts not to dwell on him, he had been in her thoughts constantly. The feeling in the pit of her stomach was not unlike the fear of going to the ball, except it was not fear but excitement at the prospect of seeing him tonight.

The carriage drew to a stop, and when the baron stepped down first, Mother Purcell took one last opportunity to offer Catherine instructions.

"Make sure you keep your shoulders back and don't slouch, dear. You've a lovely bosom, and it would not do to hide it. Many a man has been swayed by a lovely bosom. I can assure you."

Catherine forced her expression to remain carefully neutral, while inside, she suddenly saw the Purcells in a whole new light. They were so staid and practical she'd never considered their courtship might have been very different from how they treated each other now. She pressed her lips together to keep from smiling as she thought of a young Mother Purcell using a lovely bosom to entice her suitors.

The baron helped his wife down, and Catherine took a deep breath before following.

Once inside, it was clear this was a party of a different set altogether. Ladies' gowns glimmered in a wide range of jewel tones, though the unmarried ladies tended to wear white or light colors. Feathers bedecked elaborate hairstyles, and jewels glittered at ears and throats.

Not to be outdone, the men wore tightly fitted jackets of velvets and brocades, elaborately knotted cravats, and snug breeches.

Beside her, Mother Purcell shook her head. "I should have bought the more expensive shawl," she whispered.

"You look lovely," Catherine said in reassurance. Her mother-in-law glanced at her. "Besides, your manners are impeccable, and isn't that the true sign of a lady?"

Mother Purcell smiled and patted Catherine's arm. "You are the dearest child, saving us from ruin and reassuring an old woman."

Catherine's smile faded slightly as she remembered her true reason for being here tonight. She glanced around the crowded ballroom. How was she to determine which gentlemen were eligible, much less arrange an introduction to one?

"You must be Lord and Lady Tutley," said a lavishly dressed and bejeweled woman. "I am your hostess, Countess Egerton." With a sharp gaze, it seemed she noted every detail of the Purcells' well-made but simple attire. She turned to Catherine, who forced a pleasant smile and tried to appear as if this was all very natural. The countess quickly appraised her from head to toe before she took Catherine's hand.

"My dear, you are lovely. No wonder Dunsbury claimed a connection."

Catherine glanced at the Purcells, but before they could ask a question, the countess tucked Catherine's hand in the crook of her arm. "Come, my dears. Let me introduce you to the right people." She led them across the ballroom and plunged into a knot of people. She tossed out introductions so quickly,

Catherine was sure she would not remember a single name. A glance at the Purcells showed they were even more overwhelmed than she.

Catherine was spared having to make conversation when the music commenced, and a gentleman—she thought his name was Lord Fredericks—asked her to dance. Thankfully, the dance was one she knew, and after a few moments of the familiar steps, she began to relax.

"Are you new to London?" the lord asked as they promenaded around each other.

"Yes. My father-in-law recently came into the title, and we have taken up residence here for the Season."

"And where is your husband?"

"Jasper died two years ago," Catherine said, unsure of the proper etiquette for mentioning a late husband.

"I see. My condolences." The smile on his face seemed at odds with his words, and Catherine smiled hesitantly in return.

The rest of the dance passed less awkwardly, with Lord Fredericks asking what sights she'd seen.

"You haven't been to Vauxhall? Oh, we shall have to remedy that," he said as he led her back to the Purcells. "I shall arrange a party, and you will be our guest of honor as we induct you into the delights of the pleasure gardens. As a widow, you shall enjoy many more freedoms to sample such delights."

Though his tone was pleasant enough, those last words made her think he had more than a dinner picnic planned, and she decided it might be best to avoid committing to any outings with him.

"Ah, Dunsbury," the man said, sounding less than pleased.

"Fredericks," Dunsbury said before he ignored the other man and turned to Catherine. "Mrs. Purcell, how delightful to see you this evening. I believe this dance is ours?"

Catherine observed the Purcells' dazed expressions as they no doubt wondered how she knew the marquess. As he led her to the dance floor, she knew she'd have to invent a plausible tale.

Once the music began, it distracted her from that concern. "Oh! It's a waltz. I don't— That is, I've never—"

"Just follow my lead. You'll be fine."

"But—"

"You're going to step back on your right foot. It's a one-two-three count. Are you ready?"

"No. I—"

He ignored her protest and got them moving. It was a testament to Lord Dunsbury's strength as well as grace that he was able to physically propel her through the figures, all while keeping his movements smooth. She fancied he helped her move more gracefully than she would have with another partner, so only if someone were paying close attention would they be able to tell she barely avoided stumbling over her feet.

"Now relax," he said. "It's a simple pattern that repeats the entire length of the song. I shan't add any fancy embellishments this time."

"You're holding me very close," she said, a trifle breathless.

"That's one of the benefits of the waltz."

She raised her brows, and he grinned. "It's so much easier to carry on a conversation than when one is hopping about and changing partners, don't you agree?"

"No, I'm too busy counting." She stumbled as she forgot her third step, but he drew her flush against his body and whirled her around, covering her misstep before slightly releasing his hold.

"Stop counting and enjoy yourself."

She glared up at him, a retort on her lips, but the moment his gaze caught hers, she forgot why she wanted to chastise him. He studied her face. A slight crease marred his brow as if he tried to figure out something. When he dropped his gaze to her lips, she felt it as surely as if he'd pressed his mouth against hers. She parted her lips, trying to get enough air in her lungs, and at the movement, he tightened his arm against her back.

Her cheeks warmed, but the heat was not borne of embarrassment. All of a sudden, her skin seemed sensitive to the brush of her skirts against her legs, the tickle of a loose curl against her neck, and the press of his hand as he clasped hers.

She stopped counting and lost all sense of the music or placing her feet. Instead, her body responded to the slightest pressure from his hand at her back. She seemed to see in his eyes when he was going to turn her, sensed when he was going to shorten or lengthen their steps to avoid other couples. She'd never felt so attuned to another person, except perhaps to her son just after his birth. However, this was different on a visceral level. Outrageous notions filled her head. She read similar thoughts in Dunsbury's eyes and knew if they were not surrounded by several hundred people…

The music drew to a dramatic end, and Catherine wanted to beg for it to continue. Dunsbury held her a long moment, past when other couples had separated, then he visibly shook off the spell that enveloped them and released her. He offered her his arm and guided her from the dance floor before he led her to the corner farthest from where the Purcells stood so they would have to thread their way through the crowds to reach Catherine's side.

"It occurs to me your calendar is about to fill. You should receive a few more invitations."

"We received two this afternoon," Catherine said as they came to a stop.

Dunsbury nodded. "Very good. After your appearance this evening—you look quite beautiful, I might add—and especially after our waltz, I expect you will be bombarded by invitations and visitors during your receiving hours."

Still reeling from his compliment, delivered so matter-of-factly, it took her a moment to focus on his other comment.

"Why after our dance? Is there some unspoken rule that a lady must prove herself able to waltz before she is deemed fit to call upon?"

Dunsbury laughed. "It sounds like something the *ton* would do I'll grant you."

"But not the reason for your remark."

Suddenly the marquess looked a bit…sheepish.

"Would you like some punch?" he asked.

"I'm not thirsty. And don't try to change the subject. Why will dancing with you lead to sudden popularity?"

Dunsbury avoided looking at her by glancing over the heads of the people in front of them, no doubt to try and see what caused the slow orbit of guests to grind to a halt.

Catherine poked him sharply, though unobtrusively, in the ribs and was rewarded with a yelp worthy of a young girl.

"Why did—"

"Answer the question," she said, amazed at her brashness. She had no idea where her streak of bossiness had come from but supposed that once she had assumed the Russian countess's mantle, she had taken on, and kept, some of those qualities.

"You're rather imperious, you know."

"You seem to bring it out of me. I'm normally quite placid, and the only reason I can think of why you're not answering a simple question is that *you* are the reason I'll suddenly become popular. Is the great Marquess of Dunsbury such a trendsetter his mere presence during a waltz can make a lady?"

"I'm not a trendsetter, but—" He drew her to the side to avoid a herd of debutantes who were so consumed with their conversation they ran into other guests left and right.

"Yes?" She prepared to land another jab in his ribs. He glanced down at her, and she could have sworn his face was almost flushed. With embarrassment? The crowd started moving again, and he took her elbow to guide her forward.

"I told you I don't intend to marry. As a result, I tend to

avoid dancing with unmarried ladies, lest they and their mothers interpret it as…interest."

She frowned, wondering what was behind such a decision. Surely as the heir to a dukedom, he was obligated to marry and produce an heir. She forced her mind back to the conversation. "So, the fact you've broken your rule means I must be terribly appealing?"

"Something like that." He guided her around another snarl of partygoers.

"Then it sounds as if you are as influential as Beau Brummell."

"I'm no dandified trendsetter. In fact, it's not me at all—it's the dammed title. I assure you, if I were a mere mister, no one would care who I danced with."

"Ah yes, the bestowed title."

He huffed a short laugh. "The very same. In any event, it is usually a bit of a bother. The title, I mean, so I figured we may as well get some benefit out of it."

"Yes, I imagine it grows wearisome to have people bending over backward to see to your every need and desire," she said as she held back a smile.

A rueful grin tugged at the corner of his mouth. "Hush, you harpy. It does, actually."

"A harpy, am I?"

"Well, you *are* mocking me." He sounded disgruntled, though the grin still curled his lips.

Taking pity on him, she gave in and smiled. It was amazing how often she found herself smiling in his presence. "Well, I thank you for your sacrifice to the launching of my social ship. It was very noble of you."

"Are you still teasing me?"

"Not at all. I am most sincere. By the way, you said you would tell me of our first…"

"Assignation was your word choice, I believe."

Heat flooded her face. "Yes, well, unless you've a better name for it."

"I like assignation, especially in the context of meeting with the Russian countess. It sounds dangerous and exciting."

Catherine laughed at the idea of anything about her being either dangerous *or* exciting. "Very well, then, where shall this meeting occur? And when?"

"Have you visited Vauxhall Gardens?"

She smiled at the evening's second mention of the destination. With Dunsbury, however, she felt comfortable being forthright. "I will confess that the Purcells and I have not gone *anywhere*. I only managed to sneak off to the museum because Mother P—the baroness was ill that day, and I had promised Christopher he should see a Greek statue." Catherine gasped and covered her mouth with a gloved hand. With the other, she grabbed Dunsbury's arm, pulling him to a stop. "I don't know why I said such an ungrateful thing. Truly, I didn't mean—"

"Hush now. There's nothing wrong with wishing to see the sights of London, nor is there anything wrong with feeling frustrated with not being able to see such things."

"No, it was a horrible thing for—"

"You are far from horrible. You are young and vibrant and in the world's most interesting city. It's only natural you should wish to explore, just as it's natural an older couple like the Purcells would wish to stay close to home."

Catherine considered his declaration, and it seemed as if a weight lifted from her conscience. She smiled, grateful for his words.

"So, I take it that means you've *not* been to Vauxhall?"

"I have not."

"Very good. I shall take you there. How about Thursday next, barring foul weather?"

She couldn't contain her excitement as she'd read about the

myriad of entertainments at the large outdoor venue. "Yes, of course. I shall look forward to it."

"As will I." He stared at her for a long moment as if she were the only other person in the room, and her pulse quickened. She moistened her lips and watched as he dropped his gaze to them.

Unnerved by the strength of the emotions he evoked, she glanced away. They were now only a few feet from the Purcells. She tried to stifle the spurt of disappointment that shot through her.

"As I suspected, half a dozen gentlemen are waiting for an introduction," Dunsbury said, though he didn't sound terribly pleased. He stopped to allow a couple to pass in front of them, and while briefly concealed from the Purcells' sight, he bent to whisper in her ear. "I shall pick you up at ten o'clock. Will that be late enough?"

She swallowed and nodded. "The Purcells retire by nine on nights we don't go out."

He gave her a brief smile, and when their path was clear, he delivered her into the company of the baron and baroness, where he then introduced her to several men, all of whom requested a dance. To her chagrin, she did not see Dunsbury the rest of the night.

"Oh, what a successful evening!" Mother Purcell said as they climbed into their carriage several hours later.

Catherine sank wearily into the seat next to her mother-in-law. It *had* been a success. She'd met more gentlemen than she could remember, and several of them had asked for permission to call upon her. She had danced until her feet were sore and had drunk more than one glass of champagne. Ostensibly, the punch seemed to have run out, but there was no end to the sparkling wine. Catherine had even made the acquaintance of a few ladies who had invited her to call. All in all, it was everything she and the Purcells had hoped for when they came to London, and yet, for Catherine, the most enjoyable part of the evening had been the very beginning when she'd danced and conversed with Lord Dunsbury.

All the other men she'd met had been polite, flattering even. Still, only with him had she experienced that intense feeling of… She searched for the right word, but all she could come up with was "being alive."

She shook her head then glanced to the side as Mother Purcell's head came to rest on her shoulder, accompanied by a small snore. Catherine smiled and glanced at the baron who gazed at his wife affectionately.

"That was quite a bit more excitement than she is used to, poor dear. It seems we have the Marquess of Dunsbury to thank for it."

Catherine's heart lurched, and she wondered how the baron could have discovered her wicked bargain so soon. "Oh?"

"Yes. Apparently, Lord Dunsbury was familiar with the previous Baron Tutley and wished to aid his family in any way he could, so he encouraged our invitation this evening."

"Oh." Catherine's relief that Dunsbury had kept to his story sent a warm wash through her veins.

"He was the first gentleman with whom you danced this evening."

"I believe I remember him." A greater understatement she'd never made—he'd been at the front of her mind all evening. Even as she'd danced with other men, she'd scanned the crowds for a glimpse of him.

"He is heir to a dukedom, I understand," the baron said with absolutely no subtlety.

Catherine debated how to squelch his intimation. She cleared her throat delicately. "As I danced with Lord Dunsbury, he informed me that while he wished to help us, in deference to his friend the previous baron, he had no intention or desire to wed."

"He said that? Deuced odd thing to say to a lady."

Catherine heard the disapproval in his voice, and while some strange part of her wanted to defend Dunsbury as a man of impeccable character, the rational part of her brain cautioned her it would be wisest if the baron, and by extension, the baroness, harbored absolutely no hopes that Catherine ensnare Dunsbury in the marital noose. She resolutely ignored the small voice inside her that sighed with longing at the thought of Dunsbury as a potential husband. Even if she had not understood the night they made their arrangement, he'd been quite clear tonight in that assertion. If she thought to change his mind, she could very well lose his friendship, which had quickly become very important to her.

She looked out the window at the lamplit streets and tried not to smile as she thought of the squeak he had made when she poked him in the ribs.

Seven

It took every ounce of Robert's control not to slam his father's bedchamber door behind him. He paused in the hallway and took a deep breath, then expelled it as he tried to rid himself of the foul taste a session with his father always caused.

The man's temper grew stronger as his body grew weaker. Robert tried to feel compassion for his sire, the man who had once carried him on his shoulders and taught him to bait a fishhook. To be so feeble at the end of life and reliant on others for nearly everything could not be easy. His father had always been a hale, hearty man, his force of personality as strong as his body. Now, he could barely lift his head to swallow the sickroom fare his wife spooned into his mouth.

Robert shook loose his tense muscles. He might have compassion for his father's misery due to his illness, but the man still treated his only son with a hatred so deep-seated, it filled the very air like a toxic miasma. Robert studied the rug's pattern beneath his Hessians, seeing not the intertwined vines and flowers but the laughing face of his brother William. Robert could not remember a time his elder brother had been angry or out of sorts. He certainly had never argued with their father as Robert did now.

At the thought of William, the familiar ache beneath Robert's breastbone pushed against his lungs, making it harder to take a full breath. His fingers went numb, and a rushing sound filled his ears as if he stood next to a waterfall. He knew what was coming next, what he was powerless to stop.

"Robert." Rain spattered William's upturned face, but he didn't even blink, only stared straight ahead as if he already looked into the next world. His arm flailed, and Robert caught it, gripping his brother's cold hand in his own, trying to warm it.

"Rob," his brother repeated.

"I'm here, Will. Save your strength. I'll fetch a doctor."

A faint smile eased the strain on his brother's face. "No time for that, I'm afraid."

"Will!" Robert sobbed. "I'm so bloody sorry. I—" Robert leaned over him, blocking the rain with his body.

"Love," William whispered.

"Violet?" William had been on the verge of offering marriage. "I will see she is looked after. Shall I tell her—"

"No. You."

Tears blurred Robert's vision, streaming down his face with the rain. "I love you too, Will."

"Yes. No. Rob—"

Robert clutched his brother's cold hand tighter. "What is it?"

"You must love, Rob. Promise me." The shadow of a smile lightened William's expression again, and he lifted the hand he'd clutched against the gunshot wound in his belly to Robert's hair, attempting to rumple it as he'd done out of affection when they were little and to tease when they were young men. Robert grabbed his brother's hand and pressed it to his head like a benediction. He felt the moment his brother died, felt the hand on his head go lax, heard the labored breathing cease, but mostly, he felt the absence of the person who'd been his closest companion since they were babies.

Robert drew a gasping breath and looked around, scanning the dim hallway for a servant or his mother. There was no one. He relaxed and ran a shaking hand over his damp brow.

It had been months since he'd had such an episode. He didn't know what had spurred this one—his father had been no more ugly than normal today, and there'd been nothing else in particular that had reminded Robert of William. Shaking his head, he tugged on his waistcoat and took one more deep breath to steady himself before heading downstairs. He thought to bid his mother good day. Among other things, he felt guilty for leaving her to deal with his father day in and day out. He supposed since his father didn't blame her for William's death, he was not so horrible to her. Still, the man was a curmudgeon on the best of days, and Robert couldn't imagine life with him would be that delightful.

The duchess looked up as he entered the solar where she had breakfast every morning.

"Good morning, dear. Would you care to join me?"

"Thank you, Mother, but I—"

"Yes, yes. I know meeting with your father ruins your appetite." Her sardonic tone reminded him she was well-versed in dealing with the Carlisle men. "Come, I've had a letter from your sister Margaret. She is settling in nicely to her new home, and Lunceford has promised she may redecorate the entire manor if she chooses."

He was still a bit rattled from his memory of William, but mention of their sister made Robert smile. He had returned to England just in time to see her wed before she and her new husband left for his home in Scotland. Robert joined his mother at the table. He *had* been about to refuse her invitation, but apparently, he was still juvenile enough that he didn't want her to be right about *everything*. "What I was about to say was thank you, but I would like a fresh pot of coffee."

"Indeed," the duchess said, but she seemed unconvinced.

He gave her his best contrite, boyish grin, and she fought not to smile. Instead, she served him a scone and several slices of ham. He'd nearly finished with his second breakfast when his mother cleared her throat.

"I have a favor to ask."

Robert looked up from spreading jam on the last bite of scone. "Certainly."

"I should very much like you to attend the Andover ball next week."

"Andover? Of course. I generally attend—"

"And dance with Lady Eleanor Chalcroft."

"What? Why? Who is she?"

"She is the daughter of a very dear friend of mine, and the Earl of Chalcroft, of course."

"The earl is not a very dear friend?" Robert couldn't resist asking.

"What? Of course he is, dear, but I have known his wife, Elizabeth, since we were girls. We've renewed our friendship these last few years."

Robert took that to mean when he had been in exile. "Is this Lady Eleanor a wallflower needing a bit of assistance overcoming her shyness?" he asked with a smile. He thought of Catherine and wondered if he might have found a new vocation—lending his title's weight and dancing skills to young women in need of a social boost. The thought made him smile, especially as he considered having calling cards engraved. *Robert Carlisle, Marquess of Dunsbury, Launcher of Social Schooners.* He would have to remember to tell Catherine his idea tomorrow. He knew she would approve of his improvement to her "social ship" quip.

"Lady Eleanor has been considered the most sought-after young lady of the *ton* since her debut three years ago," his mother said with a frown.

"Then why would you wish me to— Ah, I see. No, Mother. I'm sorry, but no."

"Robert, it's years past time for you to settle."

He thought of his friend, Noel Wayland, who'd envied Robert for his mother's restraint in urging him to marry. He would now have to confess his mother had succumbed to the urge to direct her son's life.

"It's not as if I was in a position to be able to settle until recently." He made the remark to forestall her needling, but thinking of his years abroad trying to stay out of his father's hate-filled sight made Robert's heart pound as an anxious, angry emotion roiled in his belly. If he *had* wanted to marry, there would have been no opportunity. His father had cut off Robert's finances, and he'd lived off his inheritance from his maternal grandfather. While Robert had a roof over his head and food in his belly every night, his time abroad had not been the European Grand Tour that men had enjoyed prior to the war.

His mother laid a hand on his, which he was surprised to find balled in a fist. He relaxed his hand and glanced at her to see a sad tightness in her features and compassion in her eyes.

"I know," she said quietly.

Even though she couldn't know what it had been like to be exiled from his home immediately after his brother's death, filled with grief and guilt and nightmares, with no one to talk to, he realized she did know. Her knowledge was no doubt through the same maternal magic she'd employed when he was younger and had filched a cake from the pantry or "borrowed" the shoe black from his father's valet.

He cleared his throat to loosen the tightness there and picked up his coffee cup to give himself something else to focus on. He scarcely tasted the brew, but it allowed him a moment to regain his composure. He set the cup in its saucer and smiled grimly at his mother. He'd easily sidestepped her last suggestion to marry, but now she'd become specific in her demands, he had to tread carefully.

"I'm not prepared to marry Lady Eleanor or anyone else." He almost added "ever" but stopped himself. He realized his decision to deny his father an heir also meant he denied his mother grandchildren, but it would crush her if he told her his plan.

"Robert, you must see that—"

"Mother, I've barely begun to learn the extent of Father's holdings and finances. That was always William's duty. Pray, give me time to accustom myself to that before you ask more of me. I will dance with Lady Eleanor. That is all I will promise." He never could refuse his mother, and while she might understand what the last few years had been like for him, she could never comprehend the bitter anguish of a son hearing his father call him any number of names, including murderer, nor the burn of guilt that was a constant companion. He hated that he lied to his mother by implying he would eventually seek a wife, but he thought it less cruel than telling her the truth.

His mother seemed content with the level of his acquiescence, for she smiled and patted his hand again. "She is a beautiful young woman and quite lively. I am sure you will enjoy her company."

Unbidden, the image of Catherine's face filled his mind. He could see her impish grin after she poked him in the ribs, perfectly remember her haughty expression as the Russian countess, and he could well imagine what she would look like with kiss-swollen lips and eyes dazed with passion.

He pushed his chair back abruptly, startling his mother.

"Forgive me," he said. "I've just recalled a meeting I have scheduled for this morning."

"Not at all, dear. Thank you for having breakfast with me." She lifted her brows. "Aren't you going?"

He had, in fact, intended to stand after pushing his chair

back, except thoughts of Catherine's lips had made it necessary for him to remain seated a few more moments.

"I, um, just wanted to finish this roll. The jam is quite good."

His mother smiled at him quizzically. "Shall I have cook send some home with you?"

He washed the last bite down with the dregs of his coffee. The gritty swallow worked much as an antidote to the reaction of his lower anatomy as he focused on the bitter brew and how it made his stomach roil. At last, he was able to stand. "No, no. It's more special if I only enjoy it here. With you," he said, wondering if he'd laid it on a bit thick.

"Mm-hmm," his mother replied into her teacup. She clearly was not fooled, but thankfully she let the matter drop.

He bowed correctly, winked at her so she wouldn't think he'd completely reformed, then strode from the room, resolutely avoiding all thoughts of Catherine Purcell until he was in the confines of his carriage.

THE FOLLOWING EVENING, as Robert sat in his carriage on the way to Marylebone, he realized how much he looked forward to seeing Catherine, which was silly considering their relationship couldn't progress beyond their little game. Normally, widows had more leeway in the rules of propriety, and Robert wouldn't have been against enjoying physical delights with Catherine in addition to their mental encounters. Still, for all her unconventionality in impersonating a Russian countess and agreeing to their unusual arrangement, there was something rather...innocent about Catherine. She held herself differently than the daring widows he had met since reaching his majority.

As the city swept by, he wondered if she still mourned the loss of her husband, if they'd been greatly in love, and if no other man could take his place in her heart. She'd scarcely mentioned him when she spoke of her past, except to state that her father had arranged the union after she danced once with the man. So, either Catherine and Jasper had entered an arranged marriage as little more than strangers, or after only one dance, Catherine's father had seen his daughter and Jasper so smitten, he thought they were perfect together.

The notion made Robert uncomfortable, and he sat forward, peering out the coach window to see if they were close to the Purcells' house. He did not want to think about Catherine still loving a deceased husband, or how childishly excited he was to show her Vauxhall. He just wanted a little diversion from his life in the form of a witty companion and an entertaining venue—and that was all. The carriage drew to a halt, and a cloaked figure slipped out of the dark house.

The coachman held the door open, and Robert offered his hand to Catherine as she climbed into the carriage.

"Any difficulty escaping?" he asked when she sat back with a sigh.

"No, thankfully. It occurs to me, however, that I am clearly not cut out for espionage work. I nearly jumped out of my skin when the clock chimed as I walked past it, and I am certain my heart stopped when the stairs creaked beneath my feet. If I truly were a Russian countess here for nefarious purposes, I would give myself away within the first day, I'm certain of it."

He smiled and shook his head. "I disagree. You've already successfully pulled off three forays as Countess Alisa Bo-Bor—"

"Borodinicha, and it's only two completed forays. Tonight, I merely escaped undetected from a house of sleeping people. I still have to navigate a large outdoor pleasure garden without anyone recognizing me and sneak back into a house whose occupants are not above rising in the middle of the night for a glass of warm milk."

"I stand corrected," he said with a grin. "Let me say then that I have every faith you will prove successful in this evening's espionage escapades."

"Espionage escapades? Have you been reading penny dreadfuls?"

"I have not. Is the prose florid and alliterative?" he asked, studying her expressive face.

"Most of them are. A few I find quite intriguing, however."

"Made a thorough survey of the genre, have you?"

It was hard to tell in the low light of the carriage lanterns, but it looked like Catherine blushed, perhaps with embarrassment. "Well, it is often difficult to tell at the book seller's what constitutes such literature."

"The penny price does not give it away?" Now he was certain she was blushing, for she appeared distinctly rosy even in the dim light. A smile tugged at his lips, and he took pity on her. "You know I'm teasing, don't you? I certainly find nothing objectionable in a well-read woman."

"It's only that we had so few books at the manor in Chippenham that when I discovered the booksellers here in London, I— Well, I quite got carried away, I'm afraid."

Robert imagined a small shelf with half a dozen books on it in a provincial country manor. "How many did you read?"

"There were probably three or four hundred books in the library, though I didn't make it through half. Many were in other languages."

Robert raised his eyebrows. He certainly enjoyed a good book, but if he read a book a month, he'd be surprised. "Four hundred books weren't enough to keep you entertained?"

Her cheeks still glowed, the flush of embarrassment at odds with her compressed lips. "You've never been to Chippenham, have you?"

"That's in Wiltshire? No, I've never had a reason to go, I suppose."

"I don't doubt that. It is not the most animated society."

"I didn't realize the baron was of an academic bent." From what Catherine had told him, he assumed the former country squire was more concerned with his crops and livestock.

"I believe the books may have been purchased more for their covers than their contents."

"What do you mean?"

She shook her head and smiled. "The covers were all blue with gold lettering."

It took a moment for him to grasp what she'd said. "Wait a moment. All four hundred books had blue covers?"

"And gold lettering."

A huff of laughter escaped him. "I don't know if I'm more impressed with how that looked or how much time it must have taken to acquire four hundred blue books."

"Well, it was a *beautifully* blue room, from the wall paint to the curtains to the book covers. As to the difficulty of acquiring said color, I disagree with you. I imagine Mother Purcell simply had the gardener join her with his wheelbarrow at the book seller's." She started giggling, and he could barely understand her next words. "It wouldn't have taken long to empty the shelves of every azure tome."

Robert laughed at the image she described but laughed even more at her giggles. They sounded young, carefree, and genuine, and as if she'd kept them inside for far too long. He wondered when she'd last laughed like that. He also wondered if he could make her do so again tonight.

Catherine's laughter slowly tapered, and Robert grinned. The warm glow of shared laughter relaxed him, and they fell into a comfortable silence.

When the coach drew to a stop, Robert helped Catherine down. "You'll not need your cloak. The night is warm." He helped her remove the serviceable length of wool, which revealed a gown of heavy gold satin. He thought back to the night at the theater when he helped her out of a gold cape with worn edges. "You look lovely. Is that a new gown?"

Catherine held out her skirts and curtsied. "Do you like it?"

Her position gave him an excellent view of her breasts, but as she straightened, he forced his gaze back to her face.

She smiled impishly. "Sophie made it for me in only a week. She's quite skilled."

"It reminds me of the cloak you wore the other night."

"Does it? Well, gold is this Season's color, I'm told."

As they stepped onto the lantern-lit grounds of the pleasure garden, he noticed she'd heavily lined her eyes with kohl and reddened her cheeks and lips with whatever women used for such an effect.

She caught his gaze. "I thought to disguise my features. Is it too much?"

"Not at all." The kohl made her eyes look dark and elongated. She appeared very un-English and very alluring.

"The only thing you've left off is your accent."

"What makes you think I have forgotten?" she asked in the countess's heavy Russian inflection.

He smiled and offered her his arm. They walked through tree-lined paths strung with lamps of red, blue, and yellow. Music from somewhere ahead filled the air, as did the scent of roasting nuts and savory spices. The weather had cooperated, and while the ground was still a little soggy from recent rains, the sky was clear and the air softly warm. Though it was not as crowded as in the past, throngs of people from all walks of life made their way into the gardens.

"The gardens opened in the sixteen hundreds," Robert said, feeling the need to play guide.

Catherine smiled then stumbled on a rough patch. He tightened his grip on her arm to steady her.

"*Spasibo*. I'm not the most graceful woman on a good day. I fear when I am distracted, I am an accident waiting to happen."

Robert chuckled. "Then I shall make it my mission to ensure you remain upright this evening."

"This would be an example of your English chivalry, *dah*?"

Robert's lips twitched. She was really very believable. "*Dah*. There are supper boxes if you would care to eat, though I'll warn you, the food is not very good."

"Then it is fortunate I have already dined."

"Indeed. We can find a seat if you'd like to listen to music, or—"

"Could we simply explore the grounds?" She dropped her accent, no doubt because no one could overhear them amidst the noise. "I find watching people and walking are among my favorite activities here in London."

Robert bowed briefly. "I live to serve."

She cut a saucy sideways glance at him. "I shall hold you to that, my lord."

The huskiness of her voice and the look in her eyes sent a jolt of desire through his body. It took a moment to remember she simply played a role.

They entered a small clearing ringed by benches and lit by Turkish chandeliers. A small troupe of acrobats performed in the center. Catherine paused, and Robert stopped, more interested in watching her than the contortionists. She smiled with childlike delight, her eyes sparkling as she laughed at a comedic tumble. With her cosmetics and elaborate gown, she was an intriguing mix of sophistication and naïveté. He watched the play of emotions over her face, studied the fullness of her lower lip, the velvety texture of her cheek, and the stray wisp of hair that had escaped her coiffure.

She laughed and clapped then must have finally felt the weight of his stare, for she turned to him. "What is it? Why are you looking at me?"

He smiled, wondering what she would say if he told her he wished to kiss her. Would the ingénue or the countess answer him? He shook his head, unwilling to make her uncomfortable, especially so early in their relationship. "I'm glad you're enjoying the entertainment."

The look she gave him said she didn't believe him, but she let the matter drop. "These are far better entertainers than the traveling performers I've seen at the fairs at Chippenham. Those could barely touch their toes, much less tumble about. I used to spend the whole time worried they might dislocate a joint or break an ankle."

Robert laughed. "Shall we see what other entertainment we can find?"

She nodded and took his arm.

"Tell me about your son," he said as they wove their way through crowds of people, some dressed in rich velvets and silks, others in coarse broadcloth and rough linen.

Catherine smiled and paused to inspect an ornate wrought iron arch bedecked with lamps. "Christopher is four years old. He's quite tall for his age. I'm sure he gets that from his father."

Robert tried to discern if there was a longing for her husband in her mention of him, but she continued describing her son.

"He's very bright. I'm sure every mother must say that about her child, but he's already learning his letters and can count to ten." She chuckled. "Mother Purcell says he doesn't really know how to count, he's just memorized the words, like a nursery song, but I still think he's exceptional."

"I'm sure he is. Does he take after your late husband in any other ways?"

A slight frown marred her brow, and they walked for several seconds before she answered. "My mother-in-law says he is the spitting image of Jasper at that age, but I think he looks quite a bit like me. Mother Purcell tends to see reminders of her son in everything." She paused and clutched his arm. "I understand that, of course. I shouldn't want you to think I wasn't sympathetic to her loss. When I think of life without Christopher—" She shuddered, and he patted her hand on his arm.

"What of you, though? Do you miss your husband?"

She was silent for so long, he thought he'd crossed a line, and she didn't intend to answer. He was about to apologize for asking when she finally spoke.

"Jasper and I were married not even three years when he died. I'm sure it cannot be compared to a mother's loss."

"Of course it can if you loved him."

She avoided looking at him, and he was free to study her expressive face. It was obvious she warred with sharing her feelings versus appearing anything but respectful for her deceased husband.

"We scarcely knew each other when we wed. I told you Jasper and I had only met once before our wedding. Jasper spent a great deal of time in London. He had business to attend to, you see, and…"

Robert was confident it wasn't "business" that had drawn the man from his wife, and he wondered if Catherine was coming to the same realization.

She appeared lost in thought for a moment before turning to watch a particularly flashy woman saunter past in a gown that left little to the imagination. Vauxhall was famous for encouraging a mix of all classes of people, and that included prostitutes. Far from seeming appalled, however, Catherine appeared merely interested in the woman's low-cut gown and bold swagger.

Finally, Catherine returned her attention to him. "Jasper was unfailingly solicitous when he was home. We simply never seemed to, well, fall in with each other." She looked away again as if embarrassed. "I'm sure he found me terribly provincial."

Robert shook his head. Jasper had been a fool if he'd preferred the company of a mistress to Catherine. Robert could understand if the man resented his parents choosing his bride, but surely her appeal would have quickly become evident. Her wit and beauty should have reconciled any man to marriage.

He paused mid-thought. If his father were to imperiously betroth him to a woman, it would not matter if the lady were a royal princess; Robert would resent her very presence. Perhaps the fault did not lie so much with Jasper as the man's relationship with his parents.

"Does something displease you, my lord?" Catherine asked.

He pulled himself out of his maudlin reverie and forced a smile to his face. "Not at all. Though I'm sorry for your loss, I'm grateful circumstances arranged themselves to bring you to London."

"I'm ashamed to admit I'm glad to be here, experiencing all this." She gestured to the varied crowd.

"Why should you be ashamed?"

"Well, because had Jasper lived, we would not have come to London to…"

"Find you another husband? No, I suppose one at a time is more than enough."

"That's not what I—"

He silenced her with a finger across her lips. Though he was dutifully gloved, it was still a forward move. She froze at the contact, her pupils dilating as her breath quickened. He quickly dropped his hand.

"You did not cause your husband's death, so you have nothing to feel ashamed about. That you would seek to relish life long after his passing is perfectly acceptable."

"I suppose so."

They stared at each other for a long moment. Her widened pupils made her gray eyes appear dark, and when she parted her lips, the urge to kiss her struck him again. Had she leaned just the tiniest bit forward, he would have, but without encouragement, he would do nothing. She had made it clear she was not interested in an affair, and unless she expressed a change of heart, he would keep his attraction to her on a short leash.

A motley assortment of musicians had begun playing in the next clearing, and a wide smile broke Catherine's somber expression. "A country dance! Will you join me?"

He listened to the tune a moment and shook his head. "I don't know this one."

She gave him a look that reminded him she hadn't known the waltz when he obliged her to dance it, but she was clearly too impatient to join the circle of dancers to try and change his mind. She skipped out into the clearing and joined the group bobbing and twirling. It was a dance that required no partner; it was also a simple combination of steps that Robert could have quickly learned, but he found he relished watching her enjoy herself. In her lush gown, she stood out amongst the more muted colors of the other dancers who appeared mainly working class, but her smile was genuine and her manner unaffected as she hopped about with the other women. Joyful was the only word he could think to describe her. He felt like a fool for even thinking it, but it seemed watching her soothed his soul in a way he hadn't known he needed.

"It's not often one sees the Marquess of Dunsbury at such lowbrow entertainment as Vauxhall."

Robert turned to his right to see Viscountess Beaumont, one of the few women allowed to cross from good society to the *demimonde* and back unscathed. Her immunity to censure was partly because she refused to feel shame for enjoying her pleasures and partly because her husband had left her extremely wealthy and the mother of a four-year-old son who was his sole heir. It also didn't hurt that the woman was quite beautiful with her antique gold hair, sherry-brown eyes, and porcelain complexion. In addition, she possessed a daring and confident personality that quite bowled over those in the *ton* who would have sought to denounce her for her activities.

"My lady," Robert said with a brief bow. He and the viscountess had exchanged pleasantries but a few times since his return to England. Despite her beauty, there was an edge to her that did not appeal to him, and if they were to engage in any sort of flirtation, they'd both end up cut to ribbons.

"What brings you to the pleasure gardens tonight?" she asked as she laid a hand on his arm.

He shrugged but resisted the urge to cast off her hand. In her company, he always felt a bit like prey in the sights of a predator. He'd heard she was as shrewd a manager of her wealth and estates as at manipulating the *ton*, and though he would never begrudge Lady Beaumont her activities, he was not interested in being one of her conquests—a fact that seemed to make her pursue him with even more determination.

A loud "huzzah" from the dancers drew his attention, and he turned to see Catherine in the center of a group of people, all of whom were animatedly chatting and laughing. He smiled at her obvious delight.

The viscountess must have followed his line of sight. "Ah, our foreign visitor. I didn't have the pleasure of meeting her at Mrs. Wilson's party. Perhaps you would introduce me?"

Robert heard the edge in her voice and immediately turned to her. "She's not terribly interesting, I can assure you. I only escorted her tonight because my father owed a favor to the Russian consulate for securing him a case of vodka from his favorite distillery." His lie came easily as he did not want to subject Catherine to the viscountess's sharp tongue and cutting wit. Besides being woefully unprepared for someone like Letitia Beaumont, there was every possibility the two women could encounter each other at a society event. While the viscountess was very comfortable living on the edges of respectability, she was not so tolerant of others who did so.

"You appeared most interested in her at Mrs. Wilson's party."

Damn, the viscountess missed nothing. "Did I? Be sure and tell my father, will you?"

Out the corner of his eye, he saw Catherine begin to thread her way through the crowds toward him. He quickly took the viscountess's hand and kissed it. "I hope to see you at the Andover ball, my lady." He tried to infuse a seductive meaning in his gaze to distract her from Catherine's approach.

"Indeed, if you are not too busy playing nursemaid to the little Russian."

"I assure you, I will not be dancing attendance on her, but now I must return her to the embassy." He bowed and quickly turned to push his way through the throng of sweaty dancers.

"Oh, Robert, I had so much fun!" Catherine exclaimed.

He ignored the spurt of pleasure at her use of his given name. "We must go." He urged her in the opposite direction of Viscountess Beaumont.

"Oh? Very well." She waved at a small group who'd hopped around in the circle with her.

He led her out of the brightly lit clearing into one of the side paths less heavily traveled.

"I know it wasn't very *countess*-like of me," she admitted once they were alone. "But it was ever so much fun. It reminded me of the assemblies we would have where I grew up before Father grew ill."

"You didn't attend assemblies once you moved to Chippenham?"

"Only one before I became… Before I was expecting Christopher. Then Mother Purcell was afraid the exertion would not be good for me. After Christopher's birth, Jasper was busy in London, and Mother Purcell thought I wouldn't wish to dance without my husband present."

"Was she correct?"

Catherine took several steps before answering. "I would have rather danced and met the neighbors than sat at home in front of the fire with my needlework."

"Not your books?"

Catherine made a wry face. "I tend to keep my book reading to myself."

"Don't say your in-laws disapprove of you reading."

"It's not that. They simply don't understand how I could possibly enjoy it as much as I do. You mustn't think ill of them." Catherine stopped then turned to face him. "I know it sounds as if they had so many rules and strictures—"

"They didn't?"

"It's just— They're in perfect agreement on how to live life, and they don't understand why anyone would choose to do things differently. They've been incredibly kind to me, treating me as their daughter, and they positively dote on Christopher."

"Yes, but to make decisions about your life for you..." He frowned when he noticed Catherine had focused her attention behind his shoulder. He heard a high-pitched feminine giggle and turned to see a couple making their way out of a tunnel of sorts in the bushes. The woman stumbled drunkenly, and her escort caught her, sliding his hands over her body with excessive familiarity as they kissed passionately, albeit sloppily. There was little doubt as to what they'd been doing; the acres of unlit gardens were one reason Vauxhall was so popular, after all.

He turned back to see Catherine watching the couple with avid curiosity. Despite her intimations that she and her husband had not been close, they *had* produced a child. He wondered if she missed the physical pleasures of being married and if she was as sensuous in bed as he found her out of it.

His body tightened at the thought of finding out. If he married her, he could indulge his desire for her. He would certainly be able to help restore the baronial holdings that was her impetus for getting married. His mother would be pleased, and not just with the fact he would wed. He thought she would approve of Catherine herself.

"Catherine, I—" His mother's words, that his father would see Robert's marriage as an atonement or a pledge that he was fit to be the ducal heir, echoed in his head.

He drew himself up short and remembered the anger and pain after William's death, the bitter accusations his father had hurled at him. Robert curled his hands into fists, then forced them to relax. He'd be damned if he would do anything more to win his father's approval or forgiveness. Nor would Robert forget the vow he'd made to forsake what his brother could not have—a family. Robert shook his head. He would *not* marry Catherine, no matter how fascinating and attractive he found her.

"Yes?" She turned to face him, still flushed from dancing and no doubt witnessing the amorous couple. Her eyes, with their smoky dark lining, sparkled in the torchlight, and it was all Robert could do not to draw her close to his body and show her how she affected him.

"I think it's time I took you home. It grows late." His voice was low and tight, but he was grateful it didn't betray his turmoil.

"Oh, but I'm not the least bit tired. Can't we stay longer?"

Robert clenched his jaw then took a deep breath. He needed to stay strong because if he didn't, he'd accede to any wish of hers. "I have an early morning appointment."

"I didn't realize. Forgive me. I was thoughtless. Yes, of course we must go." She took his arm and turned to the path.

Robert hated that she'd apologized when he was the one to blame. "Please do not apologize. I—" He was a fool for not being able to control his feelings for her, especially when she seemed so unaffected by him. He let out a huff of laughter. He acted no better than a schoolboy infatuated with his governess. The absurdity of the image helped him regain his equanimity, and he guided her back to the carriage.

"Tell me," he said, trying to restore the good-natured easiness between them. "Did any of the men at the Egerton ball make an impression on you?"

She glanced sideways at him, and he knew it was ridiculous, but it seemed that glance was her immediate answer.

"Well… Mr. Skeffington was very nice. He is in shipping, I believe. Lord Stanley didn't even wince when I accidentally stepped on his foot while we danced."

Of course not. Stanley was probably too busy trying to catch a glimpse down her bodice. Robert knew of the man and his wandering eye all too well.

"I am rather nervous for the Andover ball, I will admit."

"Why is that?" Robert tore his thoughts from reminding Stanley about gentlemanly conduct.

"Well, I understand it is one of the most sought-after invitations. I still can't believe you convinced them to invite us, by the way. Suppose I make a terrible *faux pas*?"

He grinned. "There's a secret to events such as the Andover ball. There are so many people, and the rooms are so crowded, no one would notice if you spilled punch down your gown, took it off, and put on a fresh one right there in the middle of the ballroom."

She gasped then covered her mouth as she giggled like a young girl.

"People can barely squeeze from the dance floor to the refreshment table. I've walked right past my mother without seeing her at the Andover ball because I was trying to get outside for a breath of fresh air, and the flow of traffic is such that you can look neither left nor right."

"It sounds enjoyable," she said, her tone dry.

Robert laughed. He took inordinate pleasure in her sense of humor. As nothing physical could occur between them, at least he could savor her company.

᪥

A WEEK LATER, at another of Mrs. Wilson's parties, he watched Catherine as she threaded her way through the crowd, artfully dodging an inebriated playwright who begged her to serve as his muse, and the licentious Lord Wright who thought his title allowed him liberties with every woman in the room. Catherine had grown more confident during their clandestine adventures, as she called them. He smiled as she paused to free the train of her gown from beneath a portly man's heel. Her maid had grown equally more creative in transforming Catherine's grandmother's gowns. Tonight, Catherine wore the red dress again, but he only recognized it because of its magnificent ruby color.

Catherine had almost made her way back to Robert's side when yet another young man stopped her to pay an effusive compliment. She laughed, but Robert could tell the man had embarrassed her, for her cheeks pinkened instantly. It reminded Robert of a night shortly after their trip to Vauxhall. He'd taken her to a play at a small drafty theater where they sat on hard wooden benches watching a ribald comedy. It was there that Robert learned how easily Catherine blushed, even as she laughed aloud at the onstage antics.

She finally reached him and exhaled a sigh of relief. "I read an account of a form of military punishment used in the navy called 'running the gauntlet,' and I believe I know how those poor sailors felt."

Robert frowned. "Are you all right? I will have a word with—"

"No, no," she said and smiled. "I'm fine. I just never expected to be so…"

"Sought after?"

She shook her head as if amazed at the idea. Robert studied her flushed cheeks and sparkling eyes, and as usual, his body responded instantly. He should be used to it by now, but his reaction still caught him off guard.

"Come, I believe you owe me a game of chess."

"Owe you?" She smiled even as she drew her brows together.

"Yes. From the night we first met. In this very drawing room, in fact."

Catherine narrowed her eyes. "I don't recall any such agreement. What I remember is you taking my descriptions of Russian traditions as a challenge to your masculinity."

"A challenge to my—" He laughed, wanting to kiss her senseless. She made him laugh even as she heated his blood. He certainly got the better end of their bargain because he got to enjoy her company, whereas all she'd gain would be a rich husband in need of a wife with noble connections. The thought of her future husband sobered him.

"Please play chess with me." The softness of his tone made her give him another of those adorable smile-frowns.

"Very well. If you wish."

When word got out that the Russian countess, who had defeated the Duke of Newcastle, was playing, the entire party came to a standstill as people pressed around them, trying to watch. Robert could tell Catherine grew nervous that someone would recognize her. Though they'd attended a few events together, this was the first where she'd become the center of attention. So far, he'd thoroughly enjoyed their match, but he deftly threw the game, so she won within the next few moves. The second she'd checkmated his king, he grabbed her hand and ruthlessly pushed a path through the crowd. Within a minute, they escaped to his carriage out front.

"I should like to play you for real sometime," he said when they were seated inside.

Surprise flickered across her face. "After the drumming you just received? I can't recall ever having defeated an opponent in so few moves."

He laughed. "Surely a player of your talent can recognize and appreciate the skill it takes to purposefully lose a game that succinctly."

She gave him a pitying smile. "Is that what that display was?"

A slight sting pricked his vanity. "Well, of course it was. You're a good player, my dear, but no one is that good. Surely you could see I was feeding you moves?"

Her smile broadened. "All I saw was a man giving up pieces left and right, not unlike my previous game with the Duke of Newcastle."

"I must demand a rematch."

She shook her head. "It's far too late, my lord."

"Tomorrow night then."

That made her laugh aloud. "Goodness, you're quite serious, aren't you?"

"I feel my honor has been impugned."

"Because you lost to a woman?"

"Because you don't believe I threw the game to get you out of there quickly."

"Doesn't impugned honor generally require a duel to redeem itself? You already know I'm a country-bred girl. Aren't you concerned I might be a crack shot?"

Though still slightly offended she thought he'd lost the chess game, Robert was more entertained with Catherine's audacious, teasing side. He had thoroughly enjoyed their previous outings, but she had always maintained a modicum of deference in their interactions. He quite preferred this cheeky boldness, and while their verbal repartee engaged his mind, the gleam in her eye, the laughter on her lips, and the warm, sweet scent of her awoke other areas of his body—areas that were supposed to know their place in this careful arrangement he had made.

THE NEXT NIGHT, he picked her up for what he had told her was another visit to Vauxhall. Instead, he took her to the bachelor's rooms he kept, where he presented her with a chess table in his small study.

She seemed nervous at being alone in his home, which he should have realized.

"I assure you, I have no nefarious intentions. I simply wish to redeem my chess skills in your eyes." Though he spoke the truth, her presence in his home inspired a host of fantasies, and he had to remember he was a grown man and fully capable of controlling his baser desires.

For a long moment, Robert thought Catherine would leave, but she inclined her head and sat at the little table. She moved her pawn first, then Robert moved his, which Catherine quickly followed by confidently placing a knight. Robert responded with his knight, then studied her face in the lamplight, enjoying her frown of concentration as she scrutinized the board and the way she nibbled her lower lip before sliding her bishop forward diagonally.

"Ah, the Spanish game," he said.

She gave him an innocent head tilt that did not fool him. "Is it?"

After an hour, she relaxed enough to accept a glass of wine.

"This is better than the claret at the coffee house," she said after taking a sip.

Robert chuckled. "I should hope so."

Another hour of play later, he stood to stretch his muscles. "Would you like a brandy?"

"Brandy? I've never…"

Robert thought she would refuse, but then she smiled, and his stomach did a little flip at the beauty of it.

"Brandy sounds like something I'd like to try."

Robert poured her a small glass, but at the first swallow, she half choked.

"I believe you're trying to affect my wits, so I lose the game," she said, dabbing at her eyes as they watered.

"I gave you barely a splash. That's not near enough to addle an intellect such as yours."

"Flattery will gain you nothing," she said, though she seemed pleased with his compliment.

A half-hour of silent play later, Robert tried not to grin. "Are you sure you want to make that move?"

"Of course I'm sure. I'm going to— Oh." She pressed her lips together and gave him a rueful glance. "Stalemate. I suppose that still puts me ahead of you, considering I won our first match."

"As I already told you, I threw that—"

"Good heavens, it's three in the morning." She stared at the ormolu clock on the mantle as if she could will the hands to move backward. "Christopher will be awake in a few hours. I must return home."

Robert called for his carriage, and as the sleepy footman hurried off, turned to Catherine. "You don't have a nurse or governess to care for Christopher?"

"He's too young for a governess, and while Sophie does help me considerably, I wish to spend my days with him. He's the finest thing I've ever done."

Her earnest words caused an unfamiliar pang within Robert's chest. He placed her cloak over her shoulders then guided her outside and into the carriage before he followed her inside.

He wanted to ask her another question about her son but wasn't sure what to ask or how she would react, though she'd been forthcoming about her private life so far. He twisted his body to look at her, only to find her staring at him.

"Won't you tell me about yourself? You practically know my entire life story, but I know so little about you."

Though surprised at her interest, he smiled. "What do you wish to know?"

"Have you brothers or sisters?"

Robert's body tensed, and he willed himself to relax. "I have a younger sister. She married recently."

"Oh, how lovely," Catherine replied with the happy smile all women seemed to get at news of a wedding.

He could have left it at that. He knew she would assume he'd only ever had a sister, and he could simply talk about how Margaret had followed at his heels from the moment she took her first steps, despite his every attempt to lose her, and how it was so very odd to think of her living in Scotland now.

Instead, he opened his heart. "I had a brother. William. He died three years ago."

Catherine pressed a hand to her chest. Her eyes shone with unshed tears. "Oh, Robert, I'm so sorry."

"It was a gunshot." His throat tightened at the explanation, and he wished he'd said nothing.

Catherine raised her hand to her lips as if stifling a cry. After a moment, she rested her hand on his—as if transferring a kiss.

"That's how Jasper died," she whispered.

Robert looked up. "I didn't know that."

She smiled sadly. "There's no reason you should. It was a hunting accident. Is that what happened to William?"

"No. It was— There were highwaymen. Outlaws. I—" His

voice would go no further. He glanced down to where Catherine still rested her hand on his, and he covered it with his free hand. He studiously kept his gaze on the crisp whiteness of their gloves, but he could practically feel her gaze on his face, so he tried to keep his expression as neutral as possible. He only looked up when he heard her sniff.

"My father has always blamed me for William's death," Robert said, surprising himself with his confession. Catherine stared at him, wide-eyed and pale.

"That's dreadful," she whispered. "It must have been very difficult to lose a sibling. I always wished for a brother or sister when growing up. Our house was always so quiet, and I was never quite brave enough to make a rumpus on my own, but I always thought if I'd had a sibling to play with, we could have made noise together." She blotted the corner of her eyes with her other hand, the kohl around her eyes leaving dark smudges on her glove.

Robert looked back at their entwined fingers and realized she knew just how affected he was with his mention of William, and she chatted about her own childhood to give him time to collect himself. The notion filled him with a flood of warmth—a sense of being cared for that was at complete odds with what he wanted out of this arrangement with Catherine. *Or was it?* He'd only wanted her for amusement and distraction, but perhaps the distraction he really sought was from the pain he still experienced on a daily basis from William's death and his role in it…

His pulse sped up, and it suddenly became difficult to breathe. He swallowed hard, refusing to have an episode in front of Catherine.

"*Robert.*"

He glanced up to see her watching him. Without any consideration, he cupped her face. Her eyes widened in surprise just before he kissed her. His heart still pounded painfully, and he had no idea when the coach would stop, but as soon as his lips touched hers, all thoughts fled his mind. He was only aware of the soft warmth of her mouth against his, the curve of her cheek in his palm, and the utter *rightness* of their kiss. He didn't advance it beyond a gentle exploration of her closed lips. It was obvious she hadn't much experience with kissing, but he loved the pressure as she leaned into him.

When he finally released her and checked her reaction, her heavy-lidded eyes had darkened in desire.

She slowly sat back, and he followed suit, the air now cooler —or perhaps that was simply his body temperature returning to normal. He knew he should say something, apologize for crossing the platonic line they had agreed upon. However, he found himself unable to do anything other than watch her as she stared out the window. She didn't seem angry or put out or frightened—dear God, he hoped he hadn't frightened her—but she was definitely pensive. After a moment, she raised her hand to touch her lips. He relaxed at that gesture, recalling the feel of her mouth, the scent of her skin, and the curve of her face. Nonetheless, when they reached the Purcells' home in Marylebone, he sat forward.

"I find I cannot apologize for wanting to kiss you, but I shall apologize for actually doing so if you wish."

Catherine froze, her gaze on the carriage's door handle. "I'm not sorry it happened, but it would be best if it did not happen again."

She stepped down with the footman's assistance. Robert leaned out of the coach to speak quietly near her ear. "I promise not to kiss you again. Unless you ask me to." Though the gas streetlamps provided the palest illumination, Robert was fairly certain Catherine's face flushed with heat. He grinned. "Good evening, Countess."

He chuckled as she turned and fled into the house.

Eight

So, this is what a crush looks like.

Catherine stood on the steps of the Duke of Andover's palatial home just outside London. She and the Purcells waited for their hosts to greet them, but there were easily twenty people in front of them and twice that many gathered on the wide steps behind them, even though they were unfashionably early. Mother Purcell did not seem to understand that the time stated on the invitation did not mean one should be waiting to enter the house ten minutes before.

"You see," the older woman said as if reading Catherine's thoughts. "We are not the only ones to arrive promptly."

There was no point explaining the intricacies of London events to her mother-in-law, which Catherine had only recently found out herself. Anna Hamilton, a young woman who had befriended Catherine at the Egerton ball, and who Catherine had visited several times during Anna's receiving hours, had explained the only advantage to arriving early was getting some of the refreshments, which, depending on the hostess, was not necessarily a good thing.

Catherine wondered if the food tonight would be worth the early arrival and waiting for hours until the event hit its stride.

They moved up another step, and Catherine thought about Anna's other counsel. Anna had said to avoid Lord Stanley at all costs, that his title wasn't worth having to deal with the man and his predilections. However, she wasn't familiar with Mr. Skeffington but said she'd ask her husband. Anna had also promised to find Catherine many more suitors so she could have her pick.

With a sigh, Catherine glanced at the gaily-dressed ladies around her. How many of them were also looking for suitors? She hadn't confided her need for a wealthy husband to Anna, but her new friend had realized what Catherine meant when she'd confessed a desire to marry *this Season*. Apparently, according to Anna, with Catherine's coloring and figure, she should be popular because she wasn't a redundant blonde or the wrong shade of red. Anna herself had dark hair but confessed that though she was unfashionably brunette, her husband tolerated her, nonetheless.

Remembering the way Mr. Hamilton's face had lit up when he saw Anna, Catherine suspected he more than tolerated his wife. At the dull pang beneath Catherine's breastbone, she grimaced. Would she ever get to experience having a man look at her with such adoration? Probably not. Her duty was to marry a man who could save her son's birthright, just as it had been her duty to marry the man her father had chosen for her so he could die in peace.

Not for her were the marriages of romance or affection. Though she'd accepted the fact long ago, the reminder was like a vice around her chest, making it difficult to take a full breath as she climbed the last steps to the huge entry doors. She was foolish and ungrateful. She'd heard plenty of stories of well-born, gently reared yet penniless young women who had not ended up as cherished members of a husband's family. Those unwed women were reduced to a life of genteel poverty or worse.

She followed the Purcells as they entered the brilliantly lit main hall, just a few people away from meeting their hosts.

Catherine was incredibly fortunate, yet she still longed for passion and a small taste of excitement to prove that life was more than a succession of quiet evenings in front of the fire and simple days of needlework. The longing had led to mad escapades as the Russian countess, and though such behavior could ruin her, and by association, the Purcells, she relished every moment as Alisa Borodinicha and could not suppress the swell of anticipation for the next time she adopted the Slavic accent.

Of course, what she relished even more was spending time as the countess with the Marquess of Dunsbury. With him, the outspoken countess and the quiet country bluestocking merged, and she felt witty and interesting, and…desirable. She wondered if he would ask her to dance tonight, then wondered if it would be a waltz.

The group in front of the Purcells moved away, and the duke and duchess, a stately, handsome couple, greeted them. The duchess seemed to be in her late thirties, the duke a little older, but they were both striking—their good looks enhanced by their immaculately tailored clothing and that added flair that came from supreme confidence, backed by wealth and security.

As they cordially greeted the Purcells, Catherine noticed the duchess's assessing gaze. The duchess seemed as curious as Lady Egerton as to why the marquess would wish Catherine invited. Again, she suspected they did not completely believe the "family connection" excuse.

"I should like to become better acquainted with you, dear. Perhaps we may talk once I have greeted my guests."

"Of course, your grace," Catherine said with a small curtsey.

As they walked deeper into the house, Mother Purcell clutched her arm. "My dear, you must be making quite an impression on London hostesses to have a duchess wish to become acquainted with you."

Catherine smiled weakly, hoping the London hostesses didn't assume Catherine was Robert Carlisle's mistress. Thinking of him again, though in truth he was ever in her mind, she wondered what had made him so adamant about not marrying. Surely marrying was of prime importance for a man in his position, carrying on the line and such, especially considering his brother had died. Perhaps Robert had been deeply in love, even affianced. If so, she must have broken off the engagement or perished. Catherine thought of Jasper and speculated how she would have felt if they'd been in love, or even if they'd been more than polite strangers. Such a notion was so far from her experience she couldn't imagine what it would be like to truly grieve him. If Robert had deeply loved a fiancée and lost her, it might explain his assertion that he would not wed.

Catherine gasped, ashamed to be envious of a woman who may or may not exist and who may or may not be alive if she did exist.

"Are you all right, dear?" Mother Purcell asked.

Catherine's cheeks warmed in embarrassment, though no one could have known her thoughts. "It's so impressive." She gestured to the enormous ballroom they'd just entered as she surveyed the massive chandeliers, silk brocade-covered walls, and the elaborate chalk drawing on the polished wooden floor. She had learned the chalk was to keep dancers in their thin-soled slippers from losing their footing, but only the wealthiest hosts could employ an artist to create such elaborate drawings on the dance floor. It would be a blurred mess by the end of the evening, but for now, it was lovely and almost made up for their early arrival.

"Good heavens!" the older woman exclaimed. "I feel like we're in a palace."

Even the ever-composed baron seemed in awe of their surroundings. Catherine would have joined them in their gawking if she weren't scanning the crowd looking for Dunsbury. It was ridiculous, of course. He would not be so gauche as to arrive at the very opening of the doors, and if she did search for any gentlemen, it should be for the ones who had paid her court. She'd met another potential suitor just that afternoon at Anna's house. Mr. Hughes was rather attractive and had been very polite. He was perhaps not quite as witty as Dunsbury but was clearly intelligent and had not spent the entire visit talking about himself. Catherine would be far wiser to spend her time searching for him. Anna had confided that Mr. Hughes had made his wealth from his family's ironworks company that had produced the scrollwork gates at Hyde Park, but he also had political aspirations. In other words, he would benefit from an intimate connection with the nobility, even a minor one such as theirs.

A dark-haired man with square shoulders and a familiar tilt to his head caught Catherine's attention, and her heart pounded even as she realized it wasn't Dunsbury.

"Oh bother," she said under her breath. She hadn't seen him since he'd kissed her, and over the last week, her nerves had fluctuated between excitement and apprehension. He couldn't have thought about that kiss as many times as she had, but she did question if he'd try to kiss her again. She also had to ask herself if she wanted him to. Another dark-haired man caught her eye, and she craned her neck to see his face.

She stifled a sigh. Tonight would turn out to be very long indeed if she jumped every time she imagined she saw Robert Carlisle.

Two hours later, there was still no sign of the missing

marquess. *Ah, that would make an intriguing book title.* She smothered a laugh as she hopped about on the dance floor.

It was not her favorite country dance as she always ended up on the wrong foot, and there was too much waiting in a long line facing a partner with nothing to do but smile encouragingly if he was an enjoyable partner or try to avoid eye contact altogether if he was not. *Or one might search for missing marquesses and speculate on book titles, as the case may be.*

In the men's line, her partner smiled broadly, and she realized she'd been grinning at her meager wit. Catherine quickly looked away. Sir Harry Fitzgibbons was not one of the dance partners she wished to encourage. He was easily as old as the baron, and while that couldn't ultimately be a reason for discouraging him, she had it on the best authority that Sir Harry was in the market for a wealthy wife to offset gaming losses.

Catherine's shoulders slumped, and she quickly straightened her spine, hoping no one had noticed her lapse in poise. The whole marital process, however, felt so very mercenary.

It was finally Sir Harry's and her turn to travel down the column of dancers. When they took their place at the end of the line, she craned her neck to see how many couples were left until the interminable dance ended. That was when Dunsbury came into her line of sight.

She'd called him Robert the night he'd kissed her. She didn't know what had possessed her to use his Christian name, only that it had slipped easily off her tongue, and he hadn't seemed to mind.

He was engaged in conversation with the same woman she'd glimpsed him with at Vauxhall. Catherine frowned. Actually, she rather thought the lady had also been at one of Mrs. Wilson's parties. The realization brought goose bumps to Catherine's arms. What if the woman recognized *her* in return?

"Shall we visit the refreshment table?" Sir Harry inquired.

Having earlier spent a great deal of time at said table while they waited for the ballroom to fill, Catherine shook her head. "Perhaps later, Sir Harry. If you will excuse me, I need… If you will excuse me."

Thankfully, the man seemed to take her meaning and bowed politely before withdrawing. She beat a hasty retreat to the ladies' retiring room, squeezing herself through the crowds. Once there, she was loath to come out, worried she might run into the woman who'd been at Mrs. Wilson's.

"Are you all right, milady?" asked the maid whose job it was to repair torn hems and dab punch spills out of satin gloves.

"Oh! Yes. Yes, of course." Catherine realized she could not remain in there all night. "Lost in my thoughts, I suppose."

"It happens, milady," the maid said with a bob of her head.

After the relative quiet of the rest of the house, when Catherine re-entered the ballroom, she was amazed anew at the crowds. It was just as Dunsbury described. There were groups of ladies clustered around their chaperones, gentlemen weaving their way between them seeking partners for the next dance, scores of dancers twirling about on the floor, and servants trying to remove empty punch cups from every flat surface.

Why, then, was she able to pick out Dunsbury within moments of glancing at the dance floor? It was a waltz, and he danced with an exquisitely beautiful young woman. She was the epitome of English beauty with her dark gold curls, flawless complexion, and bow lips. It wasn't jealously that lit Catherine's veins; she was sure of it. She was simply disappointed because she'd hoped to dance a waltz with the marquess. He'd been such a patient instructor, and she was nervous to dance it with anyone else.

Yes, that's all I'm feeling. That wasn't the least bit true, however, particularly when Dunsbury smiled into the blonde girl's upturned face as they made their way off the floor.

Surely there would be another waltz this evening. Perhaps he will seek me out then. She had been in the ladies' room when this waltz had started, after all.

Except he didn't seek her out for the second waltz of the evening or a quadrille or a country dance. In fact, he didn't stop to pay his respects or so much as nod in recognition when she was sure he'd spotted her at the punch bowl.

Despite the dull ache in her chest, it was pointless to read anything into Dunsbury's refrainment. There were hundreds of women for him to dance with, and Catherine and his arrangement had only included socializing when she was Countess Alisa, not Widow Purcell. He'd only sought her out at Countess Egerton's ball because they'd needed to arrange their first meeting.

She chewed on her lower lip as she and her final dance partner of the night waited for the knot of people in front of them to disperse.

"Surely he'll need to seek me out tonight," she mumbled.

"So sorry, did you say something?" her partner asked.

Catherine blinked. "Just commenting on how many people are in this room. I should hate for someone to cry fire."

"It *is* the Andover ball. No one refuses an invitation," he replied, ignoring her weak jest about crying fire. It didn't surprise her; her conversation prior to and during their dance had been less than remarkable, distracted as she was with looking for Dunsbury.

The gentleman left her with a courteous but brief bow as soon as they reached Mother Purcell, and Catherine did not try to stop him. Despite the way she'd smiled and curtsied to the dozen gentlemen she'd met, she was immoderately disappointed not to have spent time with Dunsbury, which had put a pall on the whole evening.

"What's wrong?" Anna asked as they gathered their wraps.

"What? Nothing! I'm…just tired."

Anna looked at her with obvious skepticism. Though they'd only met recently, Anna felt like a lifelong friend—she could certainly read Catherine as if she'd known her for years.

Catherine longed to confide what had her out of sorts, but then she'd have to explain *why* she wished to see Dunsbury, and no matter how close Anna and Catherine had grown in so short a time, there was no way she could admit to her scandalous arrangement.

"It's simply a bit overwhelming, what with so many people and trying to make a good impression on the right gentlemen *and* remember their names."

Anna linked her arm through Catherine's and walked with her outside where the Purcells were awaiting their carriage. "You poor dear. Come over tomorrow, and I will help you figure out who to remember and who to forget."

Catherine smiled her thanks then glanced around for Anna's husband. "Isn't Mr. Hamilton joining you?"

"He's no doubt in the card room," Anna said with a wave of her hand to the house. "I'll have to go pry him away from the tables. The man never loses." She shook her head even as she grinned. "If he did, perhaps he would be a little more amenable to leaving before the hosts have to clear their throats meaningfully."

Catherine promised to visit the next day before following the baron and baroness into the carriage.

"I'd say that was our most successful event yet," Mother Purcell said once the footman had closed the door. "Catherine danced with no less than *eleven* men." She leaned toward her husband. "And I can attest they were all quite taken with her."

Catherine was certain that was untrue for at least half her partners. Even had she not been distracted looking for Dunsbury, her conversational skills were rudimentary at best. She'd spent her entire life in a tiny spot of England, whereas most men of the *ton* had toured Europe, either for edification or to fight Napoleon. So, she had no idea what she could possibly discuss or have in common with them.

Since arriving in London, she'd had a few adventures. Unfortunately, she couldn't share those with a prospective suitor. The only gentleman she could discuss anything *interesting* with was Dunsbury—the one man she'd met who wasn't looking for a wife. She sighed, then chided herself for spending so much of her evening looking for him.

"Do any of the men seem suitable for...our needs?" the baron asked. Catherine studied him in the dim light of the carriage lamp, shocked when she realized he'd lost quite a bit of weight and now exhibited deep grooves along the sides of his mouth that had been much less noticeable a few months ago. She knew he spent hours every day pouring over the books of the newly acquired baronial holdings and writing letters to various creditors assuring them he would see them paid.

Catherine was suddenly overwhelmed with guilt. Caught up in her infatuation with Dunsbury, she forgot she was not the only one beholden to responsibility nor the only one for whom the future was unknown.

"Indeed, I am given to understand several of them are quite suitable. Perhaps you can meet them when we are receiving."

Some of the tightness eased from the baron's face. "Of course. What day do you ladies accept callers?"

Beside her, Mother Purcell gasped. "Really, Mr. Purcell, how can you not know that by now? We are home a Mondays. Do you not remember the host of visitors we had just two days ago?"

The baron's expression lightened further at his wife's indignant tone. Catherine smiled at the impish look on her father-in-law's face. His expression reminded her of Christopher's when he was feeling mischievous.

"Is that what all the ruckus was about?" the baron asked with a smile.

"Honestly," Mother Purcell said, though an answering smile tugged at her mouth. "I don't think you've paid a whit of attention to our activities so far."

"Have I not escorted you to every event?" the baron asked. "Even when I had a headache?"

"Well, yes, you've been most accommodating," Mother Purcell remarked. "But really, dear, not noticing when we receive guests…"

The couple's gentle banter continued, but Catherine turned her attention inward. Of the gentlemen she'd met so far, Mr. Hughes seemed the most suited to their requirements. They met at Anna's one afternoon a few days past. He had a kind face, and Anna had told her Mr. Hughes had returned to ask about her after Anna's other callers had departed. He hadn't been present tonight because, despite his wealth, men of industry were still excluded from many society events.

Catherine frowned. She'd spent less than an hour in his company, and yet she was settling on him as a future spouse. Well, at least she could say she would know him better than she'd known Jasper when they'd wed. The thought did not bring her much comfort.

She had a sudden and unruly urge to put on her grandmother's dress, assume the Russian countess's persona and go out somewhere—*if* she had an inkling of where she could go. Maybe a party like Mrs. Wilson's. Catherine had no idea how often the woman entertained but still wanted to don the red dress and take a hired hack to that side of town. The question was whether there would be another celebration with drinking and outrageous flirtation, bawdy guests, and chess matches with statesmen. Most importantly was whether Dunsbury would be there.

Catherine sighed and pressed her forehead to the cool glass

of the carriage window. Her infatuation with Robert Carlisle was getting out of hand. Considering his utter lack of attention to her tonight, she had to remember his only interest in her was as an actress playing a role that amused him. The thought made her feel slightly ill. She forced her thoughts back to Mr. Hughes but could not even call to mind the color of his hair. All she could see in her mind's eye was Dunsbury's dark head bowed over the golden one of the beautiful young woman Catherine had learned was Lady Eleanor Chalcroft, the most popular girl of the Season.

Of course she was.

With a slight groan, Catherine gave up trying to think of anyone else.

"Are you well, dear?" Mother Purcell asked.

Catherine snapped open her eyes. "Oh, yes. My feet are just sore from dancing."

"Of course they are." Mother Purcell patted Catherine's hand. "You were quite popular this evening. Jasper would be so proud of you."

Catherine couldn't say she'd known her late husband well enough to know if her popularity would have made him proud. She smiled weakly at his mother then closed her eyes, pretending to doze the rest of the ride home.

❧

THE FOLLOWING Monday saw a gratifying number of callers during the Purcells' receiving hours. Mother Purcell was in her element, welcoming them. She made a valiant attempt at conversation for a woman who had as much experience at London small talk as Catherine. Thankfully, Anna had brought her mother-in-law, and the two older women fell in well together.

Mr. Hughes brought a small posy of delicate flowers, and

Mr. Skeffington, clearly sensing competition for Catherine's attention, far outstayed the usual twenty-minute visit. Ever the good friend, Anna sat next to Mr. Skeffington and demanded an account of all his mother's ailments so Catherine could have a moment's uninterrupted conversation with Mr. Hughes.

Light brown, Catherine realized. Mr. Hughes had light brown hair and… She ducked her head to see better. Ah yes, blue eyes. Quite a lovely blue. A color she would certainly remember. Perhaps not as striking as Lord Dunsbury's coffee-colored eyes, but very attractive, nonetheless.

Why had she gone and done that? Now all she could see in her mind was Dunsbury's brown hair, so dark as to almost seem black but with richer tones when burnished by candle-light, the mischief in his eyes, and the way his lips curved when he—

"I beg your pardon, Mr. Hughes. My mind went a-begging. What did you say?"

He smiled without the least sign of exasperation and repeated himself. "Would you care to join me for a walk tomorrow?"

"That would be lovely," she said without thought. Mr. Hughes smiled. She gave him her hand, and he bowed over it, squeezing gently. Catherine did not return the flirtatious gesture but forced herself to return his smile. As she bobbed a curtsey and watched him depart, she vowed she would stop comparing him to Dunsbury. She should be thrilled with Mr. Hughes's attentions. She'd never had anyone court her before, much less as smoothly with his tasteful bouquet, his solicitous conversation, and his offers of walks in the park. He was reasonably attractive, attentive, and apparently possessed of sufficient wealth to rescue the impoverished barony. She should be thanking her lucky stars.

As she sank onto the sofa beside Anna and pretended interest in Mr. Skeffington's conversation, Catherine realized she *would* be thankful if she hadn't met Robert Carlisle. If only she hadn't flirted with him, teased him, and walked arm in arm with him under a starry night. She might even have been able to force herself to forget the laughter and the inappropriate conversations that delighted her, *if* she hadn't kissed him. That brief press of his lips had disrupted all her good intentions. Unable to even counterfeit an interest in Mr. Skeffington's mother's rheumatism, Catherine fumed.

She cursed Dunsbury for ruining her for other men. She cursed his sly wit and his constant pushing for her to do outrageous things. She cursed him because he challenged her to learn who she was. She cursed him for making her want more from life and more from a husband, but she cursed him most of all for not wanting *her* as she wanted him.

Finally, Mr. Skeffington took his leave, and when Catherine told Anna of Mr. Hughes's invitation, Anna smiled knowingly. "I have learned, not only does Mr. Hughes see more than twelve thousand pounds a year, he also recently purchased an estate less than an hour from Haddington Manor. We shall be able to see each other frequently when we are not in London."

"Oh, that *is* good news," Catherine said. "But a walk in the park surely does not indicate an offer of marriage."

Anna, usually the epitome of good manners in public, rolled her eyes. "I already told you he returned to my house to ask after you. My husband even hinted the previous baron had not left his affairs in good order, and Mr. Hughes did not even blink. I think it's safe to say he is smitten with you."

"Or smitten with being closely associated with a baron," Catherine said, her tone bitter.

Anna laid her hand on Catherine's. "Does it matter, dear?"

Tears stung Catherine's eyes, but she refused to let them drop. "I suppose not."

"He is a kind man. I do not think you will be unhappy."

Catherine nodded and turned the conversation to the Andover ball.

Anna evaluated all the men with whom Catherine had danced, but Catherine only half-listened as she thought of Dunsbury's beautiful dance partner. As Catherine finished her lemonade, she affected a casual tone. "I was curious about Lady Eleanor Chalcroft."

"Did you meet her at the ball?"

"No, I didn't get the opportunity. I only saw her dancing, and someone told me she was considered a 'diamond of the first water.' Where did that expression come from? It sounds like a rather cold description of anyone."

Anna laughed and helped herself to the last finger sandwich. "A high-quality diamond is translucent. Like water. So, a woman who is a diamond of the first water is the most beautiful."

Lady Eleanor certainly was that. Catherine wanted to know more about Dunsbury's dance partner but didn't want Anna wondering why her friend was so curious about a woman she'd not met. Fortunately, Anna was free with her knowledge.

"I believe this is Lady Eleanor's third Season out, or is it her fourth? Surely not. At any rate, she has had dozens of offers, but she hasn't settled on any one man. Her mother is keen to have her marry a duke, but goodness knows *those* are in short supply."

Catherine's heart sank. There were few eligible dukes about, and only one very eligible heir to a dukedom.

She straightened her spine and brushed a wayward crumb from her skirts. Well, she certainly had no intention of making a complete fool of herself. She *wouldn't*.

"Are you all right?" Anna asked, leaning forward to put a cool hand on Catherine's clenched fist.

Catherine pulled herself out of her morose musings and

offered a wan smile. "I've a sudden headache. Will you please excuse me?"

"Yes, of course. You poor dear. The marriage market is a nerve-racking place to shop, is it not? Go lie down and know it will soon be over. I am convinced of it."

Catherine ignored the sinking sensation in her stomach at that notion but gave her friend a brief hug. "I'm so very glad I met you."

Anna smiled broadly in return. "As am I. Now go rest. We've the concert at Lady Taylor's this evening, and Lady Campbell's card party tomorrow, remember."

As Catherine climbed the stairs to her son's room on the third floor, she tried not to dwell on why she was so disgruntled over Robert's dance partner. Catherine considered herself a level-headed woman, and she had an enormous responsibility to see to her family's future security. She did not have time for distractions such as handsome noblemen destined to marry diamonds of the first water.

Her self-inflicted lecture did not prevent her shoulders from slumping or her eyes from watering, however.

"Ugh!" She paused outside the nursery door to roughly wipe her eyes. "Brace yourself, Catherine." It was an expression her father had often said to her as a child if she cried over a broken toy or a skinned knee. She took a deep breath and entered the nursery, where her son was finishing his afternoon snack with Sophie.

"Mama!" Christopher knocked over his chair in his haste to run to her and throw his sturdy little arms around her legs. She disengaged him and crouched to give him a proper hug.

"Are you all right, miss?" Sophie asked.

Catherine glanced up and smiled. "I am now."

Two hours of building blocks, setting up tin soldiers, and draping various blankets over chairs and tables to make tents did much to restore Catherine's equanimity. Playing with

Christopher also hardened her resolve to accomplish her goal. She wasn't simply repaying the Purcells for their care and support; she had to secure her son's financial future as well. The bankrupt baronial holdings would one day be her son's responsibility, and if she could do anything to make sure it was not an onerous one, she would. With a sigh, she decided if she saw Mr. Hughes at the concert, she would tell him she looked forward to their walk in the park and hoped he understood that meant she would accept his proposal if offered.

Decision made, she smiled at her sleeping son's flushed face. He had crawled into their makeshift tent several minutes ago, and when he grew suspiciously quiet, she'd lifted the corner of a blanket to discover him sprawled out on his belly, sound asleep. She tucked the blanket up so he wouldn't be afraid if he awoke and didn't know where he was, then she tiptoed out of the nursery.

Catherine did not scan the gathering in Lady Taylor's drawing room that evening. She started to, of course. It was hard to break the habit of looking for tall men with dark hair and sly smiles, but as soon as she lifted her head to see above the crowds, she forced her attention back to the baron. Mother Purcell had intended to join them as she normally did, but the late-night schedule had taken its toll on her, and she was no doubt already sound asleep.

"Who are we on the lookout for tonight, dear?" the baron asked. Catherine had to bite the inside of her cheek to keep from laughing. The baron was clearly trying to fill his wife's shoes, and that was generally Mother Purcell's first question when they entered a venue. Catherine had quickly learned never to tell her mother-in-law the name of any man she was actually interested in, for Mother Purcell would hunt the man down and plague him with questions about his family and assurances that Catherine was the most suitable wife a man could hope for. On the other hand, Mother Purcell had proven quite useful in ridding Catherine of those gentlemen she wished to discourage. Lord Stanley and Sir Harry Fitzgibbons had all but disappeared after enduring an hour in Mother Purcell's company.

The baron, however, had more finesse at interviewing suitors, and so Catherine decided to tell him she hoped to see Mr. Hughes.

"Hughes? Ah yes, slim chap with ashy hair."

"Ashy?" Catherine asked, perplexed.

"Well, it's not really a color, is it? It's not quite brown, certainly not blond. It's just sort of…ashy."

Catherine smiled. It was an apt enough portrayal. For herself, she would try to come up with a more enthusiastic description of the man she'd set her sights on.

"That is the very gentleman," she said in confirmation.

"Thought so, thought so. He introduced himself to me this afternoon when I ran into him at the club I've applied to. Surely that's a good sign."

"That does seem encouraging." She ignored the fact there was no flutter of excitement in her stomach at the news.

If the spacious drawing room filled with chairs was anything to go by, Lady Taylor clearly expected a large crowd to hear the quintet of musicians she had hired, but to judge by the refreshments, she only wished to feed a dozen or so people.

Catherine and the baron visited the refreshment table then mingled before taking a seat for the performance. She kept looking for Anna but saw no sign of her, and when the musicians began, Catherine closed her eyes and lost herself in the beauty of the music. This was one of the best parts of being in London—the music at nearly every event.

Halfway through the performance, Catherine was jostled as

someone slid into the seat next to hers. She opened her eyes to see Anna. Her friend smiled guiltily and leaned close to whisper, "Mr. Hamilton and I were…detained."

From the flush on Anna's face and the sparkle in her eyes, Catherine could guess what had detained them. Since arriving in London as a widow, Catherine had heard quite a bit of talk about marital activities; things maiden girls were not privy to. In retrospect, she wished she'd known more before marrying Jasper, but something told her even had she been more worldly about the intimate side of marriage, she and Jasper would have still been terribly awkward together. She turned back to the performance, unsure if she was happy for the Hamiltons or jealous. Probably both. They were so clearly a love match.

"He's not here, is he?"

Startled, Catherine turned her head sharply. It didn't matter that she hadn't looked for Dunsbury. He wasn't in the room. The air didn't vibrate with his presence, and her skin didn't tingle with awareness, but how would Anna—

"Mr. Hughes," her friend said. "I don't see him."

Catherine's cheeks flamed with embarrassment. Of course. Mr. Hughes. She took a breath to steady her pulse. "He's in the third row. Next to the blonde girl in blue."

Anna leaned to the side, oblivious to the fact she was blocking the view of the row behind her. "Ah yes, there he is. That's his sister," she whispered. "He often escorts her to events as the girl's husband is considerably older and not interested in musical evenings. Or balls. Or really any society event."

Catherine supposed she should feel relieved the woman was only his sister, but it hadn't occurred to Catherine to worry about what would happen if she had a rival. She sighed and chewed on her lower lip. She'd decided on Mr. Hughes. Therefore, she needed to focus on encouraging him.

Anna grinned. "Perhaps he intends to introduce the two of you. That would be a good sign."

"Shh!" hissed a matron behind them. The two women pressed their lips together to keep from laughing at being chastised like two girls in church.

After the musicians took their bows, Mr. Hughes did indeed search her out, then introduced his sister. Catherine ignored Anna's "I told you so" look and tried to smile warmly at the woman who could very well end up her sister-in-law. Bridgette St. George was as pleasant as her brother, and Catherine was grateful to discover they would rub along well together if she and Mr. Hughes did make a match of it.

"I am very much looking forward to our walk tomorrow, Mr. Hughes," she said during a lull in the conversation.

"As am I, Mrs. Purcell. May I inquire as to a convenient time?"

"I usually spend time with my son after luncheon. Perhaps when I put him down for a nap?"

"Oh, but he must join us. I am sure he would enjoy an outing to the park. It seems the type of activity with which young boys engage."

Catherine smiled. She wanted to ask him if he'd not been a young boy himself at some point, but touched he would make the offer, she inclined her head. "That is most thoughtful of you, my lord. Christopher would indeed enjoy a visit to the park. He is most keen on feeding the ducks."

"Splendid! We shall make sure to bring...whatever it is ducks eat, then."

"I believe that would be bread, brother," Bridgette said with a teasing grin.

"Indeed." Mr. Hughes glanced at Bridgette, then at Catherine, his face turning a little red.

"Our cook knows to save bread crusts for Christopher," Catherine said. "We shall bring the duck food."

"Very good," he said, his relief obvious.

They arranged a time for the expedition before Mr. Hughes

dutifully fetched Catherine and his sister some lemonade. The rest of the evening ended with no more excitement than Catherine overhearing someone mention Dunsbury. Try as she might, however, she could hear nothing more and wasn't even sure who had mentioned his name or if she simply heard things.

Nine

ROBERT CLIMBED into his coach and rubbed at the knots that had formed in the muscles of his neck. Once again, a visit to his father for his morning report had nearly deteriorated into a shouting match. As a result, Robert found himself in a foul mood.

He should be used to the feeling considering not a single visit with his father ended well. Still, some childish part of Robert always held out hope his father would treat him as his son rather than a pariah, and that the duke would listen to him as he once had before gently offering advice. So far, Robert remained bitterly disappointed.

It didn't help that he'd been short-tempered *before* he went to see his father. In fact, Robert had retained a simmering level of displeasure since the Andover ball last week when he'd had to dance with Lady Eleanor—a nice enough chit but clearly as uninterested in him as he was in her. The same night, he'd had to deal with Letitia Beaumont, who again coyly questioned him about the little Russian countess she still heard so much about. He had tried to brush aside her questions, but she'd grown insistent, claiming her "friend" at the Russian consulate had no idea of any Russian nobles visiting England.

Robert had shrugged, trying to look bored with the subject while he'd dismissed the viscountess's attempts to ferret out information. The woman had proven tenacious, however, offering an *arrangement* that left little doubt what she wanted. He hadn't wanted to be rude, for he generally liked Letitia. She was intelligent and daring, but he'd never found her attractive. When she'd snaked a hand down his waistcoat, clearly intending to delve further, he'd caught her hand and improvised a reason for declining her offer that involved a fictitious trip to Scotland. The viscountess had not been amused. Though she'd left in a huff, he'd caught her watching him the rest of the night. There'd been no way he could approach Catherine. Letitia was sharp. If she saw him with Catherine, there was every likelihood the viscountess would recognize Catherine as the Russian countess despite the absence of her lavish gowns and kohl-darkened eyes.

Now, as he sat in his carriage—wishing he'd ridden because the fresh air would have done him good—his thoughts returned to Catherine, and he suddenly had the feeling that only her company could remove the dark cloud that hung above his head.

He craved a dose of her quick wit, the sight of her blush if he said something suggestive, and her smile. In actuality, he craved her mere presence.

He instructed the coachman to proceed to the Purcell residence. It was rash, yes, but Robert *had* introduced himself to the baron and baroness, and he rather suspected he would not be turned away. For the endless burdens that accompanied his title, primarily that he wished it was still his brother's, there were the rare times he shamelessly used it to ease his way.

Once he arrived, already feeling better, Robert bounded up

the short walk to the townhouse, eagerly anticipating Catherine's surprise at his visit.

His rapped sharply, and a footman opened the door.

"I'm here to see Mrs. Purcell," Robert said.

"Receiving hours are on a Monday, sir."

Robert hadn't thought of that, but still… "I'm sure she will be happy to see me. Tell her Lord Dunsbury is here to see her."

"Well, sir, Mrs. Purcell is not at home."

"What do you mean she's not at home?"

The footman froze, seemingly unsure how to respond.

"Do you know when she'll be back?" Robert asked, trying to appear as if that was what he intended to say all along.

"I— That is, Mrs. Purcell did not mention her plans to me, my lord. I believe a gentleman escorted her and young Master Christopher."

Robert nodded and turned to leave, feeling a disproportionate sense of disappointment and something suspiciously like jealousy. He was halfway to his carriage when he heard a woman call after him. He turned back to see a young maid slip furtively out the front door and rush down the steps. He recognized her as Catherine's maid, Sophie.

"Lord Dunsbury. Mrs. Purcell is at the park. The big one," Sophie said.

"Hyde Park?" That park was three hundred and fifty acres. "I'll never find her."

"Aye, my lord. But she'll be near the water. Master Christopher does love to feed the ducks. Chases them too when miss isn't looking."

Robert filed that bit of information away. "Is there a favorite spot they go to?"

"Just across from that little island in the lake."

Robert touched the brim of his hat in thanks. He turned to leave but paused. "Why would you wish me to find your mistress?"

The young maid fought a smile and shrugged. "I just thought miss would enjoy your company more than the gentleman who took her there. He seems a bit dull for her, don't you think?"

Robert went through the list of the men Catherine had danced with recently. "Slim chap? Fair hair?"

Sophie nodded.

Ah. Hughes. He was a good man. Financially secure, not given to excesses of any kind, and was known to treat his mother and sister well. Robert had even heard the man provided a living for an elderly aunt whose husband had left her nothing when he died. The man was perfect for Catherine. Robert detested him.

He grinned. "You are quite right. Entirely too dull for our Mrs. Purcell. I believe I shall take the air myself."

The young woman smiled cheekily. "It is a fine day for it, sir. My mam always says fresh air will cure most of what ails you."

Robert retrieved a half sovereign from his pocket and pressed it into the astounded maid's hand. He gave her a wink and left.

Once at the park, it did not take him long to find the trio. He slowed as he approached, pretending to be lost in thought.

"I say! Dunsbury! Imagine seeing you here of all places," Mr. Hughes said with a pleased smile.

Robert pretended surprise. "Oh! Hughes, my good man. So sorry, I didn't see you there. What are you about today?" He glanced at a clearly startled Catherine.

"Mrs. Purcell. How nice to see you again."

"I didn't know you were acquainted with Mrs. Purcell." Mr. Hughes glanced between the two.

"I was acquainted with the previous Baron Tutley, and I welcomed Mrs. Purcell and the new baron and baroness at an event several weeks ago."

There was no way Robert could mention Mrs. Wilson's party even if he doubted Hughes knew anything about the woman's gatherings and her type of guests.

With the pleasantries exhausted, a strained silence fell upon them.

"Feeding the ducks, are you?" Robert asked, gesturing to the cloth bag in Catherine's hand.

"Yes. Or rather, Christopher is," she said.

Robert looked behind her to see a sturdy young boy squatting at the edge of the Serpentine, poking a stick into the mud. Robert smiled, remembering his own fascination as a boy with all things dirty, mucky, and otherwise unpleasant. He walked over then crouched beside Catherine's son.

"Tadpoles or worms?" he asked seriously.

The boy glanced briefly at Robert then resumed his perusal of the mud before him. "Worms. Tadpoles don't like it here, Mama says."

"Ah yes, the water is too turbulent. That means it moves too much for them."

Christopher mouthed the word, no doubt filing it away for later use.

"Are you hoping to catch a worm?" Robert asked.

The young boy nodded, digging more vigorously with his stick. "I thought the ducks would like worms better than dry, old bread."

"An excellent thought. I'm sure they would." Several wriggling specimens presented themselves. "Ah, there you go. Shall I help you hold them?"

At that, Christopher looked at him with amazement.

"I shan't squash them, I assure you. I've been known to handle quite a few worms in my time."

"But growed ups don't like worms."

A smile tugged at Robert's mouth. "Is your mother afraid of them?"

"Oh, she likes them all right, but she says most other growed ups find 'em disgusting." He threw a rather condescending glance at Hughes and whispered, "I think she means *him*."

Robert nodded in commiseration. "I suspect you're right. I, however, am most fond of cold, slimy insects. I even ate one on a dare when I was a good deal younger."

"You did?" Christopher asked, his eyes and grin wide. Clearly, Robert had earned the boy's respect with *that* admission.

"Indeed. Shall I prove it? Here, hand me that worm."

Christopher giggled and reached for the worm that wriggled into the soil as if aware it was about to become a snack.

"Christopher," Catherine called. The boy smoothly pretended to reach for another stick, which he then threw into the water.

Robert stood and watched Catherine approach with a cloth bag.

"Do you wish to feed the ducks or not?" She raised her eyebrows at Robert, and he grinned, unrepentant.

"All right," Christopher said. He tossed a few crusts into the water, and within seconds, a dozen ducks made their way to the shore. Christopher seemed to forget his disappointment as he laughed at the way the waterfowl squabbled over each crumb.

Robert glanced at Catherine and Hughes, amused when the man took a step away from the encroaching flock. Catherine watched her son with an expression so full of love and pride, Robert's breath caught in his throat. She was truly stunning. He'd thought her beautiful, but just then, even with the sun making her squint and a prospective husband at her elbow, she epitomized everything he found desirable. Living as he had the past three years, he'd discovered the perfect woman to be available, willing, and not interested in more than a brief affair.

However, Catherine's easy grace, good humor, and obvious love for her son called to a longing in Robert's soul. He had a vision of her standing next to the stream near Bosworth Manor, cupping a pregnant belly as she laughed up at him. No. That life was not for him. That life had belonged to William.

Robert's heart pounded as if he'd run to the park instead of ridden in his carriage.

Catherine must have felt his gaze upon her, for she looked at him, her expression quizzical. He quickly looked away, hoping his turbulent emotions were not evident.

The ducks were thick about Christopher now, but unafraid, he laughed and flung chunks of bread about. A loud honk drew Robert's attention. A swan waddled toward them, no doubt searching for his own luncheon.

Robert took a step toward Christopher. Swans could be rather aggressive, and this one looked like it would tower over Christopher if it extended its neck fully. The swan honked again, startling Mr. Hughes, who turned too quickly and lost his footing. He flailed his arms as he tried to maintain his balance. The swan, clearly believing the man was challenging him, flapped his wings and lunged at Hughes.

"Egads!" Hughes stumbled backward. His booted foot sank into the soft mud, which further threw him off balance. He tried to right himself but was too far gone. With a spectacular splash, he ended up sitting waist-deep in the water.

Robert waved his arms threateningly and growled at the angry bird who squawked before it turned tail and waddled off. Turning back to the immersed man, Robert clenched his teeth to keep from laughing—not at Hughes, per se, but his descent into the water *had* been spectacularly comical.

Catherine clapped a hand over her mouth, her eyes wide with either distress or hilarity.

"Why does *he* get to play in the water?" Christopher asked as Hughes sputtered and tried to stand.

"Mr. Hughes!" Catherine cried. "Let me assist you."

Roused from his amusement, Robert leaped to help the man before Catherine got wet herself.

Once on dry land, Hughes was clearly embarrassed. Robert took pity on him—he would hate to look foolish in front of Catherine.

"Hughes, that was most noble of you to distract that swan before it went for young Christopher." He turned to Catherine. "Though they're considered elegant and beautiful, swans can be very aggressive. I once had a swan snap at me when I was not much older than your son. Left a mark just here…" He pointed to his right cheek. "Took nearly a week to fade."

Catherine looked suitably appalled and turned to the half-drenched man. "Mr. Hughes, I can't thank you enough!"

Hughes shot Robert a grateful glance and preened a bit in front of Catherine. "Well, I can always replace my new boots," he said as he gestured to his mud-encrusted footwear. "But restoring a young boy's love of nature would not be so easy if devastated by a swan attack."

"Oh, your boots were new?" Catherine asked, clearly distraught.

Robert was glad he'd done Hughes a good turn by covering his embarrassment. It mitigated the slight guilt Robert felt over his next statement.

"Those look like Hoby boots."

"Indeed, they were," Hughes said as he cast a forlorn glance at his footwear. There was a purported six-month wait for a new pair of Hoby boots.

"They are not yet lost, then. Get them to your valet immediately. If he cleans them before the mud dries, they will be good as new. Left only with a patina of heroism." Robert was rather proud of that turn of phrase, especially when it seemed to resonate with Hughes.

Before the man could utter a word, Robert played his hand.

"I shall see Mrs. Purcell and young Christopher home to save you precious time."

Hughes looked torn between his boots and private time with Catherine, and though Robert suspected she was genuinely concerned for Hughes, she unwittingly played into his plan to evict the man from their outing.

"Oh, Mr. Hughes, do see to your boots. I should feel ever so guilty to have cost you such a fine pair. Lord Dunsbury can see us home, and you and I shall see each other this evening at Lady Campbell's card party where you can tell me if your valet was successful."

The gaze she bestowed upon Hughes was so imploring, Robert suspected she could have urged the man to jump back in the Serpentine, and he would have hastened to do so. Instead, he bent low over her gloved hand. "You are the epitome of grace and compassion, Mrs. Purcell. I shall count the minutes until this evening."

As he took himself off at a pace just short of a run, Catherine glanced at her now-soiled glove with a sigh. "I don't suppose it will matter how quickly I clean these. I doubt they will ever be white again."

Robert watched as she chewed on her lower lip. It occurred to him that she was concerned about the expense of new gloves. Money was the reason she was in the marriage market, after all. He made a mental note to have some gloves sent to her. It wasn't at all proper, but then neither was impersonating Russian nobility. Perhaps he would attach a card implying they were from the Russian embassy. They would serve as a jest and a reminder not to place too much importance on the gift. The last thing he wanted was Catherine Purcell thinking he had feelings for her, and worse, returning those feelings.

Liar. You very much want her to have feelings for you. Yes, fine, but the last thing I need is for Catherine to actually start having them.

That was closer to the truth, but before he could argue with himself any further, there was a splash behind him.

"Christopher!"

Robert turned to see the boy ankle-deep in the water, having clearly just jumped into the muddy shallows.

"But that other gent did it," Christopher said, squishing his feet back and forth.

Robert bit back another spurt of laughter.

"Mr. Hughes *fell* in trying to save you from being bit by a swan," Catherine said.

Her son frowned. "Swans don't have teef. Grandpa told me."

Robert couldn't help it; he snorted while trying to stifle his amusement, which earned a glare from Catherine.

"He has a point," he murmured.

She pushed past him and stalked to the water's edge. "In addition to ruining your shoes, you've scared the ducks off."

"It's all right, Mama. The bread was all gone."

"Smart lad," Robert said, and the look Catherine gave him this time was more incredulous than irate. "Well, he is." He strode to the water's edge and scooped the boy up, then held him at arm's length and bounced him up and down a little to dislodge as much mud as possible. Christopher giggled with delight, and Robert grinned as he gave him a few extra bounces for good measure.

"There, practically good as new."

"Except for his wet shoes and stockings. Come along, Christopher. We shall have to return you home."

The young boy set up a squall that matched Robert's inner disappointment. He thought quickly. "We've had so few sunny days lately. It seems a shame to cut short this one."

"But—"

Robert stepped closer to Catherine and lowered his voice. "He could remove his socks and shoes. They could dry in the sun while he runs around barefoot. I remember loving that when I was a boy. It was such a rare occurrence to be allowed that freedom."

They both glanced at Christopher, and he seemed to be waiting to hear if his mother would grant him a reprieve.

"You are a bad influence, my lord," she said, her voice soft.

Laughter rumbled in his chest. "I think we've already established that fact, *Countess*."

Her cheeks pinkened, and he wondered if she thought about their kiss.

She marched over to Christopher, and he gave her a toothy grin, seemingly to distract her from whatever punishment she might deliver.

"Take off your shoes and stockings. You may get your feet wet, but if you go in any deeper, we will head for home immediately, do you understand?"

The boy nodded as he hurriedly tried to untie his shoes. Catherine knelt and helped him. "You have Lord Dunsbury to thank for your reprieve. He convinced me you might enjoy running barefoot a bit."

"I do!" Christopher exclaimed as he scrambled to his feet and clenched his toes in the grass. He glanced shyly at Robert and mumbled a thank you.

Robert smiled and watched the boy run about.

"I wish there was a bench nearby," Catherine said. "He will run until either he or I am exhausted."

Robert glanced around, then knelt. "The grass seems dry. I don't mind if you don't."

"What on earth has given you the impression I am the least bit high in the instep?" she asked with raised brows, and he smiled.

She took his hand and allowed him to help her sit on the springy grass, then she arranged her skirts. "I was afraid I'd given myself away that first night at Mrs. Wilson's party when I used that phrase."

"You did, a little. I found it a particularly English turn of phrase. Do you speak Russian?" he asked, surprised he'd not thought to inquire before now.

"Alas, the little bit of Russian I do know is limited to things like asking for more biscuits and whether I might play with my dolls. I was quite young when my grandmother tried to teach me."

Robert chuckled. "And what would she think of your role as the Russian countess?"

She smiled and watched Christopher for a long moment before she glanced back at Robert. "I think she would understand why I did it. She fell in love with my grandfather and gave up her life to be with him. It must have been difficult trying to fit in to life in the English countryside after serving as a member of the Russian court."

"And your parents? You said your father was a scholar."

She twisted her lips and looked away. "They would *not* have understood. My father would have tried, mind you. He would have given me the benefit of the doubt assuming a rogue influenced me." At that, she gave him a pointed look.

"And your mother?"

"She would have expired from heart failure immediately."

Robert laughed with her, soaking in her relaxed good nature. He felt the tug in his chest again, a longing for something he could not have.

"And what of your mother?" Catherine asked. "I know your relationship with your father is strained."

"She's rather like you. She wants nothing but the best for her son."

Catherine smiled, but Robert didn't return it. "Unfortunately, her first loyalty is to her husband. She tries to ease the tension between us, mostly by asking me to appease the old man."

Catherine opened her mouth as if to speak but then pressed

her lips together. Robert knew she wanted to ask more about the rift in his family, but he would not darken this beautiful day with that story. Instead, he caught her hand and began to pull off her soiled glove.

"What are you doing?" she asked sharply.

"Relax. I'm not disrobing you. I merely sought to relieve you of a clammy glove."

She held her bare hand in her gloved one as if protecting it. When he simply laid her muddied glove aside, she relaxed. After a moment, she placed her hand next to his on the grass.

They watched Christopher in silence, the gentle murmur of the water against the shore a hypnotic melody to the drowsy, sun-drenched day, the air fragrant with the smell of crisp grass, fecund mud, and blooming trees. Overlying the pastoral atmosphere, however, was Robert's awareness of Catherine. Her huff of laughter at her son's antics and the faint fragrance of lemon verbena had his body thrumming. Without looking down, he brushed her little finger with his, then froze, not wanting to startle her. She went equally still, then shifted, covering his hand with hers. He slowly turned his hand over and laced their fingers.

Minutes slipped by. Christopher brought them treasures from time to time, such as a smooth pebble, a waterlogged blossom, and a tiny pink worm.

Robert glanced at his hand, still entwined with Catherine's, and thought of the kiss they'd shared in his carriage. It had fired his blood and hardened his body, and yet the simple touch of their hands seemed to affect him more deeply, as if, within her small palm, she held him with unconditional acceptance—something he'd not felt in years.

Catherine stiffened, then glanced behind them.

"What is it?" he asked.

"People are beginning to arrive."

He pulled out his pocket watch, amazed to discover it was

nearly three o'clock. The "fashionable hour" was upon them, and soon the roads and paths throughout the park would be full of fashionable people, there to be seen.

Robert wasn't particularly bothered by the notion, but Catherine seemed concerned, and he wondered if she worried about Hughes discovering Robert had not escorted her home right away. The thought made him scowl.

"Would you like to leave?" he asked, gruffer than he'd intended.

"No— Well, that is, I shouldn't want to put you in a, well, a difficult position," she said, plucking at the grass.

"Why? Because people may think I'm courting you?"

She glanced at him. "Well, yes. I suppose so. I can't imagine you would like that, would you? What with never intending to marry and all."

"I never said *never*." He felt like an idiot, for that was precisely what he'd said.

"I, however, can only benefit from your attention. After all, if a nobody like *me* can attract the attention of the future Duke of Dervinshire, I must be rather fascinating. Isn't that the idea?"

There was a bite to her tone. Unsure why she suddenly seemed upset, he frowned. "Catherine, you're not a nobo—"

"Christopher!" She quickly climbed to her feet. "It's time to go home. Come put your shoes on."

The boy started to complain, but one glimpse of his mother's face apparently convinced him of his folly. He obediently fetched his shoes and stockings.

Catherine seemed to be staring out across the Serpentine, so Robert got up and brushed the grass off his trousers before going to assist young Christopher with his shoes. She glanced at him and took a step toward her son. "You needn't—"

Robert waved her off and crouched beside the boy. "I'm not so very ancient I've forgotten how to tie shoes." He waggled his eyebrows at Christopher, then said in a stage whisper, "I don't remember how to tie shoes. Do you know how?"

Christopher widened his eyes and shook his head.

"Oh dear. We're in for it, then."

The young boy giggled behind a grimy hand.

"Wait!" Robert said as he tied the first knot. "I think I'm remembering. How does that look?"

Christopher nodded, never taking his gaze off Robert's face.

"I don't believe we've been properly introduced, what with the attacking swans and wet shoes. I'm Robert Carlisle." When the boy continued to stare at him in silence, Robert decided to prompt him. "And you are Christopher Purcell, I take it?"

The boy nodded again. Robert was about to stand up when the boy suddenly said, "I'm going to be a baron!"

Robert bit back a smile. "Is that so?"

Christopher climbed to his feet. "My grandfather is the baron now. When he goes to heaven, then I'll be the baron. It would have been my father, but he's already in heaven."

Robert sobered. "I know. I'm very sorry."

Christopher shrugged. "It's all right. I don't remember him. I tell my nanna I do." A worried look crossed his face. "Do you think I'm bad?"

Robert rumpled the boy's curls. "Not at all. You were very young when he died."

"Practically a baby," Christopher said.

"Just so, and babies hardly remember anything. Why, you probably don't have memories of your mother from back then."

Christopher frowned. "No. I remember Mama. She smells nice."

Something low in Robert's belly clutched tight. He'd been noticing how nice she smelled for the last hour. He pushed the unruly thought aside. "Ah, well, mothers *do* hold a special place in our hearts and minds."

"Are you going to be somebody?" Christopher asked.

"What do you mean?"

"When your papa goes to heaven. Will you be something? Or is your papa already in heaven like mine?"

"My father is still alive. When he goes to heaven, I shall be a duke."

Christopher seemed to consider that. "Is that better than a baron?"

"I believe it is a man's character that sets him above others."

"What does that mean?"

Robert laughed and would have tried to explain himself, but Catherine joined them. "Let's not talk Lord Dunsbury's ear off."

Christopher looked around. "Who's that, Mama?"

Catherine smiled. "You've been talking to him for the past five minutes."

Christopher frowned at Robert. "I thought you said your name was Robert Carlisle."

"And so it is. My title is the Marquess of Dunsbury."

"Oh," said the boy, unconcerned. "So, you are somebody then."

Catherine choked back a laugh, but Robert did not restrain himself. "If you say so, Master Christopher, then it must be true."

Catherine's good humor returned on the way home as Robert and Christopher engaged in a spirited discussion about bugs, dogs, and horses—the latter Christopher had never ridden.

"Really!" Robert said, pretending to be shocked. "And you're, what, six years old?"

Christopher giggled and held up his right hand, using his left to press down his little finger.

"Four? Oh, thank heavens, we're not too late. Nonetheless, no Englishman worth his salt reaches the age of five without learning to ride. I offer my services as an equestrian instructor, your mother's permission pending, of course."

Christopher's brow wrinkled as he tried to figure out what Robert had just said. Robert leaned forward. "If your mum says it's all right, I will teach you to ride."

"Is it all right, Mama?" Christopher asked, his excitement evident in his wide smile.

Robert looked to Catherine, surprised to see her expression shuttered once more.

"We shall see."

Christopher flopped back in the seat with a frown. "That means no."

"It means we shall see," Catherine said.

Christopher seemed to recognize it was best to drop the matter and stayed sprawled in the seat, where he promptly fell asleep.

Catherine's expression softened as she watched him.

"I'm sorry," Robert said, keeping his voice low. "I should have consulted with you before making such an offer." He observed her closely, trying to figure out what was troubling her. The idea he had said or done something to upset her bothered him more than he ever would have thought.

As if she hadn't really heard him, she nodded, still watching her son. Robert was about to say more when the carriage drew to a halt in front of the Purcells' home.

Robert hopped down then turned to help Catherine, who had gathered the sleeping child in her arms. She climbed down quite adroitly, considering her armload.

"I can carry him in," Robert said.

"I have him," she responded, her tone sharp. Robert bowed his head as she strode past him. She stopped and turned abruptly, then glanced at Robert's footman, who quickly disappeared behind the carriage.

"It is very likely Mr. Hughes and I will marry," she said without preamble. "He alluded to the notion earlier today, and he does not seem the sort of man who would mention marriage casually."

Robert's stomach sank. Nonetheless, he had no choice but to agree. "No, he does not."

"I am most grateful for your assistance in introducing us to the right circles and lending your consequence to our humble title, but…" She took a deep breath, and Robert wanted to grab her and kiss her to stop her next words.

How had he come to this state? He'd only entered into their bargain for some intellectual amusement. He'd known it was a temporary arrangement, and yet the thought of her marrying another had his heart ripped in two. It was his own fault for suggesting they not let their emotions rule—no, it was his father's fault. If not for him, Robert could have what he wanted in life. He could offer Catherine marriage. He could have children…

His throat closed. William would never marry his childhood sweetheart because of Robert, never hold a newborn babe in his arms, so how could Robert be worthy of happiness?

"I think it is time to end our arrangement," she said.

"Is that really what you want?" Robert's voice sounded hoarse, and he tried to swallow past the lump in his throat.

At that, she looked him in the eye, her gray eyes stormy with emotion. "I must consider what is best for my son. Allowing him to get to know you, to ride a horse with you, will only make it more confusing for him when he can no longer see you."

Robert intended to argue, to tell her he could still teach Christopher to ride and offer him counsel on how to train a puppy, but even as his mind made a case in his favor, his heart knew she was right. Such duties, such pleasures would belong to Hughes, not him.

"Catherine, I—" He forced himself to take a breath. "I cannot marry you." He had no idea if she'd hoped he'd changed his mind, but he had to make certain she understood he couldn't give her what Hughes undoubtedly would.

Her lower lip trembled. She pressed her mouth into a flat line, stilling it. "Could you at least tell me why?"

Why? Robert almost laughed. If only his reasons weren't so selfish, so mired in anger and a need to punish. He shook his head. "My father..." He couldn't tell her the rest. He couldn't explain his refusal to marry, to love.

The air crackled with unspoken words. After a long moment, Catherine sighed. "I think you should leave."

Despite feeling like he'd been hit by a team of six, Robert simply bowed. "As you wish, madam. I thank you for your company and conversation. I wish you and Mr. Hughes every happiness."

She looked as if she were going to say something else, but he couldn't bear to remain standing on the street like a fool, so he turned and leaped into the carriage, slamming the door behind him.

Ten

CATHERINE STRAINED with the weight of Christopher while tears flooded her eyes. She rushed past the footman who held the door for her, then made her way up two flights to the nursery. She stepped on her hem twice and nearly fell the second time. Nevertheless, she kept going despite the burn in her arms.

She laid Christopher down on his small bed and pulled off his still-damp shoes. Bits of grass clung to his toes, and as she brushed them off, she smiled through her tears. She tucked a light blanket over him and pressed a kiss to his brow. He smelled like mud, water, leaves, and that dusty, grimy smell all children seemed to emanate after playing outside.

Catherine stood a moment watching Christopher, her heart filled with overwhelming love and another emotion. Resentment? She whirled and left the nursery, then rushed to her room, feeling like the worst mother ever. What was she thinking? How could she resent having to choose her son's future over the fleeting pleasure of Dunsbury's company? She plucked at the open drapes of her window and stared unseeing at the small back garden. He'd again made it quite clear he had no intention of marrying, and her announcement that they could no longer see each other had, at most, cost her two or three more adventures as Countess Borodinicha. Nonetheless, she wished she'd prepared herself for the end of their arrangement instead of making her announcement so impulsively.

"Oh, miss! I didn't see you there," Sophie exclaimed.

Catherine glanced over her shoulder and forced a smile for the maid.

"Did you have a nice time at the park?"

"I— Yes. Yes, I did."

"What did you do?" Sophie asked as she busily put linens in a drawer.

"Hmm? Oh, well, we fed the ducks, of course. Christopher got his shoes wet, but he was having so much fun, I allowed him to run barefoot until the park grew busy."

"That's nice," Sophie said, though she seemed a little distracted. "Did you see anyone interesting while you were there?"

"Interesting? We were there very early. We left before the fashionable hour."

At that, Sophie stopped what she was doing and turned. "Oh? It was just you and Mr. Hughes with Master Christopher?"

Catherine narrowed her eyes. "Now that you mention it, Lord Dunsbury did stumble upon us while we were on the banks of the Serpentine."

"The duke's heir you've been dressing up and playacting for?"

Catherine winced at Sophie's description of her arrangement—her *past* arrangement—with Dunsbury, but she could not refute it. "Yes, *that* duke's heir. Amazing how he ran into us in all that acreage of Hyde Park."

"That was lucky, wasn't it?" Sophie avoided Catherine's gaze by refolding the linens she'd just put away.

"Sophie, did you— Did you have something to do with Lord Dunsbury's arrival at the park?"

"What, miss?" the maid asked, her tone innocent. When Catherine didn't reply, Sophie looked over her shoulder. "Oh, very well, miss. Yes. He came to *visit* all proper-like, and when you weren't here to receive him, I didn't want that to discourage him, so I told him where you went. Aren't you glad I did?"

"No. Yes! I mean—" Catherine took a breath, wondering what had possessed Dunsbury to call on her formally. "I told him I could no longer continue with our arrangement, that I would no longer pretend to be the Russian countess."

"Oh," Sophie said, disappointment evident in her voice. "Why miss?"

Catherine sat on a chair by the window and bent to unbutton her boots. "Mr. Hughes implied he would soon be offering a proposal of marriage."

Sophie came to help Catherine remove her boots. "Is that what you wish for, miss?"

"Of course it is," Catherine snapped, then instantly regretted her outburst. "It's why we came to London, isn't it? To save the baron and baroness's finances and assure Christopher's future."

"I mean, is it Mr. Hughes you wanted? I thought you fancied Lord Dunsbury."

"Well, it doesn't matter who I fancy. What matters is who will offer marriage. Lord Dunsbury has assured me he has no intention of marrying. I had thought he might have— No matter. He has made his feelings clear."

"But I thought all noblemen had to marry to get an heir?"

Catherine just stared at her maid.

"Well," Sophie said briskly. "Mr. Hughes is a fine man. Quite polished and always well turned out. You will make a handsome couple."

Catherine nodded. "I am most fortunate."

"Why don't I fix you some tea and bring you up some of Cook's jam biscuits? You can enjoy your book while Master Christopher sleeps. I know you've not had much time to read lately."

Catherine swallowed the lump in her throat. "That would be lovely, Sophie. Thank you."

BY THE TIME Catherine climbed into the Purcells' carriage that night to cross town to Lady Campbell's card party, Catherine had restored her equanimity. Paradoxically, the silly gothic novel she'd read while indulging in jam biscuits had helped. *The Misfortunes of an Italian Princess* was about a titled young lady stranded in a foreign land with only her wits and her beauty to save her from a handsome but suspicious doctor who had followed her abroad to possess her—body, mind, and coronet.

Catherine realized that women of her mediocre birth had as much chance of marrying the heir to a dukedom as the ridiculous heroine of her book had to escape the clutches of the evil doctor. Catherine had been just as silly as Princess Philodendra to even entertain the notion that Dunsbury might change his mind for her.

She smiled at Mr. Hughes as she entered the Campbell drawing room. "Please tell me you managed to save your boots," she said with a gentle squeeze of his hand as he bent over hers.

"Indeed, I did," he replied.

She told herself marriage should be based on mutual respect and mutual purpose. She and Jasper had been exquisitely respectful of each other, though beyond producing an heir, she could think of no common objective of which they'd shared. Whereas she and Mr. Hughes discussed current styles and music and… Well, certainly, those two subjects supplied a wealth of conversational topics.

Life with Mr. Hughes would deliver more excitement than her previous marriage, and she'd specifically wanted more excitement. She forced her attention back to the gentleman, who was telling her just how his valet had saved his boots.

"Positively fascinating!" She tried to sound encouraging, but her words came out ridiculously effusive.

He chuckled. "Now you're making fun of me. It is silly, I suppose, to worry so over footwear. It's only that they *were* new."

Catherine realized she probably *should* have teased him, but the fact he still discussed the blasted boots was too much.

"What are we playing this evening?" she asked. At least cards would provide some mental stimulation, and it would keep her mind off Dunsbury.

ॐ

THE FOLLOWING week was full of events as the Season wound to a close. Catherine simultaneously wished Mr. Hughes would get his proposal over with yet dreaded the moment when she committed her life to that path.

Mr. Hughes had dropped several more hints as to his intentions with references to meeting his mother in Suffolk and sending his estate manager to meet with the baron to offer advice to improve his holdings. Mr. Hughes had also mentioned "saving your son's birthright" no less than three times. Each time, Catherine tried to look pleasantly encouraging, but she began to feel she would forever have to thank him for rescuing her and Christopher. *Honestly!* She might not have a fortune to her name, but she was not without her own attributes, and the thought of years of feeling beholden to him was enough to make her slightly nauseous.

Every now and again, she wondered if she should have further encouraged the other men who had expressed an interest in her. Perhaps she might have developed stronger feelings for one of them than she had for Mr. Hughes. She tried to picture the two other men who had danced with her several times and called upon her at home. They were well-dressed but otherwise hazy, and she was unable to bring their features into focus.

Catherine stopped brushing her hair and stared at herself in the mirror. She knew why she couldn't picture those men's faces or bring herself to care more deeply for Mr. Hughes. It was Dunsbury, curse the man. He'd warned her when they began their clandestine friendship that he was not marriage material. He'd made it perfectly clear their unorthodox arrangement was simply for their amusement, which he'd reiterated after that perfect day at the park when she'd felt like there was no other person in the world who understood her like he did... Yet, here she sat, melancholy and nursing a bruised heart because she hadn't listened to him.

Even as she chided herself for her foolishness, she recalled him crouched beside her son, tying Christopher's shoes, Robert's hair rumpled, his nose reddened from the sun. She thought of their conversations, some of them scandalously flirtatious, others perfectly mundane. Or philosophical. There seemed no topic they'd been unable to discuss.

And then there was that kiss. Catherine tightened her grip on the handle of her brush as she remembered that kiss for the thousandth time. She wondered what would have happened if they hadn't arrived at the Purcells' so soon—if she'd been bold enough to have the coachman keep driving and if Robert had taken her to his rooms...

Catherine's cheeks, given to blushing at the drop of a hat

anyway, heated at the ideas running through her mind. When she pressed cold fingers to her face to reduce her blush, her fingers warmed instantly against the flames of her scandalous imaginings.

"This is not helping matters." She needed to get ready for Lord and Lady Fortescue's dance. It was a small event, with only fifty or sixty people in attendance. Just a quiet, end of Season get-together before everyone left for their country seats after Parliament closes mid-July.

❧

"WHEN ARE you withdrawing from London, my dear?" Mr. Hughes asked as they strolled around the spacious drawing room. He wanted to "show her off" and introduce her to those people she hadn't met.

"I don't believe we've set a date. We are to travel to Tutley House to assess the estate. If it is livable, we shall stay. Otherwise, we will continue to our home in Chippenham."

"I must speak with the baron before you depart." Mr. Hughes had a pleased look on his face. *Smug.* She chided herself for her uncharitable thought but wished he'd simply make a proposal or leave her be. She felt like a fish on a hook—reeled in without the knowledge of whether she'd be caught or let go.

Mr. Hughes steered her toward a beautiful woman who held court over a small group of men. "Lady Beaumont, allow me to introduce Mrs. Purcell to you. Mrs. Purcell, Viscountess Beaumont."

Catherine began to greet her, but the woman spoke first. "Have we met previously? I feel I've seen you before." Her expression was shrewd as she studied Catherine's gown and face.

Worry fluttered in Catherine's stomach. The viscountess was familiar to her as well. Had the woman been at one of the events Robert had taken Catherine to? Though her mouth was dry with fear, she forced a pleasant smile to her lips. "No, my lady. I am quite sure I would remember meeting you."

"Of course you would," the viscountess said as if quite used to standing out in people's memories. Catherine's worry lessened when the woman didn't question her further.

"Mrs. Purcell is the daughter-in-law of the new Baron Tutley," Mr. Hughes said.

"Tutley? Oh, you poor dear. The previous baron must have left you in quite a predicament. Where is your husband?"

"He passed on some years back, my lady."

Lady Beaumont gave Hughes a rather pitying glance before turning to the gentleman at her side. "This event is ghastly. I suppose we should have gone to Henley after all."

Surprised, Catherine scanned the room. She preferred the smaller gathering to the crowded events she'd attended over the past several weeks. "What's in Henley?"

The viscountess gave her an incredulous look. "The regatta, of course."

Mr. Hughes turned to Catherine. "The Henley Regatta is an annual event. A series of boat races over several days. It's but a day's drive from London."

"I loathe the event." The viscountess acted as if Mr. Hughes had not spoken. "The weather is ghastly. Hot and muggy."

Beside her, the young men nodded in agreement.

One of them leaned closer to the woman. "Although, you did look ravishing in that straw bonnet you wore last year, Letitia."

"Well, of course I did. Go fetch me champagne, Middlethorpe. I'm parched just thinking of the heat. Oh, there's Helen Wellesley. I must say hello." The viscountess cast a dismissive glance at Catherine and Mr. Hughes before sailing off with her group of admirers trailing in her wake.

"Don't mind Letitia," Mr. Hughes said. "She's a bit snifty toward any woman more beautiful than her."

Catherine smiled. "Snifty?"

"Why yes. You know, in a snit, sniffs about. Snifty."

"Of course," Catherine said with a nod. "And did you just call me beautiful?"

Mr. Hughes flushed, and Catherine was suddenly concerned for any children they might have. The poor things would not be able to say a word without going pink.

"Well, you are. Everyone says so." Mr. Hughes looked everywhere but at her face.

"It doesn't matter what everyone else thinks, but if you consider me so, I am quite content." It wasn't exactly the truth, of course. She wanted Robert to find her beautiful, so beautiful he would do anything to be with her, even give up his self-imposed restriction on marriage. She shook her head to dislodge thoughts of Robert. She needed to focus on Mr. Hughes. His compliment was the most charming thing he'd said to her, and she hoped it boded well for their potential future. She certainly wasn't trying to…recreate the way she felt in Dunsbury's company, but she hoped for at least some fervor in Mr. Hughes's and her relationship.

A shy silence fell between them, and it was with no small relief when another gentleman asked Catherine to dance. By the time she'd finished, Mr. Hughes was dancing with another lady, and Catherine found herself with a little respite. She visited the refreshment table and sipped a rather tasty punch when she overheard someone talking behind her.

"Dorothea, allow me to introduce you to the Duchess of Dervinshire."

Narrowly avoiding splashing punch down her front, Catherine quickly turned toward a group of four ladies. She wondered which one was Robert Carlisle's mother.

"We met last Season, your grace. It's so lovely to see you

again." The woman, who must be Dorothea, spoke to a diminutive woman with an elegant white streak of hair at her left temple amidst tresses the same rich dark brown of her son's. Her eyes may have been dark as well—it was difficult to discern without actually *staring* at the poor woman. Otherwise, it seemed Robert took after his father.

Catherine pretended fascination with the contents of her cup while she listened to the ladies chat.

"Did you decide not to attend Henley this year?"

Catherine recognized the lady's voice as the one who had introduced Dorothea.

"No. His grace has been unwell. I thought it prudent we not move him, and I certainly wouldn't go without him."

"I'm so sorry, Georgiana. I'd heard he'd been indisposed but didn't realize it was enough to keep him from the races."

Catherine watched the duchess closely, who tightened her mouth with worry. She quickly smoothed her expression. "Well, we are at least represented at the Regatta. My son, Dunsbury, is there."

Catherine took a tiny step closer, pretending to move out of someone's way.

"How is Dunsbury?" Mrs. Emsbury asked. Catherine had met her earlier that evening. "It seems he's been more active this year. I've seen him at no less than three balls this Season. I can't recall seeing him at one last year."

The duchess compressed her lips again. "You will recall he traveled last year. He was in Italy at this time, I believe."

Mrs. Emsbury tittered—there was really no other word for it. "Oh, how silly of me! That would explain why I didn't see him."

Dorothea shook her head slightly. "Is he glad to be back home?" she asked Robert's mother.

"I should say so. He's about to make an offer of marriage to a young woman."

The blood drained from Catherine's cheeks. It was a novel experience since they usually flooded with color, and she closed her eyes briefly, wondering if it meant she was about to faint.

"Did you say Dunsbury was going to marry?" asked someone else. The voice was high-pitched and harsh and caused the women to fall silent.

Catherine opened her eyes to see Lady Beaumont, who must have been walking by the small group of ladies. The viscountess had lost her indifference, and Catherine wondered just how close Lady Beaumont and Robert were.

The duchess did not look pleased to be interrupted by Letitia. "Perhaps. You know bachelors these days loathe to give up their freedom," she said, her voice clipped.

Dorothea smiled. "Oh, do tell us who the lucky girl is, your grace."

"Yes, your grace. We are quite starved for good gossip at this time of the year," Letitia said.

"My son's matrimonial prospects are not fodder for the gossip mill, Letitia," the duchess said.

Mrs. Emsbury practically vibrated with excitement. "I saw him dance with Lady Eleanor Chalcroft at the Andover ball. Is it her? I do hope so! They made such a handsome couple."

The fact Catherine had thought the same thing did not alleviate the lump growing in her throat. She couldn't even take pleasure in Letitia's set down.

The duchess smiled at Mrs. Emsbury. "I'll not confirm your suspicions. Although Lady Chalcroft and I have been friends since we were girls and have always thought our children would make a match of it."

Mrs. Emsbury clapped her hands. "I do hope I shall be invited to the wedding, your grace."

"I am sure when the duke's son marries, it will be a huge event," Letitia said before she abruptly excused herself.

A couple seeking refreshments jostled Catherine, and she allowed the flow of people to move her away from Robert's mother. Catherine's face and hands were numb. She wondered again if this was what it felt like before fainting, and so she sat in the first open chair she spotted, then focused on taking several deep breaths.

Why on earth was she taking the news of Robert's impending betrothal so hard? The question was rhetorical because she knew the answer. When he'd said he had no intention of marrying, what he'd really meant was he had no intention of marrying *her*. She was suitable only for amusement and a stolen kiss. For marriage, only a diamond like Lady Eleanor Chalcroft would do for the Marquess of Dunsbury. It shouldn't hurt, but it did.

Tears burned her eyes, and she closed them, willing the moisture away. When she had her emotions under control, she stood and glanced about. The party was in full swing. No one would notice if she left, and as it was a small, private event, the baron and baroness had not attended with her—no doubt to allow her and Mr. Hughes uninterrupted time together.

Thinking of the man, she decided to leave word with their hostess and simply send a note round the next day saying she had taken ill. He would understand.

During the short ride home, Catherine fumed about what a fool she'd been to pine for Dunsbury—a man who only saw her as a trifling bit of fluff to entertain him when he was bored, while against her will and better judgment, she'd begun to have feelings for him.

The irritatingly fair part of her brain reminded her she had received the better end of their bargain, for she'd now wed a man she never would have met without Dunsbury's influence. In comparison, he had only gained a handful of evenings with a false Russian countess.

"I don't care!" She felt snubbed, rejected, and far inferior to the perfect Lady Eleanor. Catherine had never been one to compare herself to others and so had never considered herself lacking, but remembering the golden perfection of Lady Eleanor, Catherine now felt gauche and unrefined.

Mr. Hughes finds me beautiful, and I'm rather entertaining company.

She'd been quite popular at the parties at Mrs. Wilson's house, and the few times Dunsbury had left her alone when they'd attended similar events had found her swarmed with attention, men and women alike eager to be seen with the eccentric but popular Countess Borodinicha.

As the carriage stopped in front of the Purcells' townhouse, an idea occurred to her. A mad, bold, ridiculous idea, but one she was going to embark on, nonetheless.

"Don't put the carriage up just yet," she told the coachman. "I'm simply changing gowns and going back out. To a… masquerade party."

The coachman merely bowed. It was not the first time he'd taken her to a second event in one evening, although she'd never had him drive her to an event as the countess.

Catherine rushed upstairs then pulled her grandmother's red dress from the back of the wardrobe. It was difficult to put on unattended, but she did not wish for Sophie to know her intentions. She could hear the maid warning of the dangers of going out alone, and Catherine couldn't very well say she was going with Dunsbury after confessing she'd ended their arrangement.

Besides, the slightest bit of doubt might make her back out of her rash plan.

Plan? She stifled a humorless laugh as she stripped off her muslin ball gown. She had no real plan. She intended to go to whatever event Mrs. Wilson might be hosting tonight to prove — Catherine paused in the act of stepping into the red velvet skirts and thought frantically for a moment. What was she trying to prove to herself? That she was still interesting, desirable, daring, even without Dunsbury? That she didn't care if she never saw him again? She drew the heavy skirts up and fumbled with the hooks at the waistband.

Yes. All that—despite Dunsbury. She went to her first event as the Russian countess without him. She would go to her last on her own as well!

The coachman didn't bat an eye at her costume, but when she gave him the address, he frowned.

"Are you sure, Mrs. Purcell?"

"Quite sure. It's a perfectly respectable part of town." That wasn't quite a falsehood. Mrs. Wilson's townhouse was in a neighborhood populated by artists, writers, and actors, though not the sort of area a gently bred woman explored on her own.

She gave the coachman a look she generally only used when urging Christopher to eat his cabbage, then proceeded to climb into the coach.

Once at the location, she dismissed the driver.

"But, Mrs. Purcell, how will you get home?"

"I am meeting friends here. I am sure one of them will give me a ride." She had no intention of accepting a ride from any of the people here but finding a hackney coach at any time of night in this neighborhood wouldn't be an issue. She would simply have one of Mrs. Wilson's footmen fetch one.

Her coachman did not look happy, but a crowd of almost respectable-looking people approached Mrs. Wilson's door. Catherine quickly joined them.

Tonight would be her last adventure. Soon, Mr. Hughes would propose, and she would embark on a new life—one that would not include late-night escapades such as this. She took a deep breath and climbed the steps. She would send the Russian countess off in style.

AFTER A DAY IN THE COACH, Robert was exhausted traveling back from Henley, where he had gone on a week-long fool's errand for his mother. She'd given him some ridiculous story about her friend's daughter being heartbroken and needing a bit of a distraction. While he and Eleanor Chalcroft clearly had as much allure between them as two rocks, she was a nice girl, and he never could deny his mother's requests. Besides, after Catherine's pronouncement, there didn't seem much point in remaining in London. He was still trying to ignore the pain that suffused his body at the thought of her married to Hughes —or anyone else for that matter.

Damn it! He clenched his fist as he stared sightlessly out the window as the streets of London rolled past. Things had gone exactly as they'd planned. Catherine had been received by the best of London's hostesses and had met far more eligible men than she would have in the Purcells' limited social circle. She'd convinced one to marry her—though that wasn't much of a feat, as beautiful, clever, and warm as she was. In return, he had enjoyed quite the most entertaining Season, escorting her to less than respectable parties, plays, and pleasure gardens. He'd certainly laughed more than he had since... Well, since before Will died.

What would Will have thought of her? Robert smiled. He knew just what his brother would have said. *"She must be an angel if she can tolerate the likes of you, Rob. You'd better marry her before she comes to her senses."* Robert's smile faded at the memory of Will's pale face as he lay dying. Robert did not deserve a loving wife, and his bitter father certainly didn't deserve to see his precious line continue.

Suddenly, Robert's guilt and vengeful vow were too much—they dragged him down like a millstone around his neck.

"Damn it."

"You all right, old man?" Wayland asked. His friend had begged a ride back to London, and they were en route to Wayland's mistress's house on Jermyn Street near Piccadilly.

Wayland was a perfect traveling companion, knowing when to chat and when to keep his thoughts to himself, which was why he'd been so quiet the last half hour. So quiet, Robert had quite forgotten his presence.

"Oh, just thinking of...something I forgot to attend to."

Wayland nodded in understanding and glanced out the window. "We're almost there," he said, unable to keep the excitement from his voice. For the past six weeks, Wayland had waxed rhapsodic about his mistress—the lovely Penny from the night Robert met Catherine. Robert would not be surprised if the man turned society on its ear by marrying the woman, for his friend was clearly in love.

Robert sobered. Wayland would not allow grief, guilt, or animosity to stop him from claiming the woman he loved. He saw life more simply than Robert, and Robert envied him for it.

With a sigh, Robert pictured Catherine's face, animated with delight as she told him about something her son had done or a new book she'd read. He remembered her moved to tears by a well-acted tragedy he'd taken her to. He could also perfectly recall her expression after he'd kissed her: dazed, slumberous, sensuous. The memory never failed to stir him. For a brief moment, he considered throwing off his shackles, finding Catherine, and asking her to marry him. She'd felt the pull between them, and even if she didn't care for him as deeply, surely his wealth and title would appeal to her practical side. Could he do it? It was a question he'd debated since Catherine had sent him packing. To give in to the impulse would be to cast aside the vow he'd made to himself. His actions had denied William the chance to marry—therefore, Robert would deny himself the same.

The coach drew to a stop, and Wayland was on the pavement before the footman could open the door.

"Thanks for the lift," Wayland called over his shoulder as he dashed up the stairs. His mistress must have been awaiting his arrival because the door opened as he reached the top step. As Robert's coach pulled away, he glimpsed the couple's fervent embrace, and he fought to ignore a stab of jealousy.

He settled back in his seat and stared out the window, his mood grim, until a flash of red caught his eye. He leaned forward and pressed his face to the window.

"Stop!" He pounded on the roof of the carriage.

What the bloody hell was Catherine doing out here? That was Mrs. Wilson's house. Did Catherine not realize how dangerous it was for an unescorted woman at night? In this area of town? He crouched on the edge of the seat, waiting for the driver to pull to the side of the street. Overcome with impatience, he opened the door, and as the carriage slowed, he leaped down, using the momentum of his landing to propel his run back up the street. Catherine had already entered the townhouse, and he forced his way through the small knot of people who waited to enter.

"I say, Dunsbury," a drunken man said behind him. "The night's still young. There's no need to push."

Robert ignored the man, though he did apologize to the women he passed.

Once inside, he scanned the rapidly filling drawing room, locating Catherine quickly in her bright Russian gown. She was laughing, and the small group of men around her wore ridiculously pleased expressions as if they'd achieved something great by amusing her. She finished off her champagne, and one of the men rushed to replace it.

Was she *trying* to become inebriated? Though she had told him they must end their arrangement, clearly what she meant was she was only finished with *him*. The realization did not improve his mood. He'd contemplated asking her to marry him, but she'd only seen him as the means to an adventure in the seedier side of London.

He watched her closely, ducking behind a tall man when she turned, clearly feeling the weight of his stare. He needed to know what she was up to. If she were here to find another man to play her game, if she had truly become tired of him and their…relationship, so be it. At least he would know the truth and would be able to push her out of his mind and his heart.

As he watched her dazzle the crowd, however, he couldn't suppress the idea she was not happy. Her laugh was brittle, and her smile never reached her eyes. There was a frenetic quality to the way she moved from group to group. His anger and hurt turned to worry.

After nearly an hour, during which time she downed three more glasses of champagne and Robert had to fend off two actresses who were clearly seeking protectors, Catherine excused herself and left the drawing room. Robert followed her. He needed to ensure she had a safe means home and warn her that the men who were so flattering to her in the drawing room might act less gentlemanly in a carriage or darkened hallway, especially if she was not in full control of her faculties. That was all he would say. He would *not* allow himself to come across as some love-sick swain, brokenhearted that his false countess had grown weary of his company.

By the time he reached the door and entered the hallway, Catherine had vacated the retiring room.

"Ah, so you weren't done with going out as the Russian countess—you were simply done with accompanying *me*," he said, instantly wishing he'd bitten his tongue. He sounded like a green lad, smitten with the milkmaid who preferred the stable hand's kisses to his own.

Catherine gasped. "Robert! What are you— That is—" She closed her eyes and took a deep breath. When she opened her eyes again, he saw the heat of anger. "I thought you were in Henley, getting yourself betrothed," she said, her tone bitter.

"What? To whom? Why would you think that?"

She moved to push past him, and he took her hand. She turned on him, and he realized her anger was tempered with hurt—emotions that apparently mirrored his own.

"To Lady Eleanor Chalcroft, and I think so because I heard your mother confide in her friends earlier tonight that you were in Henley doing just that. Do you deny it?"

"No! I mean, yes! I mean, I *was* in Henley, but not to ask for Lady Eleanor's hand. Nor would I. She's in love with someone else."

"I'm so sorry for you," she replied, her bitterness like a whip across his back.

"And I am not in love with her," he said with force.

A tipsy couple stumbled into the hallway, no doubt looking for a private alcove.

"Come this way," Robert told Catherine, and when she refused to move, he sighed. "Please, Catherine."

She allowed him to guide her down the hall and out a side door, which led to the small back garden. Robert paused by a torch and turned to face Catherine. His tongue seemed stuck to the roof of his mouth, and all he could do was stare at her.

She stared mutely back. After several awkward seconds, he finally found his voice.

"I only wanted to warn you."

She frowned. "Warn me? Of what?"

"The men you were talking to, they haven't the best reputations. I would not trust them to behave appropriately, especially considering how much champagne you've had tonight."

"Have you been *spying* on me?"

"I wouldn't call it spying. I saw you outside. I wanted to— That is, I was concerned about you. Once inside, I didn't want to bother you after you'd made it clear you no longer wished to see me, but when I noticed Gregorson and Townsend hanging about you, I thought I should warn you."

"Why?" She studied his face as though she'd never seen him.

He shifted uncomfortably. "Well, I consider you a friend. Over the course of our conversations, we've grown to know each other. It's only natural I should care for your well-being."

"You care for me?"

"Well, I mean—"

Before he finished his sentence, she launched herself at him, planting a kiss on the corner of his mouth. He quickly turned his head, and as their lips met, he slid his arms around her back, drawing her fully against him. Her kiss was as inexpert as the last time, but she was eager and warm, and she tasted so damn good, Robert's body reacted instantly. He nibbled at her mouth, and when he used the tip of his tongue to trace the seam of her lips, she parted them and darted out her tongue to welcome his. At her tentative touch, he groaned, the nap of her velvet gown beneath his fingers as soft as her lips beneath his own.

She slipped her hands from his neck to beneath his jacket before she pressed herself more tightly against him. The heat and pliant willingness of her body had him wanting more.

He kissed her cheeks, her jaw, then tasted the sweet warmth

of her neck before he threaded his fingers through her hair, dislodging pins and filling his hands with her silken locks. He groaned again as he dragged his lips along the low neckline of her gown. His cock hardened, and he tugged at her bodice.

"Robert," she whispered as if pleading for something. Reaching behind her, he found the row of tiny dress hooks and clumsily undid them. Catherine shrugged to dislodge the bodice off her shoulder. *God, she was beautiful.* Her eyes blazed in the torchlight, her dilated pupils making them dark. He dropped his gaze to the gaping décolletage of her bodice. He hooked a finger inside it, pulling gently until one pale, perfect breast popped free. He cupped it in his palm and rubbed his thumb against her nipple until it hardened.

She moaned, and he returned his attention to her mouth, feasting on her lips.

Catherine met him halfway, nipping at his lower lip, exploring the corners of his mouth with her tongue. Beneath his hand, her heart pounded, which matched his own's cadence. She plucked at his waistcoat, unfastened the buttons, then pulled the tail of his shirt from his trousers. He sucked in a breath when she slid her hands over his belly and around to his back. She drew her nails lightly over his skin, the sensation so intense, he nearly came.

He grabbed her heavy skirts and bunched them to her waist. He wasn't going to take her, not here, but he had to touch her. She widened her stance, allowing him to drag his fingers along the top of her thigh then brush her damp curls.

"Dunsbury?"

In the haze of passion, it took Robert a moment to realize Catherine had not called his name. She jerked away from him with a low cry, and his senses returned instantly. He whirled around, shielding her with his body, ready to defend her from whatever threat presented itself—which turned out to be Viscountess Beaumont.

"Letitia," he said, trying to remember if Catherine had loosened his trousers. He glanced down to make sure he was not exposing himself.

"What are you doing here?" Letitia asked, her tone tight.

He shrugged, trying to appear insouciant, though his heart still beat like a trip-hammer. "It's a party."

"Who— Who is with you?"

"No one asks such a question at Mrs. Wilson's events, Letitia. Why don't you go back inside?"

She ignored him and took a step sideways to better see who he hid. Robert shifted his body, but she darted in the other direction.

"Is that—" She stared at Catherine as if unable to believe what, who, she saw. "Is that Hughes's little widow? The one I met earlier tonight?"

Catherine had smoothed down her skirts and tugged up her bodice, but with it still gaped open in the back and her hair falling about her shoulders, there was no denying what they had been doing.

Letitia narrowed her eyes and looked Catherine up and down. "No, not just the widow. You're the Russian countess, aren't you? I recognize that dress. My God! You've been fooling us all Season, pretending to be the virtuous little country mouse in society while whoring with Dunsbury the whole time. Wait until everyone hears about this." Her voice, low and sibilant, reminded Robert of a viper about to strike.

He thought frantically. As a widow, Catherine was allowed a great deal more freedom than an innocent debutante, and as the viscountess herself had proved, a widow might even indulge in the activities of the *demimonde*. However, Letitia was a wealthy, titled widow with a long-standing in the *ton*. Catherine, on the other hand, was neither. She was also trying to secure an advantageous marriage. Robert scarcely knew Mr. Hughes, but he suspected the man might not be so indulgent of his potential bride attending a party at Mrs. Wilson's, much less engaging in questionable activities in the back garden.

If Letitia decided to be vindictive, and given he'd rebuffed her repeated advances, the possibility was high, then she could easily ruin Catherine's chance to marry Hughes or anyone else for that matter. Letitia wouldn't need to embellish to make Catherine's activities seem lurid rather than merely questionable.

Robert came to an abrupt decision that left him feeling simultaneously calm and disconcerted. He stepped aside and drew Catherine alongside him.

"Indeed, this is Mrs. Purcell. So, you met today?"

Letitia never took her gaze from Catherine's face even as the viscountess directed her comments to Robert.

"At the Fortescue's party. Mrs. Purcell was in the company of an enamored Mr. Hughes. I suspect he believes her to be a docile, conventional lady. A perfect wifely candidate," she declared with a sarcastic edge. "I'm sure he's unaware his potential bride has such prurient hobbies."

Catherine inhaled sharply, and Robert's resolve hardened.

"As it happens, Mrs. Purcell *is* the perfect candidate for a wife. *My* perfect candidate. We're betrothed and have been for several weeks. It was only as my fiancée that Mrs. Purcell and I have engaged in our little adventures outside of the *ton*."

"My lord," Catherine whispered, her tone frantic. He tucked her hand in the crook of his arm.

The viscountess's laugh cracked the air. "You can't expect me to believe that nonsense, Dunsbury. Not three hours ago, I heard your mother telling anyone who would listen that you were in Henley, proposing to Eleanor Chalcroft."

Drat my mother. Had she shouted her ridiculous announcement to the ballroom? And why did she feel the need to meddle in his affairs? He sighed. He supposed that was the nature of mothers. Still, he would need to talk to her about her premature gossiping.

"Do you really expect me to believe the Duchess of Dervinshire feels the need to tell 'anyone who would listen' anything?" Despite the wavering torchlight, Robert saw Letitia flush with embarrassment. "If my mother *did* say any such thing, it was probably to throw the gossips off my actual betrothal."

Letitia twisted her lip in a sneer. "Why on earth would she do such a thing? Why not just announce your betrothal? Surely a little nobody such as your widow there would have such a coup in the papers the very next day."

The look she cast Catherine was pure malice. Robert glanced quickly at Catherine. The viscountess had pushed the bounds of civility too far. Before his eyes, Catherine straightened her spine and hardened her gaze. She went from nervous young woman caught misbehaving to imperious Russian countess, infuriated at someone trying to challenge her. It was all Robert could do not to grin and applaud.

Before she could say anything, however, he turned back to Letitia. "As it happens, I wanted to give Catherine the opportunity to break our betrothal without any unpleasantness."

"Why on earth would she do such a thing?" Letitia asked, her tone heavy with scorn.

Robert did smile then. "Well, you see, I rather swooped her up before she had a chance to meet anyone else in London. I wanted to give her the chance to decide if her affections were settled on me before we made a formal announcement."

"That's the most preposterous thing I've ever heard," Letitia cried.

"I said the same thing," Catherine said, startling Robert. He turned to warn her to go along with him, but she didn't meet his gaze, focused as she was on the viscountess.

"I told Robert I would not find his equal were I to attend a dozen Seasons, but you know how honorable he is. He insisted

I take my time to decide. As you could no doubt tell when you came out here, I've quite made up my mind." She smiled at Robert, looking the part of a devoted bride-to-be. Despite the sticky situation, his heart contracted as if she'd reached right in his chest and squeezed it.

He glanced back at Letitia, her face a mixture of rage and hurt, and suddenly, despite the predicament she'd put them in, despite the trouble she could still cause Catherine, he felt sorry for the other woman. He bid Catherine stay where she was, then crossed to Letitia and took her hand.

"Surely now you can understand why I did not respond more enthusiastically to your…suggestions. You are a very appealing woman, my lady. Alas, my heart was already engaged."

"Do you believe me to be a fool? Your heart is no more engaged than mine. I care not if you cuckold Hughes or if your little widow is London's biggest trollop."

"Don't you dare—"

She jabbed him in the chest. "Don't *you* dare treat me like I'm a fool!"

Robert's sympathy for her evaporated. "I think you'd better leave, my lady. And I think you'd better mind what you say after you do so."

She cast him one last derisive glance before looking over his shoulder to Catherine.

"You may have caught his interest temporarily," the viscountess stated. "But remember, even if you *do* manage to get him to the altar, you'll never hold him for long. The country widow is simply not that fascinating a character. He'll eventually find his way into another's bed. Perhaps even mine."

"You—" Robert intended to say more, but she'd turned on her heel and left. There was no point in pursuing her. Instead, he turned back to Catherine, who had lost her Russian countess air and now nervously chewed on her lower lip.

"Will she tell Mr. Hughes?" she asked as he approached her.

He took her hands in his. "One can never tell with the viscountess, but it matters not. We will wed, and soon, I should think. She will not dare spread rumors about the Marchioness of Dunsbury."

Catherine frowned, horror evident in her expression. "You cannot be serious!"

Robert ignored the sinking sensation in his stomach at her lack of enthusiasm for his proposal, such as it was. "I assure you, I am."

"But you said you would never wed."

"I've changed my mind," he said, his tone firm.

"You'll regret it!"

He laughed. "Is that a threat?"

"Marry in haste, repent at leisure. Isn't that the saying? You'll regret your hasty decision, and you'll resent me for trapping you."

The knot in his chest loosened, and he took her hands in his. "I'll not regret it, and I would never resent you."

She pulled her hands from his clasp and began pacing back and forth. "Oh, I've ruined everything! What will I tell the baron and baroness?"

It was Robert's turn to frown. "You'll tell them we're getting married and that I will help the baron get his newly inherited estate back on its feet. I will make sure Christopher has the finest tutors and attends the best schools."

She stopped her pacing and stared intently at him. "Why?"

"Why what?" Though he knew what she was asking, he needed time to formulate an answer. He couldn't simply admit that every hour since the afternoon in the park when she'd told him they could no longer see each other and she would be marrying Mr. Hughes, a peculiar angst had eaten him up and had made him short-tempered and edgy. That peculiar feeling had only begun to dissipate when he spotted Catherine tonight in her red gown. It had finally melted completely when she'd kissed him. Now, an equally peculiar sense of elation, hope, and anticipation for the future filled him—but he certainly couldn't tell her all that.

For a start, it was too new a revelation. He needed time to figure out what these feelings were, what they meant, and how they could have developed when every day he felt guilty for being alive when his brother was not. Secondly, he would sound like a right idiot telling her those things after he'd gone on and on about basing their relationship on simply enjoying each other's company and nothing more. He must have sounded like a buffoon as he'd officiously told her she mustn't allow herself to develop feelings for him.

"Why have you changed your mind about marrying, and why, if you had changed your mind, would you choose me?"

Robert sighed. He had to tell her something, but there was only one truth he could reveal to her right now. "Because you are quite the most intelligent woman I've ever known. I greatly enjoy our discussions, our jests, and even our disagreements. It is important the next Duchess of Dervinshire be intelligent, you see. My mother is exceptionally clever."

"I see. Thank you?"

Her intonation made it clear she didn't know he'd just complimented her. He needed to give her more. "I'm also attracted to you, Catherine. Very attracted."

At this, her cheeks pinkened, and she toyed with the ends of her hair, though she refused to meet his gaze. He stepped closer and ran his fingers along the curve of her jaw. At his touch, she looked up, her eyes wide, her pupils still dilated.

"I think perhaps you might enjoy my company too," he said softly.

She started to speak, but he lowered his head and kissed her, trying to show her how tumultuous his emotions were.

She responded in kind, and when their lips finally parted, she seemed as dazed as he.

"Why don't I escort you home? We have much to arrange tomorrow."

She nodded and took his arm to leave. "Wait!" She turned her back so he could redo the hooks on her dress, then she tried to twist her hair into some semblance of order.

"Perhaps if you pinned it," he said when half her hair tumbled back down.

"You scattered the pins hither and yon."

"Yon?" He grinned.

She leveled a warning look at him, and he widened his grin. Perhaps his life had taken an unexpected turn, but something told him he would never be bored again.

Twelve

CATHERINE MADE her way up the darkened stairs, careful to step over the squeaky third step from the top, still dazed over the evening's events. She'd started the night determined to put Dunsbury far from her mind and focus on encouraging Mr. Hughes to offer for her hand as soon as possible, but she'd ended the night betrothed to the very man she'd sworn to forget. The very man she had most wished to wed. The very man who had claimed could *not* love her.

Jasper had not been in love with her, of course. How could he? Neither had she been in love with him. Robert, however, was someone she could easily fall in love with. In fact, she probably already was, but the pain of living day after day with him when he didn't love her back would be hell.

He did say he cared for you.

She paused in the act of unhooking her bodice. Had he said that? She closed her eyes, trying to remember his exact words. He'd said, *"It's only natural I should care for your well-being."* That wasn't the same. It wasn't the same thing at all.

She shoved her dress in a heap in the back of the wardrobe,

a throbbing in her head and a tightness in her neck making her careless of the rich fabric.

He did offer to marry me—but only to save me from ruin.

He said he was attracted to me—yet a few weeks ago, he told me he'd never marry.

Mentally throwing her hands up at her internal argument, she climbed into bed, pulled the sheets up over her head, and after an hour of tossing and turning, finally willed herself to sleep.

CATHERINE STARED AT ROBERT, who had turned up that morning to break the news to the baron and baroness. They were understandably shocked because they'd only met Dunsbury once and believed the same to be true for Catherine.

She listened as Robert smoothly explained that he and Catherine had enjoyed several dances and had encountered each other through chance meetings at the museum and the park. All of which was technically true, so Catherine couldn't fault his account of their liaisons, though she was a little bemused by the persuasiveness of his telling.

"Fancy that!" exclaimed Mother Purcell. "Our Catherine will one day be a duchess!"

Catherine smiled, though it did nothing to alleviate the confusion that still rattled around her brain.

Across the room, Robert spoke quietly with the baron. Before her eyes, a decade's worth of worry melted from his face. The two men retired to the baron's study to draw up the marriage settlement, and when they emerged an hour later, the baron was positively jovial.

"I take it you offered to singlehandedly save Tutley Keep," Catherine said under her breath as she handed Robert a cup of tea and a plate of sandwiches.

"Not *singlehandedly,*" Robert murmured. "I merely assured him I would help with his debt. Sometimes one just needs to know he's not alone in a struggle." His tone and expression were somber, and Catherine wondered what struggle he'd faced alone. Did it have anything to do with the rift with his father? Robert gave her a brief smile. "The baron still has a great deal of work ahead of him to bring the estate back. I will, of course, provide him with some advice."

"Mama!" Christopher shouted, running into the room.

Catherine caught him mid-run. "Christopher, mind your manners."

"Christopher!" the baron called, his good humor uncontained. "Come help your grandfather eat this tray of cakes."

Christopher wriggled out of his mother's clasp and darted across the room. He'd barely swallowed his first bite when he turned to Robert.

"Have you ever eaten a bug?"

"Christopher!" Mother Purcell exclaimed. "My lord, please forgive—"

"Nothing to forgive," he said before he turned to the boy. "Several, as a matter of fact. The occasional gnat—swallowed inadvertently when one's mouth is open outdoors, of course. But a friend at school dared me to swallow a worm once. Remember? I told you at the park."

"Oh yes! Was it whole?" Christopher asked, eyes wide.

"Can you imagine chewing it?" Robert gave an exaggerated shudder. "But then I read that in far off Asia, there are places where they eat beetles."

As Robert regaled her son with tales of insects as meals, Catherine smiled, even as her heart sank—not because the Marquess of Dunsbury wasn't going to be a wonderful stepfather, but because he clearly *was,* and it was one more reason to love him.

For love him, she did.

She watched his expressive face as he laughed and lavished her son with more attention than Jasper ever had. She might not have much experience with romantic love, but she had read enough to know the way her heart raced when she saw the marquess, the way he made her feel when he listened to her, the way he made her laugh, and the way he interacted with her son, all made it impossible for her *not* to fall in love with Robert Carlisle.

Again, she wondered what sort of misery she'd suffer married to someone she loved when he did not return the sentiment.

She straightened her spine. Plenty of women married with no expectation of love. She and Jasper were the perfect example. What was important was Christopher—and helping the Purcells, of course.

Robert laughed at something her son said. The man was unfairly handsome. He had flaws, of course. His nose was a bit too long and appeared to have suffered a break at least once. He had a scar along his left jaw, and his beard seemed to grow prodigiously fast as he frequently had a slight shadow of whiskers—something quite out of sorts with London's standards. Oh, who was she fooling? There was nothing she found unappealing about him. Life with him would certainly not be difficult, especially when she learned to curb her feelings for him.

So why, then, was she still twisted in knots about marrying him? She busied herself with finishing her cold tea to hide her frown. The tea was rather unpalatable, and it was only when she'd taken the last sip an idea occurred to her. It was one thing to marry a man who didn't love her but still *chose* to marry her. It was another altogether to marry a man who felt compelled to the decision by circumstances and his sense of honor.

Catherine sighed heavily. She felt like the maudlin heroine in the rather melodramatic novel she'd recently read. While self-pitying melancholia was quite dramatic on page, in real life, it grew tedious. Trying to rouse herself, she returned her attention to her son and Robert's conversation. They had thankfully moved on from the consumption of bugs to the topic of horses.

"Can I, Mama?"

"Can you what? And don't forget to say 'please.'"

Christopher sighed loudly and dramatically. "Please. Weren't you listening? He's going to take me riding tomorrow in the park."

Robert glanced at Catherine, a smile playing on those very lips he'd kissed her with so thoroughly the night before.

"You, of course, are welcome to join us," he said with a wink that made her breath catch. He certainly wasn't acting like a man forced into marriage.

"I should like that very much."

&a.

TEN DAYS after Robert had told the baron and baroness of his intentions, and Catherine had told Mr. Hughes of her betrothal, which had gone surprisingly well, she stood in the drawing room of Dervinshire House, the family's London home. The large room, lavishly decorated with flowers and candles, was a flurry of activity with liveried footmen who offered chilled wine to the wedding guests. The small ceremony and large wedding breakfast had gone off without a hitch thanks to Robert's mother, even though Catherine had yet to meet her.

When Robert had delayed introductions to his parents, giving the excuse there simply wasn't time before the wedding, she had worried he was ashamed of her, but then he'd gone out of his way to make sure she had a new wedding gown befitting a marchioness, which had appeased Catherine's anxiety somewhat.

She glanced down at her splendid gown of pale blue muslin with an embroidered net overlay and experienced another thrill at wearing it. She'd never worn anything so elaborate. She pressed her lips together to suppress a mischievous grin as she realized that wasn't quite true. Her grandmother's court gown was equally lavish. She supposed it was fitting, as wearing that gown had led her to stand here today.

"Mother, allow me to present my wife."

Catherine almost gasped as Robert's voice intruded her reverie. She straightened her spine and tried to appear poised, though her heart pounded as she waited to see if the duchess would find her lacking.

"Catherine," Robert's mother said. "Allow me to welcome you to the family."

Catherine curtseyed. "Thank you, your grace. It—it is such an honor to meet you." She cringed inwardly. She sounded like a fawning imbecile.

The duchess smiled. "I wish our entire family were here to greet you. My daughter and her husband live in Scotland, and…her condition is such that travel is inadvisable." She had lowered her voice on the last, even though no one other than Robert was near them.

"Ah," Catherine said, wondering why in London society a pregnancy was considered something to hide as if it were a contagious disease.

"And while I look forward to getting to know you, that will have to wait. Now, you must circulate and meet everyone."

"I know most of—"

"As the Marchioness of Dunsbury," the duchess said, her tone firm.

Catherine nodded, feeling like an unsophisticated provincial.

"Robert, see that you pay your respects to your father before you leave. He will wish to meet your bride as well."

Catherine glanced at her new husband, whose expression turned flat. The duke had been too ill to attend the ceremony or wedding breakfast. Robert gave his mother a short nod, and the duchess moved on to another group of guests.

"She hates me. I am certain of it," Catherine said.

"Nonsense. She's only just met you."

"I'm a nobody with no dowry or connections." Tears burned behind her eyes, and her throat tightened. Robert turned to her and brought her hand to rest in the crook of his right arm, then squeezed her hand in reassurance.

"You are not a nobody, Catherine. You are lovely and intelligent and everything she could hope for in a daughter. She is simply focused on the party and her guests." He frowned. "She is also concerned for her friend's daughter—the Lady Eleanor you heard my mother informing everyone I would marry. The poor chit has got herself embroiled in a bit of a scandal. I'm sure my mother is convinced I could have saved Eleanor from disgrace. Once that all blows over, and Mother gets to know you and Christopher, she'll be far more welcoming."

That didn't exactly sound like a ringing endorsement. Despite Catherine's personality differences with the Purcells, they'd always been supportive and protective of her. To enter a family when she was clearly not the duchess's first choice...

"Dunsbury!"

Catherine turned with Robert as a tall, lean man with wheat-colored hair joined them.

"I thought this was a joke. When I received the invitation, I was certain you were pulling off the most elaborate ruse. Didn't you tell me at the Henley Regatta you would never give that old man the satisfaction of— Oh, hello there," he said as he seemed to finally notice Catherine.

"Wayland, allow me to introduce my wife, Lady Dunsbury.

Catherine, this is Lord Noel Wayland, an old friend from school days. He's not normally a complete idiot."

"Lord Wayland," Catherine said. Wayland bowed low over her hand, then flashed her a sheepish grin.

"He's lying. I'm always a complete idiot. But I'm quick to apologize for it. May I say how very happy I am you have won Dunsbury's heart? There's nothing I enjoy more than seeing pompous bachelors succumb to cupid's arrow."

"Oh, I—" Catherine didn't know what to say to Wayland's comment. Surely, he didn't think Robert was in love with her. The thought caused a pang around her heart. The ceremony and wedding breakfast had been so lovely, she'd allowed herself to pretend theirs was a love match, at least for one day.

Robert saved her from awkward explanations. "And you, Noel? When last I saw you, you were smitten and imagining your own happily ever after."

Wayland's smile faded, and Catherine realized his leanness was not a normal characteristic. He looked as if he'd lost at least a stone quickly and recently. Dark smudges beneath his eyes added to his look of ill health.

"Wasn't meant to be. Or at least, not with me." He seemed to push his words through a throat gone tight, and Robert's expression turned somber.

"I'm sorry, old boy. Is there anything—"

"Nonsense! This is your happy day." Wayland's forced joviality made Catherine's heart ache for him. "I'm going to drink the rest of your wine and make the most of it. I just wanted to give you my best wishes. My lady," he said to Catherine with another bow.

Robert frowned as he watched his friend depart.

"Should you go after him?" Catherine asked.

He turned back to her and smiled. "He'll be fine. This is, as he said, our happy day. Let me refill your wine glass. You'll need it if you're to meet my father."

Not long after, the party began to wind down. Robert glanced at his pocket watch and sighed.

"Very well. Let's get this over with." He escorted her out into the hall and up the wide, curved staircase. Thick carpet runners muffled their footsteps, and large portraits of forbidding-looking ancestors seemed to glower at them as they passed. It was such a different atmosphere from the light, elegant drawing room that Catherine grew even more nervous.

Robert had spoken so little of his relationship with his father. She wondered if their marriage would help or hinder a reconciliation. The thought of meeting a man who loathed his own son, who blamed Robert for killing his brother when clearly Robert still grieved him—

Robert stopped in front of a wide double door and rapped sharply. Without waiting for a summons, he opened the door and led Catherine in.

"I have brought my wife to meet you," he said, his tone emotionless.

The old man in the heavily draped bed scowled. "Come." His voice was dry and raspy but imperious, and it brooked no defiance.

Robert stood still, and Catherine wondered if he had heard his father. Then after a long moment, in which Robert made it clear he would not allow his father to summon him like a servant, he took Catherine's arm and led her to the bed.

"Where are you from?" the duke asked without preamble after Robert introduced her.

Catherine pasted on what she hoped was a pleasant expression. "Chippenham, your grace."

"Were your parents anyone?"

Beside her, Robert started to intercede, but Catherine squeezed his arm. Though the duke's manner was brusque, even rude, she thought of Christopher when he'd asked Robert if he was anyone. She smiled. "They were not titled, your grace, but they were both gently bred, intelligent, and honorable."

The duke snorted dismissively. Catherine was about to say more when the door opened again, and Robert's mother entered, Christopher's hand in hers.

"Someone was missing their mother," she said kindly, and Catherine could tell her son had completely won over the older woman.

Christopher ran up, bursting between her and Robert. "Mama! Mama!" He came to an abrupt halt in front of the duke.

"Who is this impudent boy?" the duke asked, knitting his bushy gray brows together.

Catherine put her hands on her son's shoulders. "This is Christopher, my son."

Though the duke still glowered, Christopher seemed fascinated with the old man. He took a step closer and looked up at Robert's father.

"Are you my new grandfather?"

"I should say not!" the duke said.

Robert's mother stepped forward and smiled at Christopher. Catherine nudged her son, who bowed correctly and only wobbled a bit as he straightened.

"I shall be your new grandmother," the duchess said.

"Do you eat biscuits with tea? My other grandmother does." Catherine bent to whisper in his ear, and Christopher blurted out, "Your grace."

"I do enjoy a biscuit or two with my tea, yes."

Christopher turned to the duke. "Too bad you're not my new grandfather. I always give my extra biscuits to my other grandpa."

Beside her, Robert tried to stifle a snort of laughter. Her son looked up at Robert.

"I guess you'll get my extras."

"Thank you."

Catherine watched her new husband's face. He seemed more relaxed than he had since entering the duke's chamber, and she smiled, proud that Christopher had lightened Robert's mood.

"You are removing to Bosworth Manor?" Though the duke's question was directed at Robert, the older man's gaze remained on Christopher.

"We are going on honeymoon first."

"And will the boy be joining you in Leicestershire?"

"Of course he will." Sharpness had returned to Robert's voice, and his face had tightened.

The duke finally looked at his son. "There is much work to be done. Mind you don't squander another three years before you attend it."

Robert sucked in a fierce breath, but before he could say a word, Catherine threw herself into the fray. "We'd best return downstairs. The Purcells wanted to get an early start to Tutley. They don't like to travel after sunset."

She hustled Christopher away and delivered him downstairs to the Purcells, who seemed overawed at being in a duke's drawing room. Jasper's parents—she supposed she couldn't very well call them her in-laws anymore—were taking Christopher to the baronial estate to initiate renovations while Robert took her to Brighton. The Purcells would then bring Christopher to Bosworth Manor, the ducal country estate in Leicestershire. It was the first time Catherine would be away from her son for longer than a few hours, and while Christopher seemed perfectly content, Catherine was rather anxious over the prospect.

"We can take him with us if you prefer," Robert said as Catherine watched her son climb in the Purcells' carriage.

Catherine turned to him with a smile. "That is very kind of you, but Christopher is looking forward to his adventure. They are visiting the baron's new estate. Besides, it would make it harder for us to get to know each other better if he and his ceaseless questions were to accompany us."

"Indeed," Robert said with a little smile.

Catherine flushed as she realized what had made him smile, and she busied herself with straightening her skirts.

&a.

Hours later, in the small house Robert had rented very near the beach, she struggled to undo the row of small buttons down the back of her traveling costume. They had elected to travel without a lady's maid or valet. Considering Sophie had only worked as a maid for Catherine during the past few years, Catherine was quite comfortable dressing herself, but many of her new gowns required assistance to get in and out of.

Robert entered the bedchamber while she still had her arms contorted behind her back.

"I am beginning to doubt the wisdom of not bringing a maid. I don't know how you'll manage to shave," she said.

"I traveled for three years without a valet and managed not to slit my throat."

Catherine abandoned her attempts at reaching her buttons and turned to him in surprise. "Really?"

He gave her a sardonic glance. "More people than not dress themselves without help."

"Of course, but you are a marquess. I would wager most men of your station do *not* dress themselves."

Robert's expression shuttered. He picked up his leather valise and began setting brushes and cravats on the dressing table. "When I left for France, I'd been a *marquess* for but a few days." He pronounced the word marquess with disgust.

"Oh! I thought— Well, I'm not sure what I thought."

Robert was silent for a long moment as he arranged and rearranged his toiletries. "I told you my father blamed me for

William's death. His…vitriol was such that I left England not three days later. I— I was not there for the funeral."

"I'm sorry." She reached out to touch his arm but stopped at his haunted expression. Deciding to lighten the mood, she brought their conversation back to a more neutral topic.

"Well, I'm glad we don't have servants tagging along. The Purcells had a few servants, of course—that was how Sophie came to be my maid and Christopher's nursemaid, but growing up, we only had a cook and a girl who would come to clean and do the wash once a week."

Robert smiled. "How dreadful for you," he remarked, his tone teasing.

She laughed, glad to have restored his good humor, and tried again to reach the buttons in the middle of her back.

"Allow me." Robert came up behind her, and the heat of his body—or simply the force of his presence—engulfed her.

He slid the top buttons free, and she waited for him to pop the others. When nothing happened, she glanced over her shoulder. Robert stared at the bare skin of her back, his intense expression causing a wash of sensation to suffuse her body. A rush of blood flooded her cheeks and fingertips, then settled between her thighs.

Finally, he traced his finger along the line of her spine from her nape to where her gown remained fastened, where he slowly freed another button, then the next. The dress had more buttons than necessary to remove it, but she stood frozen as Robert carefully let loose each one. With the last button undone, she released her hold on her bodice and let the fabric fall to the floor.

Her heart raced as she stepped from the pool of fabric and slowly turned to face him, conscious of her chamise's transparency. She forced her gaze to meet Robert's, relieved to find him staring at her face. As a bubble of nervous laughter threatened to escape, she realized he kept flicking his gaze down to her chest. Even as she found it humorous, her nipples hardened.

"You're very beautiful." He stepped closer and took her hand.

"You're terribly handsome."

He smiled. "Terribly?"

"Wonderfully," she blurted as the heat in her cheeks rose.

"Now I'm feeling ashamed of my paltry, 'very.'" He traced the curve of her cheek with his knuckles, then bent and captured her lips in a brief, hot kiss. "How about *strikingly*?"

She laughed. "Keep trying." She drew his head down to receive her kiss.

"Maddeningly?" he inquired when their lips parted.

She shook her head before pressing kisses along his stubbled jawline. He slipped the chemise's straps off her shoulders, and she shivered as the fine fabric slid over her sensitive nipples.

"Awe-inspiringly beautiful," he whispered.

Though incredibly self-conscious of her nakedness, she lost all thoughts of embarrassment when he looked back up. "That will do."

He smiled. "I feel entirely overdressed." As he peeled off his jacket, Catherine attacked the buttons on his waistcoat. Her fingers were a bit awkward. She'd never helped Jasper undress. In fact, she'd only ever seen him fully clothed or in his nightshirt. However, Jasper had never kissed her the way Robert did, and something told her this experience would be very different from those awkward times with her first husband.

As Robert pulled his shirt over his head, Catherine tentatively ran her fingers along his chest. She didn't realize a man might have hair there, or how it might narrow into a fine line bisecting his stomach before disappearing beneath the waistband of his trousers. She stopped her exploration at his waist, unsure of what to do next.

He grinned down at her, looking more like an exuberant boy than an accomplished seducer, and an answering grin curved her lips.

In moments, Robert was as naked as she, and her embarrassment returned tenfold. She cast quick glances down, fairly certain Jasper's…endowment had not been so imposing. The marital act with him had been clumsy and uncomfortable. Catherine now wondered if intimacy with Robert would be downright painful. She'd heard stories…

"Are you all right?" Robert asked as a small frown marred his brow.

"Oh, yes. Of course." She slid another apprehensive glance downward.

Robert ran his hands up her arms and drew her in for a gentle embrace. He bent his head to speak softly in her ear. "Whatever happened in your first marriage, I promise you, I will never hurt you, and you will only find respect and pleasure in our bed."

His words broke apart her trepidation, and she leaned into him, marveling at the rough hairiness of his muscled chest. Lower still, he pressed his male hardness against the juncture of her thighs, and she wondered just what he meant by pleasure. Ripples of delight certainly spread from every place his skin touched hers, and when he kissed her again, a deep undulation pulsed between her legs—something she'd never experienced before.

Robert bent and caught her behind her knees, scooping her up against his chest to carry her across the room to the large bed.

She gasped, as much at the novelty of someone carrying her as at the ease with which he lifted her.

"You're very—" She tried to think of a more interesting word than *strong*. "Virile."

"You have no idea," he replied, his smile wicked.

She realized he had taken a second meaning to her comment, and he took great delight in teasing her. Remembering that she too had enjoyed their less-than-proper conversations, she decided to play along. She thought frantically for an amusing innuendo, but she had so little experience with marital intimacy, much less the more ribald aspects of the act.

When he set her in the center of the bed, she glanced again at his naked body, studying the sculpted planes of his chest, the flat expanse of his belly, the bush of hair between his legs, and—

"You can touch me, too, you know."

She got to her knees and lightly placed her hands on the warm skin of his shoulders before tracing down the hard muscles of his torso. She paused with her hands at his waist.

"Go on." His voice was a low rasp.

She licked her lips and glanced up at him. "I-I don't know what—"

He took her hand and guided it to his member. She took hold of it, her grasp tentative, and he let out a low groan. Encouraged, she ran her hand along its length.

"What is it called?" she asked.

He frowned. "What?"

She slid her hand down and then back up. "What is it called? Before I married Jasper, my mother only told me men and women were different beneath their clothes, and it was best if I just closed my eyes."

He let out a choked laugh but quickly smothered it. "Didn't you come across any medical texts or erotic writings in your blue library?"

Catherine shook her head, covertly studying his hard sex in her hand as she continued to caress it. "I can expound on agricultural methods of Italian farmers and recite an in-depth history of the Scottish Highlands, but the novels Jasper brought me from London never mentioned anything remotely intimate.

Oh! There was one book." She nibbled her lower lip as she tried to remember.

"Don't stop."

Catherine smirked and resumed her light strokes.

"Yes, like that." After a moment, Robert sighed. "What was the book?"

"I don't remember the name or much of the story, for that matter." She laughed. "It was not very well written, but there was one scene I believe was meant to imply a certain activity."

"You mean lovemaking?"

Her cheeks warmed, and she nodded. It was ridiculous to act like a naïve girl, but her experience with Jasper had been so awkward and embarrassing.

He nudged her to lie down, and when she did so, he stretched out beside her. "What did it say?"

Catherine giggled. "I only remember one phrase. 'His blooming tumescence.'"

Robert laughed. "Gads, that's awful."

"So, what is it really?"

"Well, there are many names for it."

When he did not elaborate, she poked his belly. "Like?"

He caught her hand and rolled atop her. Without conscious thought, she parted her legs, and he nestled between them.

His voice was a low rumble at her ear. "In medical terms, it's a penis. But it's also a prick, a maypole, a Roger, and a Thomas."

He flexed his hips and rubbed against a particularly sensitive spot she'd only dared touch a few times. She sucked in a breath. "Why so many names? And why gentlemen's names?"

He laughed again, then drew his hips back and glided along that spot once more. A sort of…tension built throughout her body that was both delicious and frustrating. It made it difficult to pay attention to anything else.

"There are a hundred other names for it, each more ridiculous than the last."

"What do you call it?"

"My cock." The low rumble of his voice combined with his graphic words and the pressure he exerted made the place between her thighs throb.

She nodded and closed her eyes to focus on the sensations he evoked. When he paused his movements to nibble at her breast, a breath of sanity returned. "What about my—" She had no vocabulary for that part of her body. She suddenly felt foolish and ignorant, but her mother had always warned her not to think of any part of her body, and most especially not...there.

Robert raised his head. "Oh, now that has some lovely names because it is a lovely organ. Lady garden, honey pot, *le chat* in French."

"In medical terms?"

"Vagina." He slid his hands between her legs and parted the folds, finding the sensitive nub he'd rubbed with his cock. "But it doesn't matter what we call our bodies."

She lifted her head. It was hard to form a coherent thought as her skin heated from the inside out. "What? Why?"

He guided himself to her opening and slowly eased into her. "It's what we do with them that's important."

Catherine dropped her head back, savoring the delicious fullness of Robert's cock inside her. He eased back and plunged again, going deeper.

"You're so wet." His voice was a hoarse whisper.

"Is that bad?"

"God, no! It means you're excited as well."

Catherine wanted to assure him she was, but then he hooked an arm beneath her left knee, lifted her leg, and surged forward, filling her completely. There was no pain and certainly no awkward embarrassment of her past experiences. As he moved within her, she widened her legs and slid her hands down to his buttocks, engrossed in the flex and release of rounded muscles. Instinct took over, and she pressed her heels into the mattress so she could thrust her hips against his.

His breath rasped like bellows. She opened her eyes, and he stared at her as if she were the most beautiful thing he'd ever seen. She licked her lips, and he tracked the movement of her tongue. She did it again, and his gaze darkened. She was suddenly a temptress, a vixen, that woman at Vauxhall coming out of the bushes. Robert groaned above her, and the sound made her feel powerful and bold.

She lifted her head and captured his small nipple between her lips as he had done to her.

"Catherine." Her name escaped on a deep growl.

She bit at his neck, his shoulder, desperate for something but didn't know what. She clawed at his back, wanting, needing...*more.*

"Easy, love. Easy."

"No! I need—"

"I'll give it to you. Just—" He pressed her back against the mattress, then reached between them and gently rubbed at that deliciously sensitive spot.

"Robert!"

"I'm here. Come with me."

He drove faster, ground harder, and the tension that had tightened every nerve suddenly shattered, turning her world white-hot. She sobbed with relief as her body shook with delicious spasms. Robert groaned and thrust one final time before he collapsed to his elbows, holding his weight while they remained fused together.

After a long moment, he eased off her and flopped onto his back. He wove his fingers through hers, and Catherine smiled, spent and satiated.

"I had no idea," she said, still a bit dazed.

Robert chuckled, then rolled to his side to face her. He

traced the line of her cheekbone before he dabbed playfully at her nose. "That, my lady, was just the beginning."

"There's more?"

Robert positioned her against his front and wrapped his arm snugly around her waist. "You have no idea," he mumbled into her hair.

After several minutes, Robert's breathing slowed. Catherine hovered on the edge of consciousness, relaxed and tired but still fascinated by what they'd just experienced.

Expressions of love, words she'd only ever said to her son, filled her mouth. She clamped her lips together and swallowed the declaration, Robert's warning about developing feelings for him chilling her heated thoughts. She tried to push the idea away. She didn't want to spoil this experience with longing for the impossible.

CATHERINE STARED out over the green expanse of lawn on the wide verandah of their rented house and wished she had more than two days left of their honeymoon.

The last twelve days had perhaps been the happiest time of her life. She and Robert took leisurely strolls, had picnics on the beach, and browsed Brighton's small shops and markets. She acknowledged their relationship had begun outside the constraints of polite society, but now, without the pressures of life in London, she simply enjoyed Robert's company, as he seemed to enjoy hers, relaxed and carefree in the casual environment of the seaside town.

Robert tutted, bringing her attention back to him.

"Raspberry jam has too many seeds. They get stuck in my teeth. I'll have to call my valet to pick them out with a pin," he said.

"But you didn't bring your valet."

Robert affected an expression of horror. "We shall have to pack up and return to London, then. You certainly can't expect *me* to pick raspberry seeds out of my teeth."

Catherine succumbed to a fit of giggles. When she regained her breath, she gazed at him fondly. He was more relaxed than she'd ever seen him, and she enjoyed his silly antics as much as his lovemaking. She grabbed up the sharp paring knife with which they'd peeled an apple. "Here, I shall do my wifely duty and remove the offending seeds."

He deftly disarmed her and tugged her out of her chair to tumble into his lap. "Your wifely duty—other than what you performed so admirably just this morning, is to ensure we only have strawberry preserves on the breakfast table."

"No, no, no. Strawberry preserves have fruit pieces that are too big. The fruit doesn't spread nicely on toast, and it makes too large a mouthful."

Robert nuzzled the tender skin behind her ear. "You didn't complain about a large mouthful last night," he murmured.

Catherine swatted his arm as her face flamed with embarrassment. Robert had spent every day showing her just how much there was to marital relations than she'd ever imagined.

"There's only one way I'll eat raspberry jam."

She dragged her thoughts from their previous night's activities. "Do tell."

In answer, he stood, tossed her over his shoulder, scooped up the bowl of jam, then carried her into the bedchamber and tossed her on the bed. "If you don't want that pretty dressed stained red, you'll remove it quickly," he said, his devilish grin making her go wet with need.

THE FOLLOWING MORNING, as they walked along the beach, the normally busy dunes empty in the pre-dawn hour, Robert spoke about the Eastern religions he had encountered during his travels.

At one particular statement, Catherine stopped and pulled her hand from his. "What do you mean I could never attain enlightenment?" she asked, offended at the idea she wasn't spiritually gifted enough to become a buddha, even though she'd only just heard of the philosophy.

Robert laughed at her affronted tone. "I didn't say you couldn't. I only said the final form before transcending to full enlightenment is thought to be as a man."

"Which I am not."

"Not now. Buddhists believe in reincarnation so you would be able to return as a man."

"Because men are so much more spiritual?" Catherine could not hide her indignation.

"Certainly not," Robert said quickly. It seemed as if he fought not to laugh, which upset her even more. He smoothed his expression. "To achieve complete enlightenment, one must release attachment from everything, from all people. Women, it is thought, cannot escape the attachment of motherhood."

"Oh," Catherine said, her ire evaporating as she thought of Christopher. "Well, that is certainly true."

She took his hand, and they resumed their walk. "I've never had conversations such as this," she said after a few minutes.

"Such as what?"

She shrugged. "Where I wasn't simply told what to think."

"Whyever would I simply tell you what to think? You're clearly an intelligent, astute woman who can think for herself."

She looked at him. "That's quite the nicest thing anyone has ever said to me."

Robert ran his free hand through his hair as if suddenly uncomfortable. "Well, it's true."

Catherine smiled, utterly enamored, though she made sure not to show it as she changed her focus to the sun that just now peeped above the horizon. Today was a new day, and so was tomorrow.

❧

As the coach drew closer to his family's manor, Robert's mood darkened. He was still unfailingly polite, ever solicitous, but his relaxed playfulness had evaporated, and he stared broodingly out the window.

When he assisted her out of the coach in front of the enormous building that qualified as his childhood home, there were tense brackets around his eyes, and he'd compressed his mouth into a tight line.

She stopped him before he led her up the steps. "If your father is that bad, there's no need for us to remain. I'm sure the baron and baroness would be happy for us to stay with them in Tutley Keep."

At that, he smiled. "We are not here because we have no other place to go." He softened his expression and briefly touched her cheek. "But I appreciate the offer. There are arrangements to be made, business to see to, instructions I need to receive before—"

"Of course." Catherine took his arm as they climbed the wide steps leading up to the house where a phalanx of servants and Robert's mother waited to greet them.

❧

"No one will ever care for your holdings more than you," the duchess said as she led the way into her private sitting room after one long day of meetings with the gardeners to discuss plans for the vast decorative gardens, evaluate the herb and vegetable production, and plan the next season's plantings.

The last few days, Catherine had followed the duchess as

they drove about the countryside delivering packets of medicine and food to tenants, and as they'd met with the clergymen who served the tenants on the vast area of the Dervinshire lands to discuss what charitable works were necessary. Catherine had also accompanied her mother-in-law as she met with the housekeeper, approved expenditures, and any new hires the estate needed.

The duchess halted at her desk and indicated Catherine sit beside her.

"As Robert has his role in overseeing the estate, so too do you," the duchess said. "You may not have needed such training for your previous marriage, but you do have much to catch up on, my dear. The life of a duchess may seem one of endless parties and countless dresses"—she glanced sideways as if she suspected Catherine believed just that—"but to truly fulfill one's duties, you must not allow one detail of the estate to slip by you unnoticed."

"I understand."

She did, though her focus often slipped to Robert. He rose early and spent much of the morning meeting with the estate manager and tenants. He met with his father after luncheon most days—an occurrence that left Robert terse and ill-tempered for several hours. Knowing he did not have a good relationship with his father, she had learned to let Robert have his space. Generally, a bruising ride or time spent out walking the grounds was sufficient to restore his good humor, then he often spent the rest of the day in his father's study, answering correspondence from his man of business and solicitors in London.

There was nothing about Robert that Catherine did not notice.

"The duke is responsible for the welfare of the estate's production and any other investments he sees fit to purchase, but we must see to the health, as it were, of the house, its many needs, as well as the people in our employ. We must also see to the welfare of the tenants. We can often learn things of great benefit to the duke that he might not otherwise hear. Now then, how are your accounting skills?"

"They are good, your grace," Catherine replied.

"Indeed?"

"Indeed." Catherine was proud of the skills she'd acquired. While the scale of the ducal estate was massive, as its newness wore off, she realized its needs were not much different than the Purcells' smaller holding in Chippenham. In the months after Jasper's death, his mother had been bedridden with grief. His father, while not as incapacitated as his wife, had still been unable to focus on the daily business of the farmland's accounts. Catherine had stepped in and managed not only the bills but had arranged for the sale of the fall harvest. It was the first time in her life she'd felt truly needed and accomplished.

The thought of the Purcells made her wonder how they were faring at the new baronial holding and when they would arrive with Christopher. The longing for her son was so great, it was distracting—as the duchess had noted several times. With a mental sigh, Catherine pulled her thoughts from how much he must have grown since last she saw him and directed her attention to the duchess's books.

Later that night, Catherine surveyed the sitting room, with its overturned chair and clothes strewn across the floor. She released a long, contented sigh as she trailed her fingers along Robert's naked back. Goose bumps of pleasure rippled in the wake of her touch, and she smiled.

Catherine had wondered if their marital…adventures would continue once they'd returned from their honeymoon, but she need not have worried. Once Robert finished with his duties, he would seek her out and chase her into their chambers, locking the door as she giggled like a schoolgirl before he tossed her into the middle of the feather bed and ravaged her, to her great, if embarrassed, delight.

Even on the days when she hadn't seen him until bedtime, they more than made up for their separation when in the privacy of their rooms. Sometimes, Robert hadn't bothered waiting until they were in the bedchamber—he'd pulled her into his lap on the small sofa in their sitting room or pressed her against the door.

The first time he'd done so, she'd been shocked, but the passionate response Robert elicited had quickly overcome her initial reaction. In fact, she'd begun to think she was a wanton at heart, for she found she spent an inordinate amount of time each day remembering the previous night's love play and fantasizing about what was to come.

"At the rate we're going, I wouldn't be surprised if Christopher has a sibling by next summer," she said as she continued her exploration of his torso.

Beneath her fingertips, Robert's muscles tensed. In the next instant, he pushed himself to his feet and gathered his clothing. She thought he was simply tidying up the evidence of their activities until he thrust his legs into his trousers and tugged his shirt over his head.

"Are you going somewhere?" she asked, unable to hide the surprise in her voice.

He waited a long moment before answering. "I've remembered something I was supposed to check in the stables."

"Can't it wait until morning?"

"I won't be able to sleep if I don't see to it now."

"What could be so important that—"

He stomped his feet into his boots, sans stockings, and grabbed up his jacket.

"Shall I come with you?" She grew concerned and stood to grab her chemise.

At that, he seemed to come out of his distracted absorption.

He crossed to her and pressed a brief kiss to her forehead. "No, no. Go to bed. I'll return shortly." Then he was out the door, the click of the latch ominous in the quiet of the room.

Catherine tugged her chemise on then picked up the remaining clothes scattered about the sitting room. She dropped them on a chair in the bedchamber then crossed to the window, drawn by the bright wash of moonlight. Below, the grounds of Bosworth Manor stretched before her in the encroaching dark, quiet and empty—except for a lone figure striding purposefully across the smooth expanse of grass. She recognized Robert's gait even as she realized he trudged in the opposite direction of the stables, so he clearly hadn't forgotten a task at the stables.

She frowned, wondering why he had fled her presence. All she had said was—

"Oh." Perhaps the idea of fatherhood hadn't yet crossed his mind. Granted, he hadn't intended to marry a few months ago, so the notion of having a baby *would* require a bit of an adjustment, but as she stared into the night, she couldn't help but worry.

She absently rubbed the flat plane of her belly. Despite her concern over Robert's reaction, she smiled as she thought of a dark-haired baby in his arms. While she would love to have his child, a part of her hoped they would have a few more months of license to get to know each other and perhaps return to the closeness they'd enjoyed in Brighton before the responsibilities of parenthood.

She climbed into bed, her body relaxed from their love-making even as her mind raced. She would have to reassure Robert everything would be fine, that he would be a wonderful father.

She didn't hear him come to bed, but when she awoke the next morning, he slept beside her, still in his shirt and trousers but thankfully no boots. She snuggled against him, and without waking, he wrapped his arm around her, tucking her in. She drowsed a few more minutes, then trailed playful fingers down his stomach to the flap of his trousers. As his body responded, she smiled. He rolled toward her, and she waited for his kiss, but he suddenly pulled away and climbed out of bed as if it were on fire.

She sat up, startled. "What's wrong?"

Robert looked flustered with rumpled shirt and hair—and an obvious erection.

"I…overslept. I've got meetings in Twycross today."

She frowned, still confused at his reaction. "All right."

Without even looking at her, he disappeared into the dressing room, and before long, she heard his valet tapping on the outer door with hot water.

Over the next couple of days, Robert appeared busier than ever, and she rarely saw him. He left before she awoke in the morning and came to bed long after she had fallen asleep. She began to suspect something greater than the distant possibility of fatherhood bothered him, but she was unsure of how to approach him, even if she could locate him during the day. Their relationship was still so new, and her marriage to Jasper had certainly not provided her with any experience discussing deeply rooted feelings.

She continued her lessons with the duchess and tried to keep her mind busy. When Christopher returned, it helped immensely, but even her love and care for him could not erase the worry that somehow something wonderful had slipped through her fingers.

ROBERT WAS AN ASS. He knew because he told himself several times a day. He would catch a glimpse of himself in the hall mirror and mutter, "You are an ass."

Mostly, though, he would tell himself he was an ass every time he left Catherine to attend to the endless tasks his father had set for him, and especially these last few days when he had avoided her. Bosworth Manor was huge and in dire need of an owner's attention after his father's failing health over the last year. Thankfully, the duke had always hired the best managers, and while there were decisions only an owner could make, the day-to-day business had continued smoothly.

Late summer in Leicestershire was idyllic. There was no reason why Robert couldn't take Catherine and Christopher riding along the maize fields, which were just being harvested, or take a trip into Leicester and view the canals that had revolutionized the river Soar, or on a picnic by the stream where Robert and William used to fish. There was no reason at all, except each place reminded him of William, and while the pain of his loss had dulled to an ache, his father did not allow a day to go by without reminding Robert that he was responsible for his brother's death.

Sometimes his father made an offhanded reference. Other times, like now, the duke's words were poisoned blades, expertly thrown.

He and his father had discussed leasing out an underused paddock on the north end of the estate. Robert had argued they could give the area over to their existing tenant farmers to accommodate growing families. The duke had clearly set his mind to leasing it to a neighbor who bred horses.

"Unless you like riding up there to gloat," the old man said bitterly.

"What on earth would I gloat over? It's a bit of pasture and some rocky hills." The tension in Robert's neck from dealing with his father began to make his head throb.

"That's not far from where you shot your brother. In one glance, you could view where you took his life as well as his birthright."

Robert gritted his teeth, his father's words making him nauseous. He stood and gathered up the map of the estate he had laid on his father's bed. They would accomplish nothing more today. He had learned long ago that when his father started down this path, there was no way to induce him to speak of anything else.

"Where do you think you are going?" the duke demanded. "We have much to discuss!"

Robert took a bracing breath and turned to leave. He started to take a step toward the door when his father said, "Your brother did not so quickly abandon his tasks. I suppose that's why you— Come back here!"

Robert used the last of his control to close the door gently, then he released his furious energy bolting down the stairs, taking them three and four at a time. He stormed to the stables then saddled his horse, much to the consternation of the stable hands.

He urged his horse into a gallop with no destination in mind, but considering his recent words with his father, Robert wasn't surprised when he ended up at the crossroads where William had died three years ago. He stumbled off his horse and made his way to the edge of the woods, where he had laid his brother in the grass.

Though it was midafternoon, the crossroads stood as deserted as they had the night he and William had ridden back from the town of Twycross, drunk from a night spent in that town's tavern. They had been singing bawdy songs and laughing over stupid jokes when a shot rang out, and Robert's hat flew off his head. In his inebriated state, it took him a moment to realize what had happened. The clouds parted, allowing the moonlight to illuminate the pale swath of the dirt road before them. The silvery light glinted off the barrel of a gun, and without thought, Robert had launched himself off his horse, knocking his brother out of his saddle. They both landed with grunts in the dirt.

Suddenly, Robert remembered that night as clear as if it were yesterday, and he could hear William, who had imbibed more heavily than Robert.

"Why'd you go'n do that?"

"Stay on the ground if you value yer miserable lives," someone *ordered from the trees behind them.*

Robert tried to see how many attackers there were, but the horses were skittish, and the only thing in his sight were their shifting legs. He started to stand but felt the cold muzzle of a gun press against the back of his neck.

"Easy, there, mate. Ye wouldn't want to lose that pretty head over a handful of coins now, would ye?"

Robert paused on his knees. "Is that what this is about?" He fumbled for the leather pouch at his belt. "Here, take it and be gone!"

He tossed it toward the gun-wielding man who let it hit the ground at his feet.

"That'll be a start, ye fat witted clot, but just a start."

The crunch of footsteps alerted Robert to a second assailant. He spun around, crouched on his heels. The second man sauntered forward; a long, elegant dueling pistol held loosely in his grasp. He'd tucked the mate to the pistol in his belt. He wore a dark cutaway, brocade waistcoat, tightly fitted trousers, and knee-high leather boots. Though he lacked a cravat, and his hair was unfashionably long beneath his top hat, he had the look of a wellborn man, and Robert wondered if the man had fallen on hard times or simply played the role of highwayman for amusement. It would not be the most profane thing Robert had heard a young man do.

"Move away from your friend, if you please." The man's accent set him apart from his cohort, and Robert revised his assumption the man had stolen the dueling pistols. Robert stood slowly, his hands up. He stepped away from William, who pushed himself to all fours.

"You may remain where you are, sir," the highwayman said conversationally.

William appeared not to have heard the instruction. He swayed drunkenly on hands and knees.

"Will, be still," Robert said.

"I've fallen off me horse, Bobby! Be a good brother and help me up!" Will bellowed.

Robert frowned. No matter how far in his cups, William never bellowed, and he never called Robert "Bobby." He clearly played the sloppy drunk to throw off their assailants. Robert's muscles tensed as he waited for some cue from his brother as to what to do. The most expedient route would be to let the highwaymen have their money and probably their horses too, but Robert knew his brother well enough to know William would never willingly give up his mount.

Robert flicked a look over to the first man who had dropped the point of his gun a few inches as he watched William's drunken display, a derisive sneer on his face. "I thought you toffs were s'posed to be able to hold yer liquor. This one's plum bosky!"

"Yes, well, it just goes to show good breeding does not guarantee good behavior," the well-dressed man said. "After all, look at me." He flourished his hands in such a way the dueling pistol twirled sideways.

William launched himself at the man and tackled him to the ground. Robert spun about on his heel and punched the first man in the face. The man's pistol went off, and a burn flared in Robert's left shoulder as the ball grazed his arm. William's horse whinnied in pain and bolted. Robert's own horse danced sideways, unsure of what to do. The less elegant assailant's nose spurted blood down his face, and when Robert took a threatening step toward him, he threw his pistol and fled into the woods. Abandoning pursuit, Robert grabbed his horse's reins and pulled his own pistol from the saddlebag.

Turning, he started to run to William's aid. His brother and the well-dressed highwayman rolled on the ground, delivering punches to any available target. Then, as one, they lurched to their feet, and the highwayman had William in a chokehold from behind, a knife at his throat.

A streak of moonlight fell on William's face, and it was impossible to miss the look and nod his brother gave him. Robert cocked his pistol just as William grabbed the knife's blade with his bare hand and threw his weight forward to give Robert a clear shot at the highwayman. Robert lifted his pistol and squeezed the trigger.

Time seemed to slow into one long, drawn-out moment. Then, the click of the hammer sounded at the same time the highwayman swung his body to the right, which changed William's forward momentum and spun him back.

Time sped up as the shot rang out, and Robert screamed, "William!"

He reached his brother as he collapsed. Behind them, the highwayman scooped up his pistol and pointed it at Robert, who waited *for the fatal shot. A loud click echoed in the otherwise quiet night, but nothing happened.*

"Right," said the thief. "That's my cue to leave." He grabbed the reins of Robert's horse and flung himself expertly into the saddle.

Robert did not watch him go. He gently lowered William to the ground and checked the gravity of his wound. Robert inhaled sharply. Even by the spotty moonlight, the spread of blood across his brother's waistcoat was visible. With an angry oath, Robert tore off his cravat and pressed it to William's side, desperately trying to stem the flow. Tears burned Robert's vision, and he roughly dashed them away.

"William! Can you hear me?"

William's eyes fluttered open. "What happened? I— Ow!" He tried to sit up but gasped at the pain and collapsed back on the ground. Robert felt a fresh surge of hot blood over his hands at William's exertions.

"You've been shot. I-I shot you, William. I'm so sorry."

His brother huffed a short laugh. "No, you didn't."

"I did! Will, it was my—"

William lifted his head and grabbed Robert's lapel. William's eyes were glazed with pain, but they focused intently on Robert's face.

"No! Rob...no." His head fell back to the road though he kept his grip on Robert's jacket. "You are not responsible for this, Rob. Promise me you'll not blame yourself."

Robert jerked. In place of the pale moonlight, the afternoon sun shone bright. No blood stained the grass at his feet where he had lain his brother after he died. Instead, small white flowers bloomed in profusion, their petals bobbing in the breeze. Only the hum of bees and the chirp of birds filled the silence. The peaceful junction would have been pleasant in other circumstances.

Only one mark indicated a great man had died needlessly in this otherwise nondescript place. Robert searched the nearest trees until he found William's initials, carved into the trunk of a birch. Robert had done it three days after William had died—

on the way out of the country after their father had told Robert to leave. He had wanted to make sure he could always find the exact spot his brother had taken his last breath.

He ran his fingers over the initials, the carving weathered brown now, and remembered William's words. *"You are not responsible for this, Rob. Promise me you'll not blame yourself."*

It was a promise he had broken immediately. A promise he never kept. As soon as he told his father and Constable Loman what had happened, he had heard his guilt. The constable, like his father, had suspected him of killing his brother to assume his title, but Robert had collected the first assailant's gun—the one that had scored his arm with a bullet—and they could not determine how Robert could have inflicted the injury himself. Furthermore, Loman had heard scattered reports from other villages of two brigands, one well dressed, the other low brow, who had robbed travelers. When William's horse turned up, sold to a farmer a day's ride away, and the constable found the highwaymen's deserted camp not far from where William died, the evidence had been more than enough to satisfy Loman. The duke, however, continued to accuse Robert of murder.

Robert pressed his forehead to the tree trunk, fighting a wave of grief. Since his return to England, he had been preoccupied with dealing with his father's unpleasantness and had not considered how coming back would make him miss his brother all the more. He stood there for long moments, remembering happy times as well as the bitter end with his brother. He thought of the girl William had wanted to marry, the family he planned to have. They were one of the reasons Robert had sworn never to marry. If his brother, who was good, generous, and compassionate, could not have a family, how could Robert, who was none of those things, deserve them? Yet now he had Catherine and Christopher.

Thoughts of William slowly faded, and Robert found himself wondering what Catherine was doing just then. He wondered if she was happy. He had certainly been a far from exemplary husband, and not just because of his absorption with the estate business. Robert had deliberately kept her at an emotional arm's length—hence his repeated declarations that he was an ass. It didn't matter that he'd told her love and emotional attachments were not for him. It didn't matter that saving her son's legacy and helping the Purcells had been Catherine's main reason for remarrying. Neither was of consequence now because they were just excuses. They were paltry, insignificant reasons not to allow himself to feel...love.

Robert pushed himself away from the tree, his heart pounding. He'd held onto his guilt for so long it had become a part of him. He was Robert Carlisle, unwilling heir to the Duke of Dervinshire, and martyr to the guilt of causing his brother's death. Refusing to marry and have a family was not just to defy his father; it was also a self-imposed punishment. William, however, had known how Robert would grieve, and William's dying breath had been to implore his brother to run toward love, not away from it.

Robert pictured Catherine's face as a haughty Russian countess and as an affectionate mother. He visualized her flushed with embarrassment as she asked him what to call his cock, then flushed with passion as she became his siren. Each vision was a facet of her allure, a glimmer of what made her the most beautiful woman he'd ever known, the woman he loved.

Robert sighed. Despite his asinine admonition not to develop feelings, he hoped she had begun to love him in return.

He mounted his horse and slowly rode home.

Entering the house through a side door, he heard his father in the small drawing room at the back of the house.

"Give that back, you miscreant!"

Even as he realized his father's voice did not sound angry, Robert took off at a run. He came to an abrupt halt just inside the doorway. This drawing room faced the back lawns and received a great deal of sunlight. As a result, his mother had filled it with a collection of exotic houseplants. It was actually Robert's favorite room, but as it was also where his father spent most of his time when not in bed, Robert tended to avoid it.

The miscreant in question turned out to be Christopher. From what Robert could discern, Christopher had taken the last jam tartlet and was trying to stuff it in his mouth—a feat made difficult by his giggling at the duke's pretend outrage.

Robert froze. It had been years since he had seen his father do anything remotely humorous. When Robert and William had been boys, their father had teased them, even indulging in the occasional prank with them. As they had grown older, he became focused on teaching William how to run an estate, but he'd never made Robert feel his worth was less than his brother's.

As he stood in the doorway watching his father growl like an old bear and pretend to swipe at Christopher, Robert wondered how a man who loved his sons and had known how close the brothers were could believe the absolute worst of one of them? How could that love simply disappear?

Robert gripped the door jamb, understanding for the first time in almost three years what had devastated him about his father's reaction to William's death. It wasn't the intense grief and resulting anger at losing a son—Robert could understand and empathize with that. It was the fact the duke had cast aside his youngest son and then recast him as the worst sort of human imaginable.

That pain went bone-deep, and he couldn't see past it. Watching his father play with Catherine's son made it worse, for it reminded him of what else he'd lost when William died.

The duke finally swiped a biscuit and stuffed his face with it before rolling his eyes comically at Christopher, who in turn laughed uproariously, his mouth still full of jam. Robert backed away, a hollow feeling in his stomach. He bumped into someone and whirled around to see his mother, who peered around the door.

She pressed a finger to her lips and drew Robert out into the hall.

"I like to watch the two of them together. Young Christopher seems immune to your father's bad moods, and as a result, I think it's actually helped your father regain his sense of humor."

"Impossible," Robert said. He cleared his throat to dislodge the press of emotion. "The man doesn't know how to smile, much less laugh."

Behind him, a rusty chuckle that could have only come from the duke joined Christopher's squeal of delight.

His mother raised her eyebrows slightly, her smile serene.

Avoiding her knowing gaze, Robert mumbled something about business to attend to and bowed before beating a hasty retreat. He locked himself in the study and tried to read the correspondence stacked neatly in the middle of the desk, but the sound of his father's laughter, coming just hours after his vicious accusations that morning, had thrown Robert's equilibrium.

More memories resurfaced of his childhood, of his father teaching him to ride a horse when he was barely old enough to walk, of the Christmas his father had presented both sons with bows and arrows despite the duchess's worry they would accidentally shoot each other, of the constant reminders that family was of utmost importance.

How could the man who'd taught William and Robert to love and support each other believe Robert capable of killing his brother?

Robert abandoned the correspondence and went to stare out the window. He rubbed his mouth roughly as if that would keep in the anguished cry building in his chest.

A movement caught Robert's eye, and he turned to see

Catherine walking hand in hand with Christopher through the lower gardens. Christopher was animated as he told his mother something. Catherine, in turn, watched her son skip and talk and gesture with all the love in the world plain on her face.

Robert frowned. Would that love for her son ever change? Or would it remain constant, unconditional, the way a parent's love for their child should always be?

Less than an hour ago, he'd realized he loved his wife. What if Catherine loved *him*? Would *that* be constant, or could some tragedy change her feelings? Could she reject him the way his father had?

Robert's stomach soured as he wondered if there was something inherently wrong with him and if that was the reason his father had turned on him. If that were true, he could never give himself over to Catherine's love. He could never risk losing it because the way he felt about her now was so intense, it was difficult to imagine living without her. If they crossed that line; if he—

No. Life was best just as it was. Their relationship was safe. It was pleasant and beneficial to both of them.

Robert returned to his desk, resolved in his decision, even as some part of him roiled, discontented.

Fourteen

CATHERINE TOOK a deep breath before going outside, where Christopher sat on the verandah with the duke. Her son and new father-in-law had struck up a friendship, which was surprising only because the duke had so little patience with virtually everyone else on the estate, and if there was one thing Christopher required lately, it was patience. For the last month, not a day went by when her son did not challenge her rules, Sophie's instructions, and even Robert's decree that Christopher could not ride his new pony without supervision. Christopher had become, to quote Mother Purcell, a handful.

She stepped outside and gently closed the French doors behind her. The duke sat in a chair facing the gardens, a shawl on his shoulders, a blanket across his lap. Christopher leaned against the arm of the chair, looking at something the duke seemed to be holding.

Perhaps her son's recent rebellious streak called to the duke's own invalid orneriness, for the two seemed to get along splendidly.

For her part, Catherine still found the duke intimidating. He rarely spoke to her and barely acknowledged her presence in the room. She wondered if it was simply because of her unimpressive lineage or because of his strained relationship with her husband. Either way, Catherine was happy to keep her distance from the old man. Though she did not know the details of William's death, she knew with a bone-deep conviction Robert was not to blame, and the fact the duke not only held Robert accountable but also punished him daily for it raised her ire. How a parent could treat their child like that, she would never know.

"Mama!" Christopher exclaimed happily. "Look! He fixed it!"

Catherine strode forward as the duke handed one of Christopher's tin soldiers back to him.

"It was broked, but he fixed it!"

Catherine surreptitiously watched the duke's expression, which went from a half-grin to a pinch-mouthed scowl, she supposed because of her presence. She straightened her spine and tried for a smile.

"Did you thank his grace?"

"Thank you," Christopher said, distracted. He busily moved the soldier's sword arm up and down.

"Mmph," the duke said, his tone brusque.

"Come, Christopher. It is time for your lessons."

"Aww," her son moaned.

Catherine gave him a look, which thankfully he heeded as he obediently came over and took her hand.

"I don't like lessons," he whispered. She didn't like them either. Her son should still learn through play rather than spend hours each day with a governess.

"Seems a bit young to be having lessons," the duke said.

Catherine bit back her surprise that he'd spoken to her. She did not refrain from responding, however. "Yes, well, her grace has assured me I have been delinquent in not starting Christopher's lessons sooner."

Despite her attempt to keep her voice neutral, she could hear the edge in her tone. Apparently, the duke could as well, for he frowned, though his gaze still avoided hers. It seemed he had nothing more to say, so Catherine led Christopher back toward the house. She had not taken two steps when the duke's voice stopped her.

"He's your son, isn't he?"

She turned back to see him still scowling as he looked out over the acres of his estate.

"Of course he's my son. What—"

"Seems you should make the decisions about his raising." The duke picked up the bell at his elbow and rang it, calling for a footman to come help him.

Catherine stared at him in shock for a moment before collecting her wits and leading Christopher inside.

"Mama?" he asked hesitantly as they climbed the stairs to the schoolroom on the third floor. She glanced down at him in question. "Why is your face all red?"

She put her fingers to her cheeks, which were hot. Normally, she could tell the instant she flushed. "It's a warm day," she said, hoping he wouldn't pick up on her lie, then she hurried him up the stairs.

He *was* her son, and the decisions about his care and upbringing *were* hers to make. When the duchess had recommended hiring a governess, Catherine had not wanted to contradict her, especially so soon into their relationship, and by the time Catherine had decided Christopher wasn't ready for a governess, the duchess had already hired one.

"Let's go fishing after your lessons," Catherine said at the door to the schoolroom.

Christopher widened his eyes. "Really?"

"Really." The boy threw his arms around her hips with such force she nearly lost her balance.

"Go learn a big word you can teach me," she urged before she watched him run into the room.

Even after the door clicked shut behind him, Catherine stood staring into space. She remembered when the Purcells tried to forbid her from reading when she was first pregnant with Christopher. With Sophie's help, Catherine had first purloined books and then implored Jasper to intercede on her behalf.

Should she talk to Robert? Ask him to intervene? They had been so distant lately. It was as if they had never snuck into *demimonde* parties together, much less spent an incredibly intimate honeymoon in Brighton.

Her cheeks heated again, not with anger, but with their remembered fortnight of passion. While Robert continued to live up to his promise to always show her respect and bring her pleasure, their encounters were not the long, drawn-out, sensuous explorations they had enjoyed in Brighton. He hadn't pounced on her like he had when they'd first come to Bosworth Manor—as if he'd been a starving man and she was his only nourishment. They no longer snuggled by candlelight afterward, talking for hours. There were no leisurely breakfasts or long walks. And they'd not played disrobe chess since that last night in Brighton. Was that simply how marriage was once the honeymoon was over?

She frowned as she thought of the Hamiltons. No, they seemed like a honeymoon couple still, and Anna had said they had been married for four years.

Catherine shook her head. She would think about Robert and her conundrum later. Now, she needed to decide if she could bring herself to ask for his assistance. Despite his aloofness, she believed he would listen to her concerns and do anything he could to aid her, even confronting his mother if necessary. Still, the idea rankled. After two years of being her own mistress, she did not want to rely on a husband to solve all her problems.

"Well, am I a Russian countess or not?" Surely the woman who could defeat the Lord Chancellor at chess should be able to stand up to her mother-in-law, especially with Christopher's welfare at stake. When she had been out with Robert as the countess, he had encouraged her boldness, egging her on to speak her mind and act in ways that shy and conventional Catherine would not.

"Countess Borodinicha, your services are required," she said, smoothing her hair and tugging her bodice into place.

"My lady?" the governess asked, opening the schoolroom door. "Did you say something?"

"Oh, no. I'm just leaving, actually." Catherine pressed her lips together. She had spoken with a bit of a Russian accent. If the governess noticed, she didn't show it; she merely nodded and stepped back to close the door. Catherine caught a glimpse of Christopher at the too-big desk looking miserable, and her resolve hardened.

She marched downstairs and asked the first housemaid she came across where the duchess was. It took another maid and a footman to track Robert's mother down. She waited outside the duchess's sitting room while she finished meeting with the housekeeper. Catherine plucked at her dress and reconsidered asking Robert to intervene, but each time her courage wavered, she closed her eyes and mentally put on her red gown, then muttered in her heaviest Russian accent, "I am Countess Alisa Borodinicha." The third time she did this, she stopped halfway through her affirmation. She didn't need to pretend she was a false Russian countess because she *was* the Marchioness of Dunsbury. More importantly, she was Christopher's mother.

By the time the housekeeper left the sitting room, Catherine's nerves were drawn tight.

"Ah, good morning, Catherine. Allow me to finish these notes."

Catherine ignored the feeling she was a supplicant waiting to beg a boon as she stood waiting for the duchess to finish. Surely Robert's mother had simply forgotten to invite Catherine to sit…

"Now then," the duchess said, closing her notebook and laying down her pen. "What may I do for you?"

"It's— Well, it's about Christopher."

"Oh dear! Is he unwell?" her mother-in-law asked with sincere concern.

"No, not at all. It's simply… Well, I *am* concerned the governess is pushing him a little too hard in his lessons."

"Really? She is quite experienced and came highly recommended. I would think she knows better than us what a child is ready for."

Bother. That was not at all what Catherine had meant to say. She became flustered. Why was she so bad at saying what she meant? She envisioned the chessboard on which Catherine had defeated the Lord Chancellor, who purported to be a brilliant strategist.

"Well, you see, I believe it is *I* who best knows how Christopher learns. He is very young, and to push him to master sums and how to read at this age may make him resent schooling."

"But dear, we must ensure he is ready for Eton. It wouldn't do to have Dunsbury's stepson—and the future Baron Tutley—fall short amongst his peers."

Catherine froze at this eminently rational argument, then stiffened her resolve. *No,* he is *my* son. "I believe there is plenty of time to prepare him for such schooling if, in fact, I decide to send him to Eton."

"He must go there," the duchess said, aghast. "It's a family tradition. Besides, he will develop friendships and contacts that will help him throughout his life."

Catherine wanted to ask how an Eton contact could possibly help her son run a small sheep-breeding estate but decided that was a question for another day. *Stay focused.* It was the same advice her father had given her when he taught her to play chess.

"Be that as it may, I believe Christopher will be better served by being allowed to be a little boy and learn through playing and natural interaction with his world around him. Perhaps next year—"

"But, my dear, the time lost in a year. If you'll consider my—"

"At what age did my husband learn to read?" Catherine asked. *Goodness, I've interrupted a duchess.*

"I beg your pardon?"

"When did Robert learn to read and do sums?"

"Well, I don't recall exactly," the duchess said, suddenly busying herself with tidying her desk.

"Surely you can recall if he was still a very young boy. Four years old is a memorable age, after all."

"Now I consider it, I believe he didn't learn to read until he was seven. But that is why—"

"That sounds an appropriate age," Catherine said.

"I simply want what's best for Christopher. I do care for him, you see."

Catherine smiled. The duchess was clearly in earnest. "You have no idea how moved I am to know that. You have been so welcoming to both of us, and we truly wish to do the family proud. But I know my son and know what's best for him."

When the duchess tilted her head in acquiescence, Catherine said, "I'll just let the governess know we won't need her for a few more years, then."

She turned to go, her hands shaking slightly—the aftereffects of standing up to the imposing Duchess of Dervinshire.

"You are very fierce in your defense of Christopher."

Catherine turned at the door and smiled at the duchess. "He is my son. I would do anything for him."

The duchess straightened the already neat stack of accounting books in front of her, avoiding Catherine's eye. "I hope— That is…" She cleared her throat, and Catherine was amazed to realize the duchess was suddenly nervous.

"I would hope such fierce loyalty would extend to others you love. Such as *my* son."

Catherine froze, her mouth dry. Suddenly, she faced not the ever-confident duchess but simply another mother who worried for her son.

"Of course it does," Catherine said. Then she decided to confess something since it appeared to be a day for monumental announcements. "I love your son very much."

The duchess gave her a brief nod and turned aside to dab at her eyes with a handkerchief.

Catherine closed the door behind her and leaned against the wall next to it. Good heavens, had she really just told the duchess she loved Robert? Catherine had certainly been thinking it since their honeymoon. Still, given Robert's warnings about his views on love, not to mention the tortuous distance that had grown between them recently, she had never intended to speak of it, much less to Robert's mother.

It suddenly felt wrong to have told his mother but not the man himself.

Well, Catherine *had* just faced down a duchess. Surely it wasn't impossible to confront a mere marquess. Perhaps… Perhaps there was a chance to bridge the gap that had widened into a chasm between Robert and herself. Or maybe she might make it worse, considering his protestations he did not desire love.

With a shake of her head, she pushed away from the wall and went to relieve Christopher of his governess. Catherine would worry about confessing her feelings to Robert later.

Now, she was going to proudly rejoice for having stood up for herself.

❧

CHRISTOPHER WAS, unsurprisingly, thrilled with Catherine's announcement that lessons would be put on hold for at least a year and declared she was "the best mama in the world!"

A day of fishing followed, which very quickly ended up being less actual fishing and more Catherine sitting on the banks of the stream watching over Christopher as he splashed in the water and lodged mud in every crevice of his small body.

If she'd had any doubt about her decision to postpone her son's formal education, watching him try to catch minnows, follow ant trails, and investigate the underside of a toadstool allayed them. Then there were the two thousand questions he asked over the course of the afternoon, which ranged from why fish didn't drown to whether dung beetles really collected—

"That's a question for another time," Catherine declared, gathering up the blanket and basket of food they had brought with them.

"Why?"

"Because it is."

Christopher threw his last rock into the water just as a loud crack in the forest across the stream rang out. It sounded like someone had stepped on a branch and broken it. Though Catherine stared, she could not see beyond the tangle of brambles and bush that clogged the far bank. She listened another minute but decided it was nothing.

"I'll ask Mister Robert. He'll tell me," he said under his breath.

Catherine fought not to smile. Though she did not understand the friendship that had sprung up between her son and the irritable old duke, she knew exactly why Christopher adored Robert.

Robert did not simply respond to her son's endless questions; he explained his answers fully and asked Christopher questions in return. In addition, Robert made jokes with her son, was never too busy to admire a new toy, and displayed unflagging energy for games of tag.

If Catherine had not already lost her heart to her husband, seeing how he was with Christopher would have been enough to make her fall in love. That brought back to mind her earlier dilemma of whether or not to share her feelings with Robert. Apart from Christopher, she had never told anyone else she loved them. Not even her parents. The idea of laying her heart out to Robert made Catherine's palms go sweaty and her heart pound in terror.

Nevertheless, her successful conversation with the duchess reminded Catherine she *was* the Russian countess, which meant she could attain anything if she were bold enough to ask for it.

With a bounce in her step, Catherine delivered Christopher into Sophie's care for a bath, then went off to ready herself for her husband.

&.

HER SCENTED BATH oil and new green gown were for naught as Robert sent word that business on the far side of the estate had compelled him to stay the night at an inn.

It was not until three days later that Catherine managed to get Robert alone and claim his undivided attention—by walking in on him while he dressed for dinner.

Amazed again at the effect his naked torso had on her as he pulled off his shirt, she stared admiringly for several seconds, enjoying the warm flush of desire that flooded her body.

He turned to face her. "Sorry. I didn't see you there."

Startled out of her sensuous reverie, Catherine blushed furiously at the way he'd caught her staring. She put a hand to her jaw, relieved to find she had not left it agape.

"Oh, hello," she said, feeling a little like an idiot.

Robert smiled. "May I be of service?"

"Yes, well…" She took a steadying breath as she scrambled to remember her plan. "You see, I wished to discuss something with you."

He raised his eyebrows in question, and she rushed on. "It's about— Well, it's about that discussion we had at that public house, when we set out the rules for our arrangement, and, um, later when you declared we would wed."

Robert's expressive face betrayed his confusion. Before he could say anything, Catherine continued. "Well, you see, I know you said it would be best for our relationship to keep our emotions in check—"

"What I meant was—"

She held up a hand to stop him. If she didn't get all her words out now, she feared she might swallow them, perhaps forever. Confessing her feelings to Robert was proving far more terrifying than confronting the duchess.

"Please let me finish," she implored. He nodded, and she chewed on her lower lip, noticing how his gaze focused on the action, the look in his eyes one of hunger. She slowly let her lip slide from between her teeth, and though she couldn't hear it, she could have sworn his breath hitched as he watched. Her body instantly reacted to his arousal, and she had to stop herself from crossing the room and kissing him.

Then again… Perhaps she could recapture some of the closeness they had shared in Brighton by way of passion. The Russian countess would certainly do that.

Her mind made up, Catherine took a deep breath and

stepped closer to him. She took the fresh shirt from his hand and tossed it onto an armless chair.

"What—" He froze when she touched his bare chest with her fingertips. She traced the ridge of muscles, and when she brushed her fingertip over one of his small, hardened nipples, he inhaled sharply.

After a moment, she scraped a fingernail lightly over his other nipple, delighting in the shudder that ran through his body. She took a step closer, then slowly, oh so slowly, leaned forward until she could press her lips into the little hollow at the base of his neck.

Movement caught her peripheral vision as Robert lifted his hands as if to grab her, but then he stopped, and she realized he wanted to see how far she would take the encounter. Emboldened, she flattened her hands against his chest, then slid them around to clasp his back as she closed the distance between them and pressed herself against him from thigh to breast.

She continued to kiss his neck, biting gently, then laving the spot with her tongue. Rising on her toes partway, she was able to place her lips on his, kissing, nibbling, and sucking on them until he parted them on a gasp. When she darted her tongue inside to explore his mouth, a low groan escaped his throat, and he pulled her even more closely against him.

His rigid arousal dug into her stomach, and she smiled against his lips before she grasped his head and tilted it to the perfect angle for a deep, soul-touching kiss that left them breathless.

They broke apart panting, and Catherine turned around.

"Unbutton me," she whispered.

Robert complied immediately, and as soon as her bodice loosened, she tugged it from her shoulders, taking her chemise with it. She hadn't loosened the lace of her chemise, however, and it would not go past her breasts.

"Damn it," she muttered. Behind her, Robert chuckled softly.

"Here, allow me." He spun her around and deftly untied the knot, then pushed both gown and chemise to her hips. Once her breasts were free, he abandoned her gown and cupped them. He placed gentle kisses along the curve of one, then lightly tongued the nipple of the other.

Catherine's desire, however, had whipped into a frenzy that did not want reverence. She quickly pushed her gown to the floor. After a few seconds of trying to untie her stays, she abandoned them and set to work unbuttoning his trousers.

"My boots…"

"Leave them." She crouched and pulled his trousers and small clothes to tangle over his boots. At face level, his swollen cock grew by the moment. Catherine grasped it and took it experimentally in her mouth.

Above her, Robert blasphemed and steadied himself with a hand against a wall.

Catherine wanted to take him over the edge, but she also wanted him inside her. She stood and pushed against Robert's chest, urging him backward. He stumbled awkwardly until the back of his legs hit the chair on which she had thrown his shirt. She encouraged him to sit, then immediately crawled into his lap and draped her legs on either side of him. She captured his mouth again while clutching his shoulders. His hardness nudged her slick folds, and she squirmed, trying to grant him access.

He grasped her buttocks and lifted her before dropping her with unerring accuracy on his cock. Catherine could just reach the floor on tiptoe, and she pushed up before sinking down on him again. She moaned as he filled her deeply, completely, the action like a spark to gunpowder.

With his hands on her hips, Robert urged her to repeat the motion over and over, faster, harder. When her thighs began to quiver with fatigue, he lifted her and continued the momentum.

Her skin became slick with sweat as he pounded into her, their bodies slapping together inelegantly. Catherine didn't care. Robert was with her completely, with no distance in his gaze, their lovemaking wild and primal. She dug her fingers into his shoulders and tensed, her muscles tight, then with an intensity that tore a scream from her throat, she climaxed.

Robert groaned and called her name, his voice raw with emotion.

Catherine collapsed on him, boneless, and nestled her head in the crook of his neck. Robert let his head hang over the back of the chair in a position that could not be comfortable. She dangled her arms at her sides, mirroring Robert as she gasped for breath while ripples of pleasure coursed sporadically through her body. Every breath she drew tasted like Robert, and she wanted to spend the rest of her days with him just like this.

When the drying perspiration began to chill her, she stirred. Robert helped her to stand, and she, in turn, held him up when it seemed his legs might not hold him. She laughed softly as they untangled their clothing.

Suddenly shy, her earlier confidence leaving her, she didn't know how to return to the topic of her feelings for him— though it should have been quite natural, given the intense connection they'd just shared.

As soon as Robert had fully dressed and finished buttoning up Catherine's gown, he smoothed her hair back from her face. "I don't know what prompted that," he said, his expression more relaxed than it had been in a long time. "But my dressing room is always open to you, my lady."

She returned his grin, her heart full. She opened her mouth to tell him she loved him, but a pounding on the door of his room stopped her.

"My lord!" someone called, urgency in his voice.

"What on earth?" Robert brushed past her to answer the door. Catherine followed closely on his heels, a sense of foreboding suddenly turning her heated blood to ice.

"What is it?" Robert asked sharply to the footman standing on the other side of the doorway.

"My lord," the footman said, his face pale. "It—" He held out an unsealed note.

Robert snatched it out of the man's hand and unfolded it, scanning the words quickly. He crumpled the note in his hand as he turned to face Catherine. The dark scowl on his face softened as he looked at her.

"What's wrong?" With her mouth so dry, she barely got the words out.

He pulled her against his chest, but she pushed away to look up at him. "Tell me."

"It's a ransom note. Christopher has been—"

"No!" Her knees buckled, and only Robert's arms around her prevented her from collapsing to the floor.

"I will get him back," Robert swore. "He will be home before breakfast." He turned to the footman. "Have a horse saddled and waiting for me out front. Now!" The young man nodded and took off at a run.

"Who? Who would take him?"

"Someone desperate for money." Robert scowled. "They've left instructions for where to leave it. Fear not, I will find him. I will deal with these men as they deserve."

"Christopher…" Catherine pressed a hand to her mouth to keep from sobbing.

"He will be safe. They will not dare risk him. They simply want gold."

"But I haven't any!"

He drew back slightly and frowned. "He is my son now as

you are my wife. I would give every last farthing were it required."

Tears flooded Catherine's eyes—her heart as full of love for Robert as it was with fear for Christopher. "Bring him home, Robert."

He nodded, then set her aside to grab his coat and a brace of pistols. She followed him as he raced downstairs and into the study, where he opened a lockbox. He then pulled out a thick wad of bills that he shoved in a leather wallet.

"Where are you to meet them?"

Robert paused in the doorway but did not turn around. After a long moment, he turned his head to the side, his back still to her. "A crossroads north of the estate. It's about an hour's ride from here." He strode down the hall toward the front door.

The thought crossed her mind that if something terrible happened, this could be the last time she saw him, and she ran after him. "Robert, wait!"

He opened the door and paused. Outside, the peaceful sounds of a late summer evening and the lush scents of fresh-mown grass and night-blooming flowers gave the illusion all was well with the world.

Robert's determined frown told her he was anxious to be gone, but she couldn't risk not telling him.

She stopped in front of him and studied his face, memorizing every curve, every line, every stray bit of stubble. "I love you, Robert. I have for so very long I can't even say when it first started."

He looked like he had been poleaxed, and she rushed on. "I know what you said about…emotions, and you needn't say anything. I just needed you to know."

She kissed him on the cheek then quickly stepped back. He touched his cheek as he looked at her, still a bit stunned. He nodded then turned to stride down the steps. He paused at the bottom and half-turned. She took a step forward, thinking he had something to say, but he simply threw himself onto his horse and galloped down the long curving drive.

She watched him until even the puff of dust from the horse's hooves settled, then she slowly closed the front door and turned to find her mother-in-law standing in the entry to one of the drawing rooms.

"What's happening?" the duchess asked.

"Did he go after the boy?" The question came from the duke, his voice weak though still imperious.

Robert's mother gestured Catherine into the room where the duke sat in a large, upholstered chair, a blanket across his knees.

Catherine was in the middle of explaining what Robert was doing when Sophie burst into the room.

"Miss! Miss!" She panted as if she'd been running. Her hair was a tumbled mess about her shoulders, her left cheek bore a long scratch, and there were rents in her clothes.

"Sophie!" Catherine exclaimed, rushing to the maid. "Are you all right?"

Sophie shook her head, gasping. "It's the young master! I can't find him! We were playing hide and seek down by the stream. He told me to count to fifty, so he could find a really good hiding place. I searched and searched for him. I didn't worry at first because he's become so familiar with the grounds. I thought he was just really well hidden, but then I called him, told him he won the game, that I gave up, but he didn't come out." A sob escaped her, and she shook her head again, clearly distraught.

"I searched everywhere—even went across the stream into the woods, though I knew you told him never to go there. But I couldn't find him! I only came back to get help, but I—" Sophie broke down completely, and Catherine gathered her close.

"You couldn't have found him, Sophie. Christopher has been—"

"Someone took him, and it's your fault!" the duke shouted hoarsely before succumbing to a fit of coughing. The duchess tried to calm him.

Sophie wailed miserably and tore at her hair. "Miss, I'm so sorry—"

"You will leave this house immediately!" Spittle flew from the duke's mouth, and though his eyes were red and watery, fury filled them. "You are terminated without a reference. You are to blame for Christopher's—"

"Enough!" Catherine bellowed, surprising everyone in the room, herself included. "Sophie is not to blame. The attack was clearly well-planned. Whoever they are would have taken Christopher regardless of whether he was with Sophie, me, or even Robert. Furthermore, Sophie is in *my* employ, and her terms of employment are up to *me*."

Complete silence reigned for several moments, broken only by a sniffle or two from Sophie, who clung to Catherine's hand.

Finally, the duchess nodded. "You've put the duke and me in our places within the span of a week." She turned to her husband. "I told you she would make a fine duchess."

Despite the terror and fury racing through her veins, a bubble of laughter rose. She tried to suppress it, but it came out as a half-snort, half-giggle.

"Now," said the duchess, her tone practical. "Though I'm sure none of us are hungry, a spot of tea, fortified, to be sure, is clearly in order."

Fifteen

Robert rode north with a cold fury that paradoxically made him acutely aware of every tree and cottage he passed, even as he focused intently on the looming confrontation. The ransom location was not lost on him. It was the same crossroads where his brother died—the very spot Robert had recently visited. His stomach was in knots at the thought another person he loved might die there.

The ransom note had said to deposit the money at the base of a large oak tree at the northwest corner of the crossroads and then leave. Once he did so, they would return Christopher by dawn. The note did not say how or where the kidnappers would return the boy, but Robert had no intention of taking the risk they'd simply drop Christopher on the road to fend for himself. Nor did Robert trust they would not merely keep the boy and continue to demand money.

No, as soon as Robert left the money and appeared to depart, he'd then circle back to look for their camp. He felt sure they would not be far as the area was heavily wooded, and anyone without knowledge of them would soon become hopelessly lost. He, however, knew the woods like the back of his hand, and he would regain custody of Christopher at any cost.

As he approached the crossroads, he deliberately did not look at the birch tree on which he had carved William's initials. Nor did he glance at the side of the road where his brother had died. Instead, he scanned the surrounding woods, looking for any trace of movement.

Dusk had fallen by the time he placed the thick wallet at the base of the oak tree, the evening light a pale periwinkle that at any other time would have made him stop and stare in awe. Now, however, his only thought lay with Christopher. Robert stood and cupped his hands around his mouth.

"The money is here! Bring the boy!" He waited a full minute and then another, but beyond the twitter of a bird settling down for the night and a field mouse rustling through the grass at his feet, no sound penetrated the cool air.

Robert mounted his horse and headed back down the road he'd just traveled. He knew of a small clearing about a quarter of a mile back. He and William had discovered it when they were following a game trail years ago. As thick as the surrounding woods were, it would make an excellent camp for someone trying to remain hidden.

When he reached the trail, he dismounted and pretended to examine his horse's hoof while he surreptitiously checked to see if anyone observed him. Scarcely any light filtered amongst the trees as he led his horse off the road and along the path to the empty clearing where a small spring bubbled at the base of a boulder. Robert tethered his horse there and tried to think of where else an outlaw could set up camp. He took his pistols from his saddlebag then tucked them in his jacket pockets before heading north through the woods. He and William had explored these forests in every direction when they were boys, and this particular area had been their favorite outside the safe confines of their father's lands. There were two more clearings he would check before returning to the crossroads.

Robert moved slowly until his eyes adjusted to the dark. He had to travel mostly by instinct as he moved around ravines and through thick clusters of brush, and he estimated he was nearly even with the crossroads when some kind of light flickered to his left. He crouched, straining to see what it was. The light flickered again, and he realized it was a lantern, and someone had crossed in front of it.

Remembering a shallow cave in the rock face of a hill, he slowly and carefully crept toward it. When he stepped on a stick, he paused, his heart hammering, but luckily, the occupants of the camp seemed busy. Within minutes, he could see a rough sort of camp set up in front of a small collection of boulders. One man packed up blankets and stuffed things into the saddlebags of a horse that placidly grazed. Another horse looked about as if smelling a newcomer, but the man didn't notice and turned to address someone.

"Here, now, there's no need to cry. Be a little man. I'm sure your parents will follow instructions, and you'll be home before breakfast."

After shuffling a little to the side, every muscle in Robert's body tightened at the sight of Christopher crouched at the base of one of the boulders. He hugged his knees, his face streaked with dirt and wet with tears. Robert wanted to scoop Christopher up in a hug and assure him he was safe. Robert also wanted to grab the man who had taken Christopher and thrash the bastard to a bloody pulp.

Infuriated, Robert took a step forward, unsure of what to do first, but a crash to his right stopped him. A second man stumbled into the small clearing—the leather wallet clutched in his hand.

"It's a good thing we're so far off the road, Tom," said the first man. "As loud as you are, you'd have been caught long ago, or else shot by a hunter as a wild boar."

"Ain't no one live anywhere close, and ain't no one use that road. Don't know why you made camp in the middle o' the bloody forest."

"And that is precisely why you will not make a sustainable living as a highwayman. You always want to take the easiest path. I, however, will go down in history as the great gentleman bandit who was never captured."

Robert's blood ran cold as he recognized the man's voice. This was the villain who had held up William and him three years ago. The urge to tackle the man was so strong, Robert found himself taking a step forward. A sniffle from Christopher stopped him, helped him rein in his rage.

"What ails him?" Tom asked, handing the leather wallet to the gentleman bandit.

The man shrugged as he opened the wallet and began counting the thick stack of bills. "Probably missing his nurse. No boy from an estate like his even knows his parents. Nurses and servants are all he sees." He pulled out a handful of bills and thrust them at Tom. "Be a good man and don't spend it all on drink this time, all right?"

Tom grunted and moved to one of the horses, where he stuffed the money in a pouch. Robert edged through the trees, watching both men. The gentleman bandit crouched in front of Christopher.

"Stop your snuffling, lad. Imagine what a fine adventure you'll have to share with the other boys when you go off to school. You should thank me for giving you a story worth telling!"

While the man continued to explain what a favor he had done for Christopher, Robert came up behind Tom. The man pulled a bottle from his saddlebag and took a long pull from the contents. Robert moved swiftly, drawing back the butt of his gun to strike the man hard at the base of his greasy skull. Tom crumpled like a marionette whose strings had been cut, and Robert rolled him into the bushes beside the horses.

"Bring me that bottle before you drain it, eh, Tom?"

Robert surged into the small clearing, cocked his pistol, and fluidly drew up his arm. "Step away from the boy," he snarled.

The man whirled around, still in his crouch, and reached into his coat.

"Pull your hand out!" Robert strode forward and pressed his gun to the other man's forehead.

"Easy, brother," the man said, raising his hands. "There's no need to be hasty. You'll be wanting the lad, I assume. Take him —he's not a scratch on him."

Robert glanced at Christopher, who still sat on the ground, his eyes squeezed shut.

"Are you all right, Christopher?" Robert asked.

At the familiar voice, the boy opened his eyes then launched himself at Robert. "Papa!"

Robert was about to tell him to stay put, but the highwayman grabbed Christopher around the waist, and as he stood, held the boy in front of him. In an instant, Robert found his gun pointed at Christopher, whose small body shielded the villain. Cursing beneath his breath, Robert quickly lowered his arm.

"Put the boy down. I've lowered my gun. You have your money. Now leave."

The man laughed. "You don't last long in this profession falling for lines like that. Toss your gun aside."

Robert paused. He wanted nothing more than to shoot this man between the eyes. William was dead because of this man— because Robert had—

He quickly uncocked the gun and tossed it over by the lone lantern. As he moved, the light played over his face.

"Say, I believe we've had this conversation before," the man said. "What was it? A carriage raid? Or were you the unlucky one I robbed while he had his pleasure with a whore against a wall?"

Robert clenched his hand into a fist. "You shot at my brother and me while we were on horseback," he said through gritted teeth.

"Oh, those are always my favorites! You never know if one will make a run for it. Did you stay, or did you run?" At Robert's silence, the man continued. "Ah, so you stayed. Must have been deep in your cups. Ah well, at least you had an exciting tale to share. Probably embellished it a bit for the ladies, aye?"

Robert took a lurching step forward. "You killed my brother!"

The bandit stepped back, and a knife appeared in his other hand. He studied Robert carefully.

"Easy there, mate. I remember you now. Only as *I* remember it, I wasn't the one who pulled the trigger. Seems to me you did that yourself. I was only defending myself."

An agonized growl escaped Robert's throat just as Christopher began struggling against his captor's grip. Time crawled to a snail's pace all over again as Christopher lifted both legs high then kicked back with all his small but sturdy weight. One of his booted heels caught the man squarely in the crotch, and the man doubled over, dropping Christopher in the dirt.

Without a moment's hesitation, Robert stepped forward and delivered a jaw-breaking uppercut to the highwayman. The man's head snapped back, and he took two staggering steps to keep from falling. Robert followed and punched him in the nose. A sickening crack preceded a gush of blood, and Robert continued the attack with a cuff to the man's ear.

As blood poured down the man's face, his knees buckled. Robert caught him and forced him upright so Robert could deliver blow after blow with a berserker's rage. He didn't know how long he pummeled the man before Christopher's small voice cut through the red haze.

"Papa! Papa!"

Robert dropped his hands, and the highwayman crumpled to the ground in a heap.

Christopher threw his arms around Robert's legs. Robert lifted him then hugged him tightly. Years-old sobs escaped Robert's chest as he held the boy and the memory of William, not willing to let either go.

At Christopher's teary sniffles, Robert sought to soothe him, and for a moment, he forgot his own pain. "You're all right. I've got you. I'll keep you safe."

After several long moments, the boy calmed. He lifted his head from Robert's shoulder and put a grimy hand on each of Robert's cheeks.

"Don't tell Mama I cried. She won't think I'm a brave boy."

Robert half-laughed because his face was as wet as Christopher's.

"She will certainly think you are a big, brave, young man regardless. Tears are not a sign of weakness." As he said the words, they sank into his brain, and for the first time, he believed them. He hugged Catherine's son once more while a few more tears of relief and grief slipped into the boy's curls.

A few minutes later, Robert set Christopher down and set about binding both unconscious men. Tom started to wake as Robert threw him over the back of the bandit's horse but quickly passed out again, though for real or pretend, Robert couldn't tell and didn't care. He tied the hands and feet of the gentleman bandit—who, with torn shirt and bloodied face, did not appear as gentlemanly as the papers had described him.

"Let's go home, shall we?" Robert asked Christopher.

"Yes! I'm so hungry I could eat an elephant!"

It was a bit of a trick getting Christopher and the two laden horses out to the road then the quarter of a mile back to

Robert's horse. Robert ended up having to carry Christopher on his back, but as soon as they had recovered his horse and were finally on their way home, the boy fell soundly asleep, curled up against Robert's chest.

Robert looked down at the tawny curls, just visible by moonlight, and his heart swelled. So guilt-ridden that William would not have a family, so angry with their father, so determined not to marry and produce an heir, Robert had never thought to consider what he wanted—what it would be like to have a child. Catherine had cracked his obstinate shell.

The swell of emotion for Catherine's son, who slept trustingly in his arms, could be nothing less than paternal love. Robert thought about what it would be like to have a child with Catherine, and the idea made his vision go a little blurry. He roughly dashed at his eyes. Despite having told Christopher there was nothing wrong with tears, they were an unfamiliar occurrence for Robert, and he wasn't sure how he felt suddenly becoming a bit of a watering pot.

He shifted Christopher, so the boy lay more comfortably across Robert's lap, though why he bothered, he wasn't sure. The boy seemed content to sleep sprawled in whatever position he found himself.

Robert smoothed the tangled curls from the boy's face and thought again of Catherine and what she told him before he left the house.

"I love you, Robert. I have for so very long I can't even say when it first started."

He silently replayed those words over and over, feeling the surge of emotion race through his veins with every repetition. Catherine had said he needn't say anything back, she simply wanted him to know, but suddenly, he needed to tell her she was everything to him, that she'd made his life worth living, that he would protect and care for, and yes, love her as long as his body had breath.

Robert urged his horse to walk faster, tugging the other two beasts along.

It had been a tumultuous, transformative night, and he was not yet comfortable delving too deeply into his emotions after facing the bandit responsible for William's death. Still, Robert could recognize that doing so, and saving Christopher from the highwayman, had done much to soothe his soul.

By the time Robert rode into a small town just north of Market Bosworth, his left arm had cramped from holding Christopher's sleeping weight for an hour. He stopped in front of the house of Alder Hobson, a yeoman who often assisted the local constable.

In short order, he turned the now-conscious bandits over to Hobson to deliver into the constable's custody.

"Tell Mr. Loman I'll visit him first thing tomorrow to settle the charges on these men, but he should know murder and kidnapping are among them."

"Aye, milord," Hobson said, taking the reins of the two horses.

"Keep the mounts for your trouble," Robert stated—to the loud complaints of the gentleman bandit.

"This beast is too fine to be pulling a plow! I demand—"

Robert stopped right in front of the man, who still hung upside down. The man craned his neck to look Robert in the face, and whatever he saw caused him to drop his head without further complaint.

After settling Christopher on his other shoulder, Robert mounted his horse for the final leg of his journey. Less than half an hour later, he gently shook Christopher as they rode up to Bosworth Manor.

"We're home," he said. "Wake up so you can tell your mother what a brave lad you've been."

The boy rubbed his eyes with his fists and looked around groggily. "I'm hungry!"

Robert laughed as he stopped his horse and dismounted before setting Christopher on his feet. "We will get you as much food as you can eat."

The front door opened, and Catherine cried out as she ran down the steps. She fell to her knees and enclosed her son in a tight hug, tears streaming down her face.

"I was brave, Mama!" Christopher said, wriggling in her grasp to look at her.

"I'm sure you were, my darling."

"Papa, I mean, Lord—"

"You can call him Papa, Christopher. Your father will understand," Catherine said as she smoothed the boy's tangled hair.

"Papa was even braver! You should have seen him fight that man!"

Catherine looked up at Robert. Love and gratitude shone in her eyes as tears continued to flow down her cheeks. "He is indeed a brave man."

Robert's throat tightened, and a now familiar burn stung his eyes. He shook his head to clear it of the emotions that were still too raw.

Catherine's smile faded, and Robert realized she must have thought he'd shaken his head at her. She stood and led Christopher into the house before he could think to explain, to tell her…

He slowly followed them into the entry hall, where his mother stood in the doorway to the front drawing room. She smiled broadly, one hand at her heart, the other wrapped around her waist. "Oh, thank heavens!" She looked over her shoulder. "He's back! Robert brought him back."

"I'm going to call for a tray for Christopher upstairs," Catherine said.

His mother indicated the drawing room. "Oh, no. Have it brought in here. That way, we can all hear what happened."

Robert followed Catherine and Christopher into the drawing room, where his father sat beside a fire. The room was stiflingly hot as a result, so Robert opened one of the windows, ignoring his father's grumble.

Sophie screeched and ran across the room. She threw herself to her knees and gathered Christopher to her in a very un-servant-like manner. Robert's father scowled and opened his mouth to say something, but then the oddest thing happened—he glanced at Catherine, who returned his gaze with raised eyebrows. Robert quickly looked back to his father, who had apparently swallowed his words.

A smile tugged at the corner of Robert's mouth as he wondered what was going on between the two. He had not known his father to hold his tongue in years.

"Robert, what happened out there? Where did you find Christopher?" his mother asked.

Unsure where to begin, wanting to spare the details in front of Catherine, Robert was grateful when a maid and a footman arrived bearing two enormous trays of food and tea.

As Christopher tucked in, he began recounting the story of his kidnapping from the woods by the stream. With the resiliency of the very young, his greatest complaint was that his kidnappers had not provided adequate food.

"Two bits of bread! And no jam or butter!"

"Uncivilized!" Robert said with a grin.

Christopher started to nod, but when the duchess put an enormous serving of treacle tart in front of him, his eyes grew round, and he abandoned both the story and the roast beef his mother had tried to encourage him to eat. Robert watched her smile indulgently and found he couldn't look away.

He had always found her beautiful, had always experienced a strong physical attraction to her, even when he insisted their relationship was strictly platonic.

Now, she was like his lodestone. He found he could not

look away. He studied the curve of her nose, the reddish-brown sweep of her silky brows that were a darker shade than her magnificent hair, which glinted in the candlelight like amber, warm and rich.

He stared at her mouth, remembered the taste of her from just a few hours ago, and craved her lips against his. He watched her dab at her son's face with a serviette, then move the cup he was in danger of knocking over. She moved with an economy of motion that was quintessentially graceful. There was no ostentation in her movements to draw attention to herself. If anything, he suspected she tried to go unnoticed as she cared for everyone around her, except, of course, when she acted the role of the Russian countess.

Then, she was perfectly happy to be the center of attention. Robert smiled as he wondered if she would ever realize she *was* the Russian countess. Despite having spent most of her life outside the urbane confines of London, there was nothing provincial or unsophisticated about Catherine. Grace, intelligence, and wit were a natural part of her. What was more, he loved her. With every fiber of his being, he adored her. He wanted to fill her every day with love and happiness. His conflict with his father was petty and trite compared to how he felt about Catherine and how she made him feel. Suddenly, some of his brother's last words came back to him.

"You must love, Rob. Promise me."

He glanced at Catherine's son—now his son—as the boy laughed around a too-full mouth of pudding. Christopher was simply an added benefit of marriage to Catherine. Today's misadventure had woken Robert to so many things he had been too stubborn to realize before now.

"Time for bed," Catherine finally said to her son. "Though how you'll be able to sleep after having eaten so much food is anyone's guess."

Sophie cleared the boy's empty dishes. "I'll sleep in a cot in his room tonight, my lady."

"That's not necessary," Catherine said.

"I won't sleep a wink with worry if I can't hear him breathe tonight."

After a small moment, Catherine nodded. Robert started to follow her and Christopher but paused at the doorway. He wanted to help put the boy to bed then tell Catherine how he felt, but first, he had a need to put a few things to rest with his father.

He turned around and took a few steps toward the older man. His mother glanced at him and must have read the resolve in his face, for she excused herself and hurriedly left the room.

His father, who had been downright pleasant while Christopher had relayed his story, screwed his face into an unpleasant scowl. "What is it?"

Robert took a breath and sent a silent prayer to his brother for patience.

"I shot William."

His father's face took on a mottled shade of maroon. "I know you bloody well—"

"I shot William, but I did not kill him. Highwaymen attacked us. I tried to kill the one who fought with my brother. It was a terrible accident." Robert had described the details three years ago. He would not go into them again now.

"The men who took Christopher today are the same who attacked William and me."

At this, the duke inhaled sharply. His hands trembled as he gripped the arms of his chair.

"I believe one is the 'gentleman bandit' who's been in the papers for the past few years. I captured them both, and they are in Constable Loman's custody now."

His father seemed to try to speak, but no words came out.

Robert pressed on. "You may question them if you like, hear their account of the night William died. They may or may not corroborate my story."

"May not?" the duke asked, his voice an angry rasp.

Robert shrugged. "They are highwaymen. I doubt honor and integrity are their strong suits. The point is, I loved my brother. I would have died for him that night. I also know he took his role as my older brother very seriously. If anyone had asked, he would have given his life to save me.

"I bitterly regret he died at my hand. I will regret it and miss him for the rest of my life. However, I will no longer listen to your constant tirades about that night. You don't have to act like my father, but you will not continue to berate me."

The duke frowned, his face suddenly resembling a dried apple. "Or what?"

Robert laughed shortly. "Or else I leave. I take Catherine and Christopher, and we go to the Tutley estate. Or the continent. Perhaps even America. The point being, I will let your title rot. If that doesn't show you how little I've ever wanted it—"

Robert took a deep breath because his speech was devolving into a tirade of his own. He had said enough.

"Sir." He bowed and turned on his heel, then went to find his wife.

Sixteen

CHRISTOPHER HAD BEEN PARTICULARLY energetic when they reached the nursery, making Catherine wonder how she would get him down, but she had no sooner tucked him in bed and kissed his brow than he was sound asleep. She watched him for several minutes, noting how the baby roundness had left his cheeks. He was sun-browned, and there was still a bit of treacle on the corner of his mouth.

Her heart clenched as she remembered the hours of terror she had experienced today. To think what could have happened — Fighting the tremor in her hands, she tucked the covers more snugly around her sleeping son then left the nursery.

She would be forever grateful to Robert for rescuing Christopher, and so she would never trouble Robert again with declarations of a love he had never wanted. Though she hadn't really expected a return of the sentiment earlier when he was leaving to save Christopher, his silence then, and the shake of his head when she'd been about to say it again at his return, told her his resolve to avoid emotional entanglements was still strong. She would not put him, or herself, in such an awkward position again.

She quietly closed the door to the nursery and pushed aside the ache in her heart at the notion of never mentioning her feelings to her husband again. As she reached the second-floor landing, she met Robert, who was coming up from downstairs. She smiled, though it was tentative at best.

"I'll never be able to thank you for what you did," she said, her voice hoarse.

"Shh." He drew her to him and hugged her.

She absorbed the warmth of him. He smelled of dirt and horse and his own indescribable *maleness* that she found viscerally appealing.

"Do not thank me," he whispered into her hair. She shuddered to think how badly the situation could have gone. If there had been even one more highwayman, Robert could have died. Though he was solid and safe in her arms now, horrible visions continued to play out in her head, and her body trembled uncontrollably.

"It's all right." He ran his hands over her back. "We're safe."

She nodded, though she kept her face pressed into the open collar of his shirt. He murmured something before he tilted her face and took her lips, softly at first, reassuring, soothing, but then his kiss quickly sparked into something more scorching—an elemental celebration of being alive. Catherine moaned when his tongue tangled with hers, and she clung to his neck, suddenly lightheaded. Robert moved to support her fully, and she pressed closer to him. His arousal was palpable through trousers and skirts, and her body quickened in response.

Just as Robert slid his lips along her jawline, the sound of several people climbing the stairs interrupted them. Robert spun around, shielding her from view, but she peeked around his shoulder to see two footmen carrying the duke in a chair. The footmen paused as they reached the landing, clearly surprised to find her and Robert simply standing there.

The duke, however, smiled. "Goodnight," he said before he waved the footmen on down the hall to his room.

A huff of laughter escaped Robert. "Well, that was unexpected."

Catherine moved to face him and started to ask him to elaborate, but he placed a finger gently over her lips.

"I'll explain soon, but first, there's something I need to tell you."

The footmen returned from delivering the duke to his chambers. As they tromped downstairs, Robert took her hand. "Not here," he said, his tone and manner cryptic. He led her to their room, where a maid had lit candles and turned down the bedcover.

Robert stopped in the middle of the room, suddenly looking like Christopher when he was about to confess to something he wasn't sure was allowed.

A flutter began beneath her ribcage, which made her think... No, the sense of excitement was no doubt a result of their passionate kiss in the hall. She smiled and tried to look encouraging.

"What you said earlier..."

Catherine frowned, trying to remember what she had said. "You mean about thanking you?"

"No, um, earlier than that."

"I don't know what you—"

"On the steps. When I was leaving to fetch Christopher."

"Oh." She suddenly understood. "I..." She had to assure him she wouldn't declare herself again, but it proved exceedingly awkward to admit she had lost her heart to him after he had warned her not to. She cleared her throat and forced herself to speak. "I must apologize for that. I know you said—"

"No, that's not what I... I don't wish for you to apologize. That is—" He stepped closer and gathered both of her hands. "I'm doing this with all the finesse of a green schoolboy. What I am trying to say is that when you told me you loved me, I should have said I love you too. I love you so much. I almost can't breathe for how greatly you fill my heart. You said you didn't know when you started loving me, but I now know the exact moment I fell in love with you. It was that night in Vauxhall when I watched you dancing, so full of life and joy. Then once I kissed you, I knew I could never kiss another woman. At the time, I told myself I was just infatuated with you. I even pretended I was doing the noble thing of saving your reputation when Letitia caught us in Mrs. Wilson's garden. I couldn't accept I'd fallen in love when I'd sworn for three years I never would."

Tears filled Catherine's eyes. Her cheeks flamed, and the skin of her body grew flushed, but she didn't care she was a crimson, wet mess. Robert's love shone in his gaze, and her own love—free from restrictions and free to shine—reflected back at him.

She laid a hand on his cheek, and he turned his head to press a kiss into her palm. "Kiss me, Robert." He wrapped his arms tightly around her and kissed her as if she were the most important person in his life.

Several minutes later, she drew back, panting. He pressed his forehead to hers, his breath warm puffs on her face.

"What made you change your mind? About loving anyone?" she asked.

He chuckled. "Not just anyone. Only you." He glanced around the room. "Shall we…get more comfortable?"

Catherine kicked off her shoes, and Robert shrugged out of his jacket. They climbed atop the bed, heedless of the crisp sheets and smooth satin coverlet. Catherine sat cross-legged like a girl and grinned foolishly at the man she loved who miraculously loved her back. The notion had just begun to sink in, and she had the feeling life was about to become more wonderful.

Robert stretched out beside her, propped up on his elbow. "I told you my father and I had a brutal falling out after my brother died, and how the duke blamed me for William's death."

She nodded and took his hand in consolation. He smiled and gave her hand a squeeze.

"What I didn't tell you was that my father accused me of murder."

"Why that's—"

Robert put a finger to her lips. "In a way, he is right. I shot my brother."

Catherine's mind reeled as she tried to assimilate this information with the man she knew. "But I thought you said highwaymen attacked you."

He nodded, then told her about the night he lost his brother. Tears, only recently dried, flooded her eyes again, but she remained silent, realizing he needed to get the words out, uninterrupted. When he finished, she stared at him for several long moments before she shook her head.

"You're not responsible for William's death."

"There's more," he said.

What more could there be?

"The men who took Christopher were the same who attacked William and me."

"What?"

"I'm sure you've heard of one—he's known as the gentleman bandit. There have been several stories about him in the paper over the years, generally romanticizing him." Robert twisted his mouth into a grim line of distaste. "Well, I nearly beat him to death tonight. It was Christopher who stopped me. I hugged him tight then, and something in me just…let go, as if I finally realized I could grieve my brother's death without *ruining* mine. I had forbidden myself from falling in love and beginning a family as penance to my brother and in anger at my father. But you and Christopher found your way into my heart anyway. It just took a while for me to realize it. Does that make any sense?" he asked, finally looking her in the eye.

She nodded as tears continued to flow, tears of grief, happiness, and relief.

"I love you, Catherine."

"I love you too."

He smiled and drew her head down and pressed his lips to hers. Catherine pushed him back and climbed on top of him, cradling his face in her hands as she kissed him. She took the initiative in their lovemaking, using the lessons he'd taught her to give them both pleasure. This time was different, though. She did not have to hold back her words of love as she took him within her. She rode him slowly, rocking her hips to bring him deeper. She sobbed as her orgasm rolled through her body and as he urged her faster. He dug his fingers into the soft flesh of her hips and bucked as he came, his body convulsing, his voice raw as he called out her name.

Later, as she lay draped against him, Catherine thought of the fateful night they had met. If she hadn't been so desperate for something more out of life, if she hadn't had the mad courage to put on her grandmother's dress, she might never have met this man who so completely filled her heart.

"When we have a daughter, I should like to name her Alisa. After my grandmother."

Robert sat up abruptly. "A daughter? Are you—"

"No, not yet. I meant if we ever have a daughter."

Robert flopped back against the pillows and drew her against him. "Of course. Yes. Absolutely." He chuckled softly. "Forgive me. It has been a day of shocks and revelations."

Catherine kissed him and smiled. "It just occurred to me we would never have met if not for her."

Robert drew in his chin to look at her, his expression quizzical. "Aside from borrowing a name and a gown from your grandmother, the Russian countess is completely you. You do realize that, don't you?"

"I don't think I did know when we first met. I thought I was playacting a confident woman." She paused and thought of her recent confrontations with the duke and duchess. "However, I've come to realize I could not have acted that way without having a bit of that confidence inside me. It's somewhat disconcerting, actually, to find I am more than I ever thought."

He rolled onto his side and nuzzled the soft skin of her neck just below her earlobe, causing goose bumps to rise on her arms. "I suspect you have hidden depths and strengths we have yet to discover." He ran his hand down her back and cupped her bare bottom. "And I look forward to a lifetime of such discoveries."

The world had suddenly opened in front of Catherine. Not long ago, she had been a shy widow, unable to voice her opinions or thoughts, swaddled in a life of safety and predictability.

Now, she stood at the helm of a life full of love and adventure, next to a man who'd encouraged her to push her boundaries and question her limitations—a man who made her *feel* more than she thought possible.

"*Spasibo,*" she said to her life.

Ballad of Discord

TARAH SCOTT AND SUMMER HANFORD

Sneak Peek at Ballad of Discord

Sneak peek at book one in the Songs of Rebellion series, **Ballad of Discord** by Tarah Scott and Summer Hanford

If the man you love won't trust you with the truth, how can you ever again trust him?

The pieces of Elizbeth McKinley's world scatter when her father, in an act of pure madness, joins forces with a mysterious Frenchman in an attempt to claim the Scottish crown. Now, pawns in a game far vaster than they can imagine, Elizbeth and her sister must flee or be shipped off to France to wed strangers. To make matters worse, the one man who should most wish to help her, the man Elizbeth loves, refuses to believe she's in danger. His betrayal will cut deeper than any sword.

One

GIGGLES and rapid footfalls sounded in the corridor outside the sunny parlor. Elizbeth smoothed a stitch in her needlework while she waited for the bittersweet prick of tears to subside. It had been two years since their mother died. Laughter and joy were long overdue in their household.

"You know we ought to chide her for running," Aunt Davina said.

Elizbeth glanced at Davina, who sat across the parlor.

"She's nineteen," Davina went on. "A child no longer. When the two of you come out this autumn, we can hardly have her running about in company."

Elizbeth nodded as her strawberry-haired little sister charged into the room. Elizbeth wouldn't reprimand Margarette, and she doubted their aunt would, either. Only four years Elizbeth's senior, Aunt Davina was more an older sister than a matronly aunt and was as apt to join in their schemes as curtail them.

"The mail came," Margarette cried. She slid to a halt in the center of the Kidderminster carpet and waved a handful of letters.

Aunt Davina smiled down at her book, her bowlike lips pressed closed, her only censure to ignore the display.

"Oh?" Elizbeth looked up with feigned disinterest even as she tried to discern familiar handwriting on the flapping envelopes.

Her dear friend, Mister Robert McFarlan, was away on business for their father. Their three-week separation was the longest they'd been apart since…she fought down a blush… since he'd kissed her a month past. Although writing her was inappropriate—they weren't officially engaged—she considered a letter far less scandalous than his single, decidedly unchaste, embrace. So, she'd wheedled from him a promise to write. Though he was due to return that evening and she'd searched the mail for such a letter every day, he had been remiss thus far.

Smile wide, Margarette twirled on her toes, letters held aloft. Somehow, she'd noticed Elizbeth's recent interest in the mail and was determined to tease.

"Margarette, dear, shouldn't you be at your lessons?" Aunt Davina asked sweetly.

With a final spin, Margarette twirled over to the settee and plunked down beside their aunt. "After I see who's written." She began shuffling the envelopes. "Father," she said, and tossed two in a pile. "Father again." Another followed. "And again."

Elizbeth returned to her stitching. Attempts to contain her sister would only fuel her teasing. Perhaps Aunt Davina was correct and they should try to instill more decorum in Margarette. What man wanted a wife who ran giggling up and down the corridors of his home?

An intelligent one, she decided, who wanted a home full of joy. Not the same sort of man who would marry their aunt, but similar. She suppressed a grin. Little did Aunt Davina know, but as Elizbeth had already settled on a suitor, she planned to use her delayed season to find a man for Davina. It wasn't right that one disastrous romance, undertaken nearly a decade ago when Davina was just seventeen, should prejudice her against all gentlemen.

Margarette's sudden silence caused Elizbeth to look up. Her sister's blue eyes sparkled, her grin full of mischief. She'd finished her sorting and held two letters back from the pile for their father. Seeing she had captured Elizbeth's attention, Margarette pried one open and unfolded the pages within.

"Now, this one is interesting," Margarette drawled. "Great Aunt Saundra writes that she's returned from Italy for another visit."

"Has she?" Aunt Davina raised one delicate brow. "What is she now, eighty? I am surprised she made the journey."

"She says she wishes to see us, when we can." Some of the joy left Margarette. "She's of the opinion this will be her final visit to Scotland." Margarette blinked rapidly. "She means then to return, to die in Italy and be laid to rest there."

Aunt Davina plucked the letter from Margarette and scanned the page. "I know she's pious, but I will never understand how a good Scottish noblewoman grew so enamored of Italy."

"She is not even our real great aunt," Margarette said with a sniff. "It's not as if we will lose a real family member." Margarette's unspoken words echoed through the room: *as we did when mother died.*

"True enough, but our families were close, and she has never forgotten that." Aunt Davina folded the letter. "She's been Great Aunt Saundra since before I was born, and we shall visit her as she asks."

"Yes, of course, we shall," Elizbeth said. "What is the final letter, Margarette?"

As hoped, her sister's frown disappeared and mischief lit her eyes. "This?" Margarette held up the envelope, careful not to reveal the handwriting. "This letter must be an error. I shall have it returned. After all, only an engaged miss would receive a letter such as this one."

Elizbeth smiled before she could stop herself. Robert had written? Her soon-to-be betrothed cared more for her than for propriety, and more than he feared her father's wrath. Not that Father had ever indicated displeasure in their courtship… assuming he'd noticed.

Margarette popped to her feet. The pile of letters for their father toppled in her wake and spilled across the settee toward Davina. "In fact, such a letter as this is so scandalous, could do such harm to a lady's reputation, that I say we must burn it." Margarette whirled toward the tall fireplace at the far end of the room.

"Margarette," Elizbeth cried before she could help herself.

Her sister turned back with a victorious grin. She thrust the letter behind her back and took two steps backward toward the hearth. Elizbeth didn't know if she should laugh or shriek. She felt caught between the girl she was at twelve, tormented by her little sister, and the woman she'd become at twenty-two.

"For Heaven's sake." Aunt Davina laughed, her chocolate-colored curls a jumble as she shook her head. "Give me that letter and take yourself off to your lessons, Miss. I believe 'tis Italian today."

"French," Margarette said, then clamped her lips closed with a grimace. She crossed to their aunt and proffered the envelope, which Davina accepted with a smile.

Although she still didn't have her letter, Elizbeth couldn't contain a smirk. Margarette hated French.

"Well, off you go to the library." Aunt Davina made a shooing gesture. "I will quiz you later."

"Yes, Aunt Davina." Margarette made a great show of becoming somber before she smiled and skipped from the room.

Aunt Davina gathered the scattered letters, placed Elizbeth's on top, and held out the stack. "Will you take these to your father? He likely wishes to have his mail."

Elizbeth set aside her needlepoint and stood. Eyes on the top envelope, she took the pile and hurried from the parlor. She reached her father's office to find the door closed. The thick wood panel shutting him away meant he didn't wish to be disturbed, so Elizbeth deposited his mail on the small table outside his office door. She couldn't help but recall a time when their golden-haired mother had been alive and his door was always open. Elizbeth sighed. Mother was not alive, and their father's office door was nearly always closed.

She turned from the door to find Mary hurrying toward her. The maid took in the closed office and proffered a card. "There is a Frenchman here to see your father, Miss. Claims he's a lord of some sort, or I wouldn't have let him in."

Elizbeth took the card. Etched on the surface was simply *Seigneur Faucon.*

Lord Hawk, she thought, her French considerably better than Margarette's.

She looked at the maid. "Do you think he truly is a French lord?" A lord would be worth disturbing her father.

"Well, Miss, he seems quite fancy, to be sure, and very French." This last, Mary delivered with a wrinkle of her nose.

"Show him to my office," came her father's clipped voice behind the closed door.

Elizbeth winced. She'd forgotten about her father's keen hearing. She offered the card back to Mary. "Bring him to Father."

"Yes, Miss." Mary took the card and scuttled away.

Elizbeth stood for a moment, gaze on the door. Should she ask her father if he needed anything? He had a bell pull, and servants to fetch for him, but since their mother's death, he'd taken to skipping breakfast. Now, they rarely saw him outside the dinner table, if then. She shook her head. He knew she was there. If he wanted to see her, he would ask her in. Besides, she had Robert's letter to read.

Elizbeth turned on her heels. Though guilt assailed her, she went to the little room that had been her mother's office. She withdrew the key from her bodice—a key none knew she possessed—opened the door, and slipped inside.

Stuffy heat warmed her arms. Her mother had kept the window open nearly year-round. Elizbeth preferred the fresh air, as well. Today, however, she dared open the curtains and beveled panes just enough for a sliver of light and a flicker of breeze. She couldn't risk being caught. Her father, who thought he had the only key, would be livid.

Elizbeth understood his feelings. He wished this room, where Mother was once so often found, to remain undisturbed, in some fruitless hope to preserve a glimmer of her spirit. But it didn't. When mother was alive, light poured in through the open window. Her household notes and correspondences lay scattered about the desk and the second table, which overcrowded the little room. Father had pressed her to take one of the parlors for her office, but Mother liked her cramped little space with its lavender walls and flowery upholsteries.

Now, desk and table were bare, their papers long since sorted by Aunt Davina. After Mother's death, Aunt Davina arrived with their wayward, unpredictable Uncle Graham, and she'd taken over running the household. While Elizbeth appreciated Aunt Davina and was daily grateful for her competence, she had no real notion why Uncle Graham was there. All he did was soak up Father's whisky—when he could pry himself away from his harlots long enough to come home.

Shrugging off her now-grim mood, Elizbeth settled into the armchair by the window. She ran a finger along Robert's concise handwriting then, carefully, she opened the envelope.

This was her first letter from Robert and she wished to cherish every word.

ELIZBETH:

As promised, I am writing. I comply only because I abhor breaking a promise. However, I must remind you how inappropriate it was for you to ask me to write. Your father would be displeased not only that you asked me, but that I allowed you to extract my promise to write. Be warned, in the future, I will not give in to your pleading.

ELIZBETH ROLLED HER EYES. If there was one little flaw in Robert, it was that he was too serious, but that was also what she cherished about him. His seriousness drew her in. To call forth his laughter made her heart sing, and she knew, when Robert spoke, he meant each word. Still, he could stand to be a touch less severe.

Her eyes went to the final line.

With the very greatest affection, yours always, Robert.

Elizbeth pressed the letter to her chest. Those words made the rest of the letter worthwhile. Her gaze caught on the quill sitting on the desk. The quill had been her mother's favorite. Tears unexpectedly pricked. It was terribly unfair that she had died without seeing Elizbeth fall in love. Elizbeth recalled the delight in her father's eyes whenever her mother walked into the room. Elizbeth wanted a love like that. She'd found a love like that.

"You would have loved him as much as I do, Mother," she whispered.

Elizbeth held the page back in the line of sunlight to reread the short missive.

"This request to speak in the garden is ridiculous," her

father's voice, speaking French, emanated from somewhere outside, near the window.

Elizbeth snapped her head up.

"Not ridiculous, but necessary," a man replied in the same tongue. "The manor has ears."

"I assure you, none of my staff speak your language," her father snapped back. "Half of them barely speak English."

Movements slow, least the chair creak, Elizbeth grasped the window and drew it back toward the sill. Father would not appreciate being made a liar of.

"Humor me, *Seigneur*, for my news is life shaking," the Frenchman said. "Any who hear it will face mortal danger."

The window clicked quietly closed, muting her father's reply into unintelligibility.

Face mortal danger? Elizbeth would have laughed had *Seigneur* Faucon's tone not been deadly serious. What news could possibly be of such importance? Her fingers tightened on the latch. She hesitated a heartbeat, then drew her hand back.

Eavesdropping was unacceptable. Doubly so when the two men were going to great lengths not to be overheard, and especially if the information they shared was truly somehow dangerous. If the Frenchman's words were for Father's ears alone, Father alone should hear them.

A thought struck. The library windows also opened onto the garden. Margarette!

Elizbeth surged to her feet. She folded and tucked Robert's letter into her skirt pocket as she crossed the room. She poked her head into the corridor—empty, as hoped. She slipped from the room and hurried down the hall.

Halfway to the library, she came up short. Lord, she'd forgotten to lock the door. Elizbeth hurried back and secured her mother's office, then again headed toward the library. She pushed the door open, stepped in, and nearly collided with Margarette. Elizbeth stumbled back.

Her sister recoiled. "Elizbeth," she cried. "You cannot believe what I heard."

Elizbeth contained a sigh. She leveled a frown on her sister. "You listened in on Father's private conversation."

Margarette gaped. "How do you know?"

"I heard them talking and came to stop you." Elizbeth grasped her sister's arm and pulled her into the center of the large room, away from windows or door, then realized the Frenchman's words had truly rattled her. "It is wrong to eavesdrop."

Margarette yanked free. "I do not care. 'Tis a good thing I heard. I don't want to go." Margarette's voice broke off in anguished tears.

Elizbeth stared. "Go where?"

"To France," Margarette cried.

"Why would you be going to France?" Elizbeth asked, unable to follow Margarette's tearful declarations.

"The Frenchman said we must." Margarette rubbed at her eyes. "He said we are to marry Frenchmen so Father can have an army."

"What under Heaven are you talking about?" Elizbeth demanded. "What do you mean, 'we'?"

"You, me and Aunt Davina," Margarette said. "Father is going to send us to France so they will send back an army to help him become king of Scotland."

"Margarette," Elizbeth hissed. "Do not say such things. That is treason. Stop making up stories."

Margarette lifted her chin. "It is not a story. The Frenchman said Father is the secret descendent of the Jacobite kings, and so we are princesses—which would be great fun—except that France sent him with a ship to take us away."

Elizbeth planted her hands on her hips. "Did you fall asleep over your lessons?"

Margarette grimaced. "Aye, because French is so boring, but that is *not* the point."

"It is exactly the point," Elizbeth corrected. "That is what you get for eavesdropping—and for not studying properly. Your French is terrible, which is why you so badly misunderstood their conversation."

Despite her admonition, a thread of unease wound through Elizbeth. Margarette might not speak French well, but Elizbeth did, and she hadn't misunderstood the Frenchman's warning about mortal danger.

Margarette's gaze sharpened. "You heard something, too."

Elizbeth groaned inwardly. Margarette eschewed books, but she was too intelligent for her own good.

"If I am wrong, why were they talking in the garden rather than Father's office?" Margarette demanded.

"There could be many reasons," Elizbeth said, but doubt persisted. While Margarette's story was obviously a mad mixture of dream and miscomprehension, the meeting was odd. Why was a French lord speaking with their father to begin with?

"My French may be atrocious, but I comprehend much more than I speak," Margarette said. "I know what I heard. We cannot let Father send us away to France. Especially you. What about Robert?"

"Mister McFarlan," Elizbeth corrected absently as she sought to make sense of Margarette's story.

"We must warn Aunt Davina," her sister urged. "The Frenchman said they want her, too." Elizbeth shook her head and started to tell Margarette to return to her French lesson, but Margarette grasped her hand. "Please, we must tell Aunt Davina."

The fear in Margarette's eyes stopped the refusal that leapt to Elizbeth's lips. Margarette feared nothing.

Elizbeth gave her hand a gentle squeeze. "You must try to see that you dreamed up this silly story."

Margarette stubbornly shook her head. "Aunt Davina can decide."

Elizbeth bit her lip. Their aunt was forgiving, but eavesdropping on Father's private conversation was a graver transgression than running down a hallway.

Margarette's hand clutched harder. "Elizbeth, I am afraid."

"We may have to tell Aunt Davina," Elizbeth allowed. "Or we may be able to keep your misbehavior between us. Tell me everything you think you heard, as near the original as you can, in French, and I will decide."

Margarette hesitated, then nodded and launched into her tale.

Two

Davina closed Debrett's *The New Peerage*. She weighed the etiquette book in her hands. Debrett's, and all of Britain, agreed that a proper chaperone must be wedded or widowed.

Due to Bhradain's betrayal, Davina was neither.

Mister Haywood, she corrected. He never should have been Bhradain to her. After nine years, some other woman must have the honor of addressing Mister Haywood by his Christian name.

She rubbed eyes tired of reading Debrett's dry, restrictive words. Across the room, the mantle clock ticked off slow minutes. The dinner hour approached, and Elizbeth hadn't returned. Margarette wouldn't. She would hide from a French exam for as long as possible. If the girl devoted as much effort to learning the language as she did to avoiding her lessons, she would be fluent.

Elizbeth, though, should have returned to her sewing. The envelope from Mister McFarlan had been thin. How many words could the page contain, and how many times could Elizbeth possibly read them? Davina considered fetching her niece.

A smile flittered across her lips. Elizbeth, as conscientious a young woman as Davina had ever met, thought no one knew where she hid when she wished to be alone. Sweet Elizbeth had no idea Davina—who had never been very well behaved—routinely followed, snooped, and spied on her nieces. In their best interests, of course.

She drummed her fingers on the book in her lap. Nae, Debrett would never condone her as a chaperone. But she was all her nieces had, and she was determined to safeguard their wellbeing.

Which brought her to Mister McFarlan. A kind man. Intelligent. An attorney. Not a true gentleman, though from a genteel family. Born the same year as Davina, so not too old for Elizbeth, nor so young as to be foolish. In truth, she felt him a good match for her niece. There would be no trouble there, except that Davina had no idea how her eldest brother felt about the notion of his daughter wedding one of his attorneys.

One might assume, as James permitted the courtship to continue, he was pleased. That would be, if one didn't know James. Or rather, the man he'd become since Maryanne's death. With his wife's passing, James had lost all attachment to the world. Like as not, he hadn't noticed the glaringly obvious affection between his daughter and the attorney.

Hurried footfalls, growing in volume, sounded in the hall without. Davina stilled her fingers. The footsteps were too heavy to be Elizbeth or Margarette. Her brother James burst into the parlor. His gaze darted about the small room, minnow-like. A strange pallor had leached all color from his face and his normally neat brown hair was wind tossed, as if he'd been outdoors. Of late, James never went outdoors.

"Whatever is the matter?" She set the book aside and rose. "James?"

"Where are my daughters?" he barked.

"Not here, as you can see. Is something amiss?" In view of his distress, she tried to keep a check on her temper, a thing more easily accomplished were it not the case that James was continually brusque these days. "James?" she repeated.

"What? Nae. Nothing is amiss." He raked long fingers through his dark hair.

At forty, James was still a handsome man. Only a hint of gray touched his temples and his broad shoulders and arms were well muscled. Unlike many other men his age, he had no paunch. She saw the way women looked at him, even young women. He could find happiness again. If only he would try.

He looked about the room again. "Where did you say they are?"

"Margarette is most likely in the library." She would not betray Elizbeth's secret. He would be furious should he learn his daughter possessed a key to her mother's office. "I have no notion where Elizbeth is."

James's mouth thinned. "Is not your one purpose in this household to know where my daughters are?"

She tamped down harder on her anger. "Indeed. Shall I launch a search, or would you rather wait an hour and see if they join us for dinner?"

His frown deepened into a scowl. "A husband would have curbed your tongue years ago. But I suppose it's better this way." He turned on his heel and stomped from the room.

Davina stared at the empty doorway. "That was rude even for James," she murmured.

Should she go after him? Was something truly amiss, aside from his self-absorbed sorrow over Maryanne? Before she could decide, new footsteps filled the corridor. Recognizing both sets, Davina retook her place on the settee. Perhaps the answers were on their way to her.

"Aunt Davina." Much as her father had, Margarette hurtled into the room.

Behind her, Elizbeth entered, her lovely face marred by worry and her steps considerably more graceful. Instead of sitting, they stopped before Davina. She looked up at them, expectant.

"Aunt Davina, Margarette has overheard something that concerns us," Elizbeth's voice was grave.

"Overheard?" Davina cocked a brow. "How did you manage that, dear?" Davina understood all too well how one *overheard* things.

Margarette had the grace to blush. "I did not do it on purpose. I was in the library, studying French. I truly was."

Davina nodded.

"The window was open, and Father and that Frenchman started talking in the garden."

"Frenchman?" Davina asked.

"Yes," Elizbeth said. "He arrived shortly after we left you, and asked to speak with Father. He gave the name Seigneur Faucon."

"Lord Hawk?" Davina didn't like the sound of that. The name was obviously false. She turned back to Margarette. "What did this Lord Hawk have to say to your father, and how does it concern you both?"

"It concerns you as well." Margarette popped up on her toes as she spoke, hands clasped before her. She shot Elizbeth a look.

"Tell her," Elizbeth ordered. "Only, do try to make sense."

"He said it all in French." Margarette scrunched her nose. "Elizbeth says I must repeat it as nearly as I heard, so you may interpret the words for yourself, since my French is abominable." This last, she accompanied with a supplicative glance upward.

Davina didn't know if she should be amused or alarmed. James's harried visage came to the forefront of her thoughts. "Let's have it, then."

Margarette embarked on a monologue. She used two voices, one apparently her idea of her father and the other the Frenchman. Some of the syllables that left her mouth resembled no language.

As Davina took in the half-intelligible babble, her pulse quickened with each word. Lord Hawk had told James he was the descendent of Henry Benedict Stuart, Cardinal-Duke of York, and the last of the Jacobite kings? Davina clenched her hands in her lap, for the tale grew even stranger. Seigneur Faucon had asked, and James agreed, to be given custody of her, Elizbeth and Margarette. He planned to take them and their considerable dowries to France and marry them to men of power. Their new husbands would raise an army, and return with it to Scotland, to fight for James, the Jacobite king. Davina stared up at her nieces. Tall, lovely young women whose hands would be a prize for any man but…princesses?

"And then they went deeper into the garden," Margarette concluded.

Davina looked at Elizbeth. "You heard none of this?"

She shook her head. "Nae, but I did hear the Frenchman say they must discuss something very secret and dangerous."

Margarette stared, her blue eyes filled with uncharacteristic worry. "Aunt Davina, what are we going to do?"

Davina shook her head, dazed. She had no idea. "You are sure that is what they said? You weren't dreaming? I know how French puts you to sleep."

Margarette blew out a frustrated breath. "I repeated the words to you—badly, I might add. How could I have dreamt all that? I don't even know some of those words. Please, I do not want to go off to marry some horrible French lord."

Davina scrubbed at her forehead. It couldn't be true. They were not royalty, not even gentry, though possessed of considerable wealth. Even if Margarette had heard correctly, it simply couldn't be true. The most shocking part was that James might believe any of the tale. His frantic eyes, his pallor, rose in her memory.

"Let me think on this. Please," she murmured.

"Yes, of course," Elizbeth said.

"But, what if Father tries to send us away?" Margarette demanded.

"He will hardly have us abducted," Davina soothed. "Go ready for dinner. We will see how your father is then. Like as not, he'll tell us the tale of this strange Frenchman and his bizarre ideas, and we will all laugh together. Tomorrow, Seigneur Faucon will be but a memory."

Elizbeth smiled. "You are quite correct, of course." Margarette looked mutinous, but Elizbeth caught her arm and tugged her toward the door. "We'll see you at dinner, Aunt Davina."

"Yes," Davina murmured absently as they stepped from the room into the hall.

She hadn't wanted to further alarm her nieces by speaking of their father's odd behavior, but there was someone to whom she could report the entire series of events. Her brother, Graham. Davina rose and went in search of him.

Davina found her brother sprawled face down and shirtless atop his bed. Beside him, curled to one side and, blessedly, fully clothed, though grass clippings decorated slippers and hem, lay a blonde woman Davina had never before seen. Nor, if she knew Graham, would she ever see the woman again.

Nose wrinkled at the stale sweat that permeated the chamber, Davinia crossed the room to the window. She yanked back the curtains and unlatched the windows. As fading daylight and fresh air spilled in, a groan sounded behind her.

"Davinia, what the devil are you doing?"

She turned to find Graham seated on the edge of his bed.

The blonde, snoring softly, didn't stir. Graham blinked rapidly, eyes bloodshot in a face still striking, despite his lack of sleep and what had undoubtedly been an abundance of whisky. Bare chested as he was, Davinia was reminded why her brother remained a favorite of the ladies. She would have thrown a shirt at him, but the one discarded on the floor looked too sweat-infused to touch.

"What am I doing?" she repeated. "I am here to tell you to ready for dinner. You have avoided consciousness long enough for today."

He pushed a hand through tangled brown locks, then cast a look over his shoulder. When he turned back, he wore a perplexed frown, as if he didn't quite know what to make of the unconscious blonde.

"Consider me told, sister dearest."

"That is not all," she said in clipped tones. "I must also, though Heaven knows why I bother, ask your opinion on a matter that may be significant."

Graham groaned and fell backward onto the bed. He fumbled for a pillow, found one, and pulled it over his face.

Davinia hurried back to the bed and kicked him in the shin. "Graham, this is important."

He lifted one half of the pillow. "I'm listening." He dropped the down-stuffed fabric back into place.

"I cannot very well discuss this in front of her." Davinia waved at the woman on the bed.

Graham lifted the pillow and craned his neck. Again, that perplexed look crossed his face.

"You *do* know her?" Davinia's voice dripped sarcasm.

"I suppose I must." He stretched out an arm and poked the slumbering woman in the shoulder.

Thick lashes fluttered open. Blue eyes focused on Davinia. "Hello."

With one word, the woman revealed her English

origins. Davinia grimaced. Leave it to Graham to bring home an Englishwoman. Offering Davinia a shrug, he tucked the pillow under his head. The Englishwoman sat up and looked about, appearing just as perplexed as Graham.

"Hello, Miss…" Davinia let her voice trail off in question.

"Ingram." She offered a bright smile. "Anastacia Ingram. And you are?"

Davinia bit back a sharp retort. "Miss McKinley. If you could excuse my brother and me, Miss Ingram, I should like to speak with Graham alone."

Miss Ingram's head snapped toward Graham. "*You* are Graham McKinley?" She frowned. "I was told to stay away from you. You're a terrible rake."

"Posh." Graham smiled his most charming smile and tucked his clasped hands behind his head. "If I am such a rake, why are we clothed?"

Miss Ingram looked about again. "If you aren't a rake, why am I in this bed?"

"I haven't the foggiest." Graham shrugged. "But if you would care to remain, I can think of several ways to test my fortitude. We must put this rake business to rest."

"Graham," Davinia snapped. Between James's half-madness since losing Maryanne and Graham's devotion to sin, Davinia sometimes felt as if she were responsible for the entirety of their family's wellbeing—and sanity.

Graham pointed toward the door across from the bed, leading to an antechamber. "Go in there, sweetheart, and ring for a servant to ready you a bath. I will come to you shortly."

Miss Ingram stood. She tugged her skirt straight and squared her shoulders. She was tall for a woman, her build slender. "I will give you your privacy, but you will not find me waiting for you in the bath." Her blue eyes snapped. "Just because we ended up in this bed, does not mean I am here for your frivolous pleasure, sir." She cocked her chin in the air and marched from the room.

Graham watched. A slow smile stretched across his face.

"You have no idea who she is or how you both ended up here?" Davinia asked once the door clicked shut behind the woman.

"You heard her. She's Miss Anastacia Ingram."

Davina had a few choice things to say about that, on the heels of which, she launched into the details of both their nieces' story and her encounter with James. Halfway through, Graham's brow furrowed. By the time she finished, he sat upright on the edge of the bed, his features hard with thought.

"I suppose it is possible," he murmured.

"That we are decedents of the Stuart family and James is a Jacobite king?" Davinia snorted. "Hardly. My only fear is James might believe the mad tale and turn our nieces over to some strange Frenchman. Likely, this is some sort of ransom plot to get at his wealth."

Graham regarded her with worried eyes. "And you."

"Me what?"

"If he really believes the Frenchman's tale, he could turn you over as well."

"I am six and twenty. I am no more subject to James's will than I am to that of a random passerby." *Unlike Elizbeth and Margarette.*

Graham shook his head. He levered himself to his feet, towering over her. "I cannot imagine James being taken in by some Frenchman's tale. Besides, Margarette likely dreamt the whole thing."

Davinia nodded. For all his debauchery, Graham was dependable when it came to family, and he, if anyone, knew their older brother well. "Of course, you are correct. I am going to prepare for dinner." She glanced toward the door through which Miss Ingram had departed. "Do not let your English harlot keep you."

"She is not a harlot. She is Miss Anastacia Ingram."

Davinia raised her brows. "Graham, I found her asleep in your bed. She is a harlot." Without another word, she left the room.

Three

ELIZBETH ENTERED the dining room arm in arm with Margarette. As with every informal meal, Aunt Davina sat at her place to the right of their father's seat, which, as usual, stood empty. A small measure of relief loosened the knot in Elizbeth's stomach at sight of her Uncle Graham. He occupied his place at the opposite end of the table. He met her gaze and gave a reassuring smile.

Elizbeth's pulse skipped a beat.

He knows.

Aunt Davina must have told him what Margarette heard. That meant Aunt Davina was worried. Was Uncle Graham there to ensure their father didn't send them to France? Elizbeth took her seat to the left of her father's chair. Was it really possible he might agree to marry them to strangers? What of Robert? Surely, her father wouldn't tear her from the man she loved. Robert would never permit it. Her stomach cinched tighter. Could he stop Father?

Margarette sat beside her. "Father isn't here," she said, tone relieved.

Elizbeth fought to keep her thoughts clear. His absence had

to be a good sign, didn't it? She exchanged a glance with Davina. Her aunt smiled encouragingly.

Margarette leaned close to Elizbeth. "Do you think he has already ordered our trunks packed?" she whispered.

"Hush," Elizbeth hissed.

Three maids entered, each carrying platters of food, but Elizbeth scarcely paid attention as they filled her plate.

"You appear refreshed, Graham," Davina said.

He laughed. "I always appear refreshed."

Davina gave him a look Elizbeth couldn't interpret. Were they mentally communicating about Father?

"Aren't you hungry, Elizbeth?" Margarette asked.

"Are you ill?" Uncle Graham regarded Elizbeth.

He waited, expression gentle. He was a good uncle. He looked out for them, particularly since her mother's death and their father's retreat from the world. He would never allow Father to send them to a foreign country to marry strangers.

She shook her head. "Nae. I am just not particularly hungry tonight."

His eyes twinkled. "I smelled blueberry buns baking earlier. Surely, you want one? No one makes a better bun than our Missus Henderson."

She smiled. Uncle Graham always made her feel better. "I do love blueberry buns."

He winked. "I know. At least taste a bit of the pheasant. It is quite good."

"I will."

She was being silly. She'd allowed Margarette's dream to influence her reality. She forked a piece of pheasant and lifted it to her mouth, then halted when Father strode into the room.

"Well, this is a pleasant surprise." Uncle Graham lifted his glass of wine and downed a mouthful.

Ignoring his brother, James looked about the room. His gaze fell on the waiting servants. "Leave us, and ensure neither you nor any other stand outside these doors, on pain of death," he said, voice grim enough to send a shiver down Elizbeth's spine. "I will ring when you may return."

Eyes wide, the staff hurried out. Elizbeth watched them depart with mounting fear, a fear reflected in Margarette's eyes. Aunt Davina stared at their father through narrowed eyes. Uncle Graham leaned back in his chair, expression sober.

Her father went to the hall door, then to the servants' door, peering out each before closing them firmly. Finally, he took his seat. "I am glad everyone is here. That will save me the trouble of having to repeat this announcement."

Aunt Davina exchanged a look with Graham.

Elizbeth's uncle turned and met her father's gaze. "You look far too serious, James. Have some wine." Graham lifted his glass again and emptied its contents.

To many, the action would appear cavalier. Elizbeth knew better. Her uncle's keen mind seldom dulled, even with great quantities of liquor.

Her father reached for a nearby platter of potatoes and spooned some onto his plate. "You could use with a dose of responsibility, Graham," he said. "But that will come soon enough." He reached for the decanter of wine.

"Responsibility?" Graham repeated. "It's rather too late for that, don't you think?"

Her father slowed in filling his glass and flicked a glance at his brother. "You had best hope not." He set the decanter down, stabbed a slice of pheasant, and transferred it to his plate. He began cutting the meat. "What I am about to tell you, remains between us." He flicked a glance at Graham.

"Surely, you are not accusing me of being a gossip monger?" Graham laughed.

"No man can be assured of keeping his own counsel when he drinks too much."

Uncle Graham laughed again. "I heartily agree. Luckily, I

never drink too much." He reached for the decanter and refilled his glass.

Aunt Davina shot him a warning look.

James forked pheasant into his mouth. "I will get straight to the heart of the matter. Our great Aunt Saundra is not truly our aunt."

"If that is your big announcement, then it is you who have been drinking too much," Uncle Graham said.

Her father didn't so much as glance at him. "In fact, Saundra is our" –he pointed his knife at Davina, Graham and himself— "grandmother, and you girls' great-grandmother." The knife darted menacingly toward Elizbeth and Margarette.

Aunt Davina gasped in unison with Margarette's cry of surprise. Elizbeth could only stare. What they'd overheard indicated nothing like *this*.

"What could possibly give you that idea?" Graham asked.

"I have seen the ledgers, records of marriages, of real names and births," her father replied.

Graham regarded him. "Why are we only learning of this now?"

Her father ate more pheasant. "Because her husband, Henry Benedict Stuart, Cardinal Duke of York, was still living."

Even Elizbeth couldn't refrain from a loud gasp this time.

"*James*," Davina breathed, "Henry Stuart never married. He was a priest, sworn to celibacy."

"Davina is correct," Graham said.

"She might be naïve enough to believe that would stop a man, but not you, Graham," Elizbeth's father said, his attention on his food. "He would not be the first priest to marry in secret."

Elizbeth's mind raced. Henry Benedict Stuart was the last legitimate descendant of James VIII, and younger brother to Charles. What year had Charles Stuart last tried to take the throne? Her thoughts muddled. 1759. Yes. To the Jacobites, he had been the Young Chevalier. Dear God, Margarette hadn't dreamed the conversation between their father and the Frenchman. It was true. Nae, it wasn't true. It was ridiculous to think they were descendants of kings. But their father believed the Frenchman's story.

"Birth certificates can be forged, James," Graham said. "Where did you get this information?"

"That is not important at this time."

Graham snorted. "I beg to differ. Never has it been more important than now."

Her father took a drink of wine. "You may take my word. It is all true."

Elizbeth held her breath in anticipation of Graham's demand of proof.

Graham picked up his wine glass, leaned back in his chair, and studied her father. "What has Father to say of this?"

"He knows nothing of it," James replied.

Graham's brows rose. "I should think a man would like to know that the woman he called mother *isn't* his mother."

"He will be told when the time is right."

"When will that be?" Graham asked.

Under the table, Margarette's hand found and clasped Elizbeth's.

Their father laid down his utensils and looked at them. "Once I have laid claim to the Crown.